Love Finds You™
IN
SILVER CITY
IDAHO

Love Finds You™ IN SILVER CITY IDAHO

BY JANELLE MOWERY

summerside
PRESS™

Summerside Press™
Minneapolis 55438
www.summersidepress.com

Love Finds You in Silver City, Idaho
© 2010 by Janelle Mowery

ISBN 978-1-60936-005-4

Scripture references are from The Holy Bible, King James Version (KJV).

The town depicted in this book is a real place, but all characters are
fictional. Any resemblances to actual people or events are purely
coincidental.

Cover Design by Koechel Peterson & Associates | www.kpadesign.com

Interior Design by Müllerhaus Publishing Group | www.mullerhaus.net

Photo of Silver City by Jimmy Emerson, www.flickr.com/photos/auvet.
Used by permission.

*Summerside Press™ is an inspirational publisher offering fresh,
irresistible books to uplift the heart and engage the mind.*

Printed in USA.

Dedication

....

To my Lord and Savior, Jesus Christ,
who looks at our hearts with a love that knows no bounds.
To my wonderful family,
whose love, encouragement, and prayers
helped make my dream of writing novels come true.

Acknowledgments

....

Thanks to Susan Page Davis and Bill Tompkins for providing pictures and information about Silver City.

Thanks to Lisa Ludwig, Nancy Toback, and Marcia Gruver, whose assistance made this story shine.

And last, but certainly not least, a special thanks to my cheerleaders, MerriDee Shumski and Rachel Moon. Your prayers and support are greatly appreciated.

For the LORD seeth not as a man seeth;
for man looketh on the outward appearance,
but the LORD looketh on the heart.

~1 SAMUEL 16:7

Silver City, Idaho

WHEN GOLD WAS DISCOVERED ALONG JORDAN CREEK IN 1863, the rush to the Owyhee mountain range began in earnest. Dozens of mining camps sprang into existence, one being Silver City. The activity was first limited to the creek, but rich deposits of gold and silver were soon discovered in the nearby War Eagle and Florida mountains. At the peak of the town's success, Silver City had about twelve streets that were anything but level, seventy-five businesses, and three hundred homes with a population around twenty-five hundred. Some extremely rich mines caused intense battles. One required the U.S. Cavalry's arrival to bring the dispute to an end. It is believed that over sixty million dollars' worth of precious metal, at the value of that time period, was removed from the area. The living ghost town of Silver City receives thousands of visitors each year seeking a taste of what the Old West and mining towns of the past were really like. Many hike the mountains still peppered with mine shafts. About seventy-five original, privately owned structures, dating back to the 1860s, still remain and are well maintained. Some visitors are fortunate enough to spend a night in the Idaho Hotel. Restored for use, the hotel is filled with history, antiques, and atmosphere.

Janelle Mowery

Chapter One

....

Summer 1869

"The next time I get my hands on him…"

Whump.

"…he won't stand a chance."

Rebekah Weaver took careful aim at the dark green oval in the center of the rug, then swung the beater with all her strength.

Whack! That was better. Right on target and sure to be felt. She struck the rug two more times for good measure, then stood back and observed her handiwork with a satisfied smile.

"You keep hitting the rug that way, Rebekah, and there won't be much of a pattern left."

At her mother's voice, Rebekah's smile dissolved. She turned and lifted her apron to wipe the perspiration from her forehead and neck. "I didn't hear you get back." She must look a sight—what with all the dust she'd removed from the rug reattaching itself to her skin. "Do you need help unloading the supplies?"

"If it keeps you from stripping my favorite rug of every thread, yes." After setting one large basket on the porch, her mother headed back for another. "What's got you riled? I know that poor carpet is innocent."

Rebekah leaned the rug beater against the house and emulated her mother's regal walk as she followed her to the buggy. "Your son..." She blew out a breath that could start a windstorm.

Laughing, her mother handed her a sack of flour before grabbing the sugar and a package wrapped in brown paper. "Well, let's see. Since Michael is studying law in St. Louis, I guess you must be talking about Andrew."

"Who else? Mama, trouble sticks to him like stink on a pig."

"Now, Rebekah, he's only ten."

"I'm serious." They plunked their loads beside the basket on the porch and returned for the last of the supplies. "Andrew doesn't have to go looking for trouble—it stays with him like they're best friends."

They each carried a basket inside the house, through the entryway, and on into the kitchen. Mama set her provisions on the table before dropping onto one of the chairs. She lifted the apron hanging from the back of the seat and dabbed at the moisture on her face.

"All right, tell me what happened."

Rebekah's shoulders relaxed. She'd thought Mama would never ask. She needed sympathy and quite possibly an ally. For emphasis and drama, Rebekah remained standing. She set her basket next to her mother's, pressed her hands on the smooth, hand-carved table, and announced, "Andrew put a snake in the basket of clothes I planned to hang out on the line."

The humorous twitching at the corners of Mama's mouth was the exact opposite reaction Rebekah had hoped for.

She stood upright and crossed her arms. "It's not funny, Mama. I nearly shed my own skin, I jumped so fast. Not to mention that most vile of creatures touched all those clean clothes. I had to rewash them."

Mama leaned back, looking weary. Maybe the heat was too much for her today. The sun coming out full force after buckets of rain the last couple days made the humidity unbearable. A breeze would do wonders but had yet to make an appearance. Worry for Mama wormed its way into Rebekah's heart. She shrugged and buried her anger. She'd deal with Andrew on her own. Besides, a full-grown woman of twenty-one ought to be able to best a ten-year-old boy.

"I'll admit putting a snake in with the clean clothes is going a bit too far. I'll talk to him about that." Mama rubbed her hand over the polished tabletop. "But I thought you'd be used to Andrew's antics by now."

A shiver started at Rebekah's scalp and raced to her toes. "I'll never get used to snakes."

Mama chuckled. "I'm guessing he knows that. But you've got to admire his creativity."

"I do?"

"Sure. Most days, you're the only playmate he has. What's more fun than making a girl scream, especially if it's a sister?" Mama shrugged. "It makes you pay him some attention, even if it's bad attention."

With a loud sigh, Rebekah plopped onto the chair across from her mother. "I never thought about it that way. He's gotten worse since Michael left for St. Louis. I guess Andrew misses him and is using me for his amusement. Now I miss Michael more than ever." She propped her chin in her left hand and traced the scar on her cheek with her forefinger. "So either I get used to snakes and frogs to keep from reacting to his pranks, or I find time each day to play with him."

"That sounds like a wise decision." Mama got up from the chair and shuffled to put away the supplies. "Now, if you aren't mad at Andrew anymore, maybe you can take Misty and the buggy out to the barn, then try to find your brother and let him know you're no longer in the mood to cause him harm."

Rebekah laughed as she stood and gave her mother a quick hug. "Sure. But first I'll bring in the rest of your purchases."

After releasing their horse Misty into the fenced pasture, Rebekah returned to the barn and called out for her brother. She silently listened for a snicker or shuffle of hay.

Nothing.

That left his second favorite place to check. She headed for the creek, hoping he wasn't full of mud. Or worse yet, that she'd end up muddy. No longer did she cringe at the thought of walking so far. It had taken months to get used to the high elevation of their new home, but thankfully the hike no longer winded her.

The breeze she'd begged for earlier finally arrived but only in a short burst, rustling the leaves of the few aspen trees and the shiny needles of the pines and firs lining the creek. A second waft soon followed but died as swiftly as the first. The massive trees provided plenty of shade from the burning sun. The thought of burning made her finger the scar on her cheek, no longer so tender after a year of healing. Still, she should have worn her bonnet to protect the sensitive skin.

The scratching of denim against bark drew Rebekah's attention. Andrew must have seen her and was trying to hide. That meant she'd probably be scrubbing pine sap from his clothes again. She left the lane's edge and tiptoed her way through the patchy grass, trying to avoid any muddy areas, stopping well short of the swollen creek.

"Andrew," she called in a singsong voice as she peered up into the trees. The little bugger could sure hide well. How high did he climb? "I'm not mad any longer." Maybe that would make him show himself.

The words worked as planned. The sun glinted off his towhead as he peeked down from a branch midway up. His sweet, angelic face was the perfect disguise for the little imp dwelling inside. Andrew had a charming side that could warm the coldest heart. With his wide grin, long lashes, and pleasant personality, he'd lure her tender side to the fore—right up until he pulled one of his pranks.

Andrew's face screwed into a frown. "Are you sure you're not mad? You looked ready to turn my hide inside out."

Rebekah lifted an eyebrow at his colorful, though grisly, description. "Fear of that snake nearly did the same to me." She shuddered. "But I'm not mad anymore. Why don't you come down and we'll talk about it?"

Andrew shook his head. "I don't believe you. It's a trick to get me down so you can give me a good whipping."

Rebekah held up her empty hands and wiggled her fingers. "See? No switch. I'm telling the truth. You're safe to come down."

Andrew grinned. "Watch what I can do, Bek." He lowered himself to the next branch while keeping hold of the one above, moving farther toward the end. Her heart stopped as he started to bounce, making the branch dip lower with each lunge. "It feels like I'm flying."

Heart inching into her throat, panic struck harder than when she'd smacked the rug earlier. She speared a glance at the water and couldn't see bottom. Terror brought her eyes back to her brother. "Careful, Andrew."

More words of warning swam through her brain but somehow refused to leave her mouth. "*Stop!*" finally forced its way through but was drowned out by the cracking of the branch.

The horror that made her breath catch in her lungs was reflected on Andrew's face as he began his descent, the rotten branch leading the way. "Bekah! Help!"

Andrew landed in the swollen creek with a hard splash. Rebekah ran forward. All she saw in her mind's eye was Andrew tangled in branches as they pulled him under water. She had to get him out. Without another thought, Rebekah jumped into the numbing cold and landed right where Andrew had disappeared. Gasping for air, she swallowed water.

"Andrew!" she screamed, kicking and reaching till she latched onto her brother's shirt. As her sodden skirts dragged her toward the bottom, panic set in. Then she remembered: she didn't know how to swim.

* * * * *

Nathaniel Kirkland watched and listened with amusement to the exchange between the woman and child, right up until the woman thrashed in the water like a frightened cat. Her gulps for breaths as she struggled and clawed the air to keep her head high proved her inability to swim. Nate had yet to see the boy reappear. He heeled his mount into a gallop and raced to the creek's edge, stripped off his gun belt and hat, then lunged from the saddle into the water.

Chapter Two

....

Nate surfaced to get a breath of air, gasping at the shock of cold water. The boy's head bobbed near the top, his small arms flailing. Nate reached for him, only to have the boy elude his grasp. Furiously kicking his feet, Nate lunged and grabbed an arm.

With a hard yank, the boy's head appeared. Gasping and sputtering, the youngster sucked in several breaths. He bobbed like a piece of cork, before the wailing began. In between gulps, he repeated one word.

"Bek!" Another gasp. "Bekah!"

Nate made an instant decision. Get the boy to shore, then look for the girl. As Nate tugged and kicked, neither of them moved. He pulled harder. The boy screeched. Nate figured his leg was hooked to something.

Running his hand down the boy's leg, Nate found another arm. He grabbed and hauled with every ounce of strength he owned. The weight was incredible, but the girl's head finally broke the surface.

She blasted a breath of air, then gulped several in succession before she sobbed, "Andrew?" She had released his leg and grasped for him again.

Nate couldn't wait any longer. He was running out of strength. If he didn't hurry, they'd all drown. With everything left in him,

Nate kicked his legs, dragging his two burdens with him. Progress was slow, but the shore was coming into reach. Now to get the boy and girl on dry land.

An arm wrapped around Nate's neck. He couldn't breathe. He had no strength left. They went under. In that instant, his neck was released. He felt the girl and boy struggling. Begging for strength, Nate pushed for the surface. In one smooth move, he flung the boy to the shore, the current having swept them to where Nate could finally touch bottom and still keep his head above the waterline. He grabbed the girl with both hands and pulled her out of the water.

He dropped to the ground beside them both, where they all lay gasping for air, completely spent. Within moments, the boy started to cry. The girl rose on one elbow and reached for him. They sat up and hugged, weeping, while they shivered.

The girl examined the boy's face. "Are you all right?"

The boy nodded. She grasped him by his shoulders and gave a shake. "Don't scare me like that—ever again." She pulled him back into her arms. "You're going to be the death of me yet, Andrew."

The boy struggled to be let loose, then stared at Nate. Thankful for the sun warming his chilled skin, Nate finally pushed to his knees and shook off the excess water from his hair.

The girl turned and held out a trembling hand. "Thank you."

Nate gaped at the red splotch on her cheek. "Are you hurt?"

Her hand flew to her face for only a moment before returning to grasp Andrew's hand. "I'm Rebekah Weaver. This is Andrew." Her voice cracked. She took another gulp of air. Her throat worked. "Thank you so much for your help. I don't know what—"

"You're welcome." Poor girl. The strain of what she'd just been through caused her much distress. "I'm glad I was here."

While she scrutinized Andrew's face, Nate studied hers. He'd never seen such an odd scarring before. Had she been burned?

She swung around and caught him staring. He could feel his face flame as he looked away. To cover the awkward situation, he yanked off his sodden boots, dumped the water, then pulled them back on. The way she fussed over the boy, Nate assumed she was his mother. But up close, she appeared much too young to have a son his age. Except for the scar on her cheek, her skin looked as smooth as a girl in her teens.

Discomfort at the silence made him stand. Time to move along. "I'm looking for the town called Silver City."

The boy jumped up like he'd been stung. By the wide eyes and full grin, he appeared fully recovered from his dunking. "I can take you. It's right over the hill."

"Andrew."

The girl's motherly side kicked in again. Rebekah, was it? She stood and put a protective arm around Andrew's shoulders, which he tried to shrug off. Nate hid a smile. He remembered trying to extricate himself from his mother when she tried to coddle him for too many years. Boys that age wanted to be considered men. On their own terms, of course. They also still wanted to avoid responsibilities and play like children. A confusing time. Nate felt for the lad.

"Your name is Andrew?"

"Yes, sir."

"I'm Nathaniel Kirkland." Nate stuck out his hand and the boy shook it, now standing as tall as he could stretch his spine. "Friends call me Nate."

Andrew grinned and shook Nate's hand harder. "Hello, Nate. You can call me Andy. Only ones who call me Andrew are my parents and Bekah." He hooked his thumb over his shoulder toward his sister. "Especially when they're mad. Then they add my middle name."

This time, Nate couldn't stop his smile. He understood about adding the middle name. He'd gotten to the point that he nearly hated his by the time he was grown. "And what's your middle name?"

Andrew made a face like he wondered if he really wanted to share that information. Then the grin returned. "I guess I can trust you with it. It's Robert. Named after my grandfather."

"That's a mighty fine name." Nate crouched down and lowered his voice. "Just be sure to watch out when they start tacking on your last name."

Andrew peered up at him, his head cocked, one eye closed as he squinted against the sun. "Really?"

"Trust me." Nate scooped up his hat and gun belt, putting them back on before settling a hand on Andrew's shoulder. "Now, where did you say I could find Silver City?"

Nate knew he was close. He should have followed the road from California, but the quiet ride through the mountainous country was more to his liking. He still couldn't believe his superiors had given him the assignment. Sending a twenty-five-year-old man was unheard of, so they told him. A task such as his normally required an experienced man. He had to fight for the job, but he'd turn himself inside-out to prove himself worthy of the deputy marshal post. With effort, he forced his mind back to Andrew's directions.

"Other side of the hill. You'll go past our barn and house. Just past that you'll find the start of Silver." Andrew shrugged. "Or you can follow the creek."

Sounded like he'd missed the place by a mere mile. Yep, the town couldn't possibly be much to speak of. But then many mining towns in the mountains rarely were. Too difficult for family men to get to, let alone stay on to forge out a profit worthy of their effort. Most women didn't cotton to rough living and rougher neighbors.

"Thank you, Andy."

Andrew nodded and hiked up his dripping trousers. "You gonna stay awhile, Nate?"

He hoped not. "For a bit. Probably not long."

He finally turned to Rebekah. He'd avoided facing her long enough and still couldn't look her in the eyes. Her neck was as far as he made it, which was when he first noticed the small scar there, what looked to be another burn. Curiosity nudged his mind for the first time, but he tamped it down. He wouldn't be around long enough to care.

Drawn to a glint at the base of her throat, Nate found an odd-shaped piece of flat metal. The high shine made him guess it to be pure silver. The facing nestled against her dress, keeping him from seeing what might decorate the front. When her hand went to the ornament, he again felt heat in his face. He needed to stop staring.

She appeared to be all right, but he figured it wouldn't hurt to ask once more. Still uncomfortable, he scratched the back of his neck and worked his way to his chin before shoving his hands into his pockets. "You, ah, you're not hurt or anything, are you?"

He glanced at her eyes long enough to catch the mirth in them. His anxiety must amuse her. He found that interesting, especially since she stood in a puddle from her dunking, shivering while wringing out her light brown hair and soiled apron. Odd that she didn't hide her scars. Most ladies he knew would cover their face or at least turn away.

The smile in her eyes finally reached her mouth. "Thanks to you, we're both fine. Again, I appreciate your help, Mr. Kirkland."

Her formality didn't sit well. "I sure wish you'd call me Nate."

"Well, I reckon that means you should call me—"

Gunshots drew their attention westward. The sound of trouble ricocheted off the surrounding hills, reminding Nate of the task before him and why he'd come to Silver City in the first place.

Chapter Three

....

Rebekah's heart could have been hit by the bullet; it lurched so hard at the gunshots. Nate had taken a step toward his horse but stopped to look at her, a question in his eyes.

Understanding dawned. "We're fine. Go!"

She said a silent prayer for the town as he flew to his horse. In one smooth move, he slid onto the saddle and reined his mount around. His easy action betrayed years atop a saddle. Rebekah had spent enough time around her father's livery to recognize a skilled horseman.

Curiosity about the stranger started the moment he treated Andrew as a young man. Most men considered him a nuisance or ignored him altogether. Her interest bloomed as if watered by the moisture still dripping from her hem. Men often had difficulty looking her in the face, so Nate's reaction was no surprise. But this man's aversion bothered her. There was something in his eyes that drew her. Kindness, perhaps, with a tinge of sadness.

Andrew yanked on her arm. "Come on, Bek. Why you just standing here? Let's go."

Remembering the gunshot, Rebekah raced after her brother, ignoring her squeaking and squishing shoes, and gasped a prayer for Mr. Kirkland's safety and that of all the other families in town.

* * * * *

Nate vaguely noticed the house and barn he sped past—Rebekah and Andrew's home. He felt bad about leaving them behind with no escort, but it couldn't be helped. If the gunshots came from the men who'd been causing all the trouble, he could catch them and be done with this place. Besides, Rebekah told him to leave and get to town.

What seemed an eternity later, Nate galloped around a corral attached to the livery and headed into the main part of town. The first street he came to looked quiet with merely a handful of people lingering on the boardwalks and alleys facing west. He urged his horse down a narrow road, only to have to rein him around several wagons lining the dirt street. Muddy was a better description. A crowd gathered in front of what appeared to be the biggest saloon on the sprawling street. He heeled his mount as close as he dared and dismounted.

Wading through the group, excusing himself several times over, Nate finally made it to the center of the ruckus. Two men stood toe to toe, fists raised. The sheriff and an older gentleman tussled off to the side with another young man whose wild swings cut harmlessly through the air. The sheriff finally pulled his pistol and stuck the barrel in the man's face.

Nate moved to help since everyone else seemed more interested in watching than lending a hand. "You can stop right now." His gruffest voice didn't stop the punch headed his way. Nate ducked and landed his left fist on the young man's nose. With his right hand, he pulled his pistol and aimed it at the other man. The first man ended up in the mud with a bloody nose.

The second man raised his hands and backed away. "Hold on. I was just trying to protect my sister's honor." He moved next to a very young and terrified woman. Wide-eyed, she all but climbed under her brother's arm.

Nate glanced around, taking note of several faces in the crowd. Some looked completely innocent, while others wore hard expressions that caused suspicion. He'd try to seek them out later for further investigation.

The sheriff had his man by the collar, the older gentleman at the ready if needed. The sheriff motioned to Nate. "Put your gun away." When Nate obeyed, the sheriff holstered his own and reached down to grab the other man, who jerked away.

The young man eyed him with a crooked grin. "You like swimming with your clothes on?"

Nate ignored the comment and yanked the young man to his feet. "Sheriff, I'd be happy to help you get these two to your office." Under orders not to reveal who he really was, Nate did his best to act like a concerned citizen and nothing more.

The sheriff eyed him a moment, then nodded. "I'd be obliged." He looked around before scooping up a pistol from the ground and shoving it in his gun belt. He pushed his man into motion. "What'd I tell you two about drinking too much?"

"Aw, Sheriff, we was just trying to tell the girl she was pretty."

"Yeah, well, you crossed the line when you grabbed her, and you landed yourself in jail when you pulled your gun and tried to shoot her brother."

Nate gritted his teeth, fighting the desire to flatten the young men again. Fools. Actions like this would be the worst part of his job as a deputy marshal. Patience wasn't a strong character trait for him lately. Maybe one day he'd get it back.

The way the young men meandered into the cell and flopped

onto the cots told Nate this wasn't the first time they'd called the place home. If they didn't take this time to learn their lesson, they just might see the rest of their life through bars—that is, if they managed to keep their necks off the end of a rope. The door clanged shut and the keys rattled in the lock. The boys never flinched. What a waste.

The sheriff dropped the keys in a drawer of his battered desk. After slamming the drawer closed, he scrutinized Nate from head to toe. "Appreciate the help." He held out his hand. "Sheriff Caldwell."

Nate accepted a firm, strong handshake. "Nathaniel Kirkland." He crossed his arms, ready to get some answers to his questions. The sooner the better—especially from the sheriff. He'd been told to keep an eye on the lawman and consider him a suspect. "I would imagine you're always on the ready for scuffles like this. Or worse?"

The sheriff didn't look happy. "Meaning?"

That didn't come out right. Sounded like he'd questioned the sheriff's abilities. Nate needed to smooth the ruffled feathers. "I just meant that you probably have to stay on guard since miners bring their finds into town much of the time. I imagine the less-than-honest are always looking for easy money."

"And what would you know about that?"

This wasn't going well at all. He shrugged, hoping for nonchalance. "I read the papers."

The same gentleman who helped the sheriff swung in off the street. "You just passing through?"

Glad for the interruption, Nate shrugged. "Not sure. Thought I'd rest up here a bit. Maybe work for some pocket money before I move on."

"Good. We could use more men like you around here." The gentleman held out his hand. "Perry Weaver."

The name sounded familiar. Nate searched his mind as he shook the man's hand. "You Rebekah and Andrew's father?"

Mr. Weaver frowned. "I am. How would you know that?"

Nate motioned to his damp clothing. "I fished them out of the river earlier. Andrew is quite a character."

"He is that." Mr. Weaver cocked his head. "Why were they in the river?"

"Oh now," he said with a smirk, "I wouldn't want to take away the boy's chance at telling his own story. Whatever he embellishes on, I'm sure your daughter will rein in toward the truth."

Mr. Weaver grinned. "Sounds like you were able to get to know them both well during your short visit."

"I doubt that, but I have some knowledge about how it goes between siblings."

Crossing his arms, Mr. Weaver leaned against the desk. The sheriff looked annoyed, but Mr. Weaver didn't appear to care. "You say you'd like a job?"

This was getting interesting. His trip here might work out exactly as his superiors had hoped. "Possibly."

"I own the livery and the dry goods store next to it. I could use some help in the livery if you're willing. Do you have experience?"

Nate's heart thumped. Fortune was smiling on him, which was good since the Lord sure didn't. "As a matter of fact, I used to help my father work the forge. We did our own shoeing and wagon repair, along with any other metal work that was needed."

"Well, if God isn't full of blessings." Mr. Weaver stood and clapped Nate on the shoulder. "Come to supper tonight. We'll talk wages. You find a place to stay yet?"

"Ah, well, no sir." This was moving too fast.

"You're welcome to use my oldest son's bed until you find a place."

Way too fast. "No, sir, I couldn't do that."

"No? Then you can stay in our barn or livery. Up to you." He turned and reached to shake the sheriff's hand. "Time to get back to work, Paul. I'd invite you to supper too, but it appears you'll be busy for a while." He cocked his head toward the cell, then strode to the door and held out his hand. "After you, Nathaniel."

"Please call me Nate."

Mr. Weaver nodded. "Nate it is. Follow me and I'll introduce you to your new workplace before you meet the rest of the family."

Nate trailed behind his new boss. In the span of a few short hours, he'd fished two people out of a river, broken up a fight, and agreed to a job offer. All three left him feeling like he'd been swept up in a twister and had yet to find out just where he'd land.

Chapter Four

Rebekah's belly quivered as she struggled to force herself to turn around. Daddy had brought guests home for a meal many times before but never one that could steal the words from her mouth with a mere look. His eyes—the pale green shade such a sharp contrast to his dark hair—

"Rebekah, honey." Amusement colored Daddy's voice. "You gonna keep those potatoes all to yourself, or do you plan on bringing them over here for all of us to enjoy?"

Heat worse than the flames that puckered her skin flooded her neck and face. Now how was she going to be able to join them? And how could Daddy embarrass her like that? The only good thing about this whole evening was that she'd had time to clean up from her dunking before they arrived. She took a deep breath, prayed her face wasn't as red as she figured, and headed to the table. Her mother's sympathetic expression helped. At least someone in the house understood.

"Well, my goodness, Daddy." She set the bowl on the table. "If I'd known you were near to starving, I'd have rushed a little faster."

As she took her seat, she caught her father's smirk and wink. The rascal. He knew exactly how his comment would affect her. But did he realize the effect his guest was having on her? More than likely, especially if her mother recognized her turmoil.

After blessing the food, her father speared her with another teasing look. "So, Rebekah, Nate tells me you decided to learn to swim today."

What was Daddy trying to do to her?

Andrew laughed and banged the table with his hand. "You shoulda seen it, Daddy. I think she scared the fish so bad, they won't come back for months."

Daddy stabbed a slice of meat and passed the platter to Nate. "And what exactly were *you* doing in there, Andrew? Trying to catch them barehanded?"

The entire meal passed with Andrew giving his version of the day's misfortunes. Poor Nate didn't get to say a word unless their father specifically asked him a question. He sat, one forearm on the table, chewing and smiling as he shoveled in the meal. He appeared to be enjoying himself, but Rebekah hoped he wasn't eating as fast as he could because he was miserably bored and couldn't wait to escape.

Her mother went for the dessert while Rebekah cleared the table. The fact that Nate's plate was all but licked clean made her feel good. He must have liked her potatoes. In the midst of the clanking of plates and clinking of silverware as she collected them, Andrew kept on talking. If only Daddy would stop Andrew, she could learn more about Nate.

As if reading her mind, Daddy leaned his elbows on the table without touching the pie Mama placed in front of him. "So tell me, Nate, what brings you to the area?"

Rebekah paused halfway to the counter at Daddy's question, then rushed the remaining distance, shoved the dishes onto the counter, and hurried back to the table, not wanting to miss a word.

Nate already had a bite of Mama's dried apple pie in his mouth. He swallowed quickly.

SILVER CITY
1869
ID

"The gold and silver."

Rebekah's heart fell. Another fortune seeker. She'd hoped for something a bit more exciting, fascinating even, from the man who'd risked his life to save theirs. A down-to-earth reason would have been more admirable than his answer. Too many men had come to town with a sparkle in their eyes to match that of the treasure they sought, only to leave more broke and broken than when they arrived. She wanted better for Nate than for him to leave town with nothing to show for his efforts except calloused hands and a stiff back.

Daddy nodded. "Understandable. We get a lot of men coming through town with that very purpose in mind. Almost as many leave for the same reason. Making a living in the mining business is difficult at best. I know firsthand. That's why I had to start the livery. It's not as exciting as finding gold, but the income is a bit more steady."

"So I've heard." Nate looked thoughtful as he took another bite. "I've also read about trouble in the area. Fires, explosions, cave-ins—some think they're done on purpose. Do I need to be wary?"

Rebekah held her breath as she glanced at her mother. Her parents often discussed the new dangers that came with mining. Fights over claims and labor wages had worsened over the years. Worry deepened the lines on Mama's face every time Daddy spent a day working in the mine he owned with his partner, Reuben Buckley. Most miners hounded the sheriff about investigating the so-called accidents. So far, the sheriff wasn't in too much of a hurry to do his job.

After several moments of silence, Daddy picked up his fork. "It's always a good idea to be on the alert when mining, Nate. Never forget that." His head dipping, he took a large bite and chewed thoughtfully, his gaze carrying him far away.

Other than the clink of forks against plates, not a sound was made as Daddy's heavy words of warning continued to roll through the room like echoes of thunder.

With a helpless expression, Mama held the pie plate out to Nate. He promptly waved it away, shaking his head. "I couldn't possibly eat another bite, Mrs. Weaver, but thank you. This was by far the best meal I've had in a mighty long time."

Mama smiled her pleasure. "Do you have family nearby, Nate?"

Anyone not watching with Rebekah's interest wouldn't have noticed the immediate change in Nate, the way his eyes hardened and his body tensed. She caught all of it, even the tightening lips and clenching jaw. She blinked to make sure she wasn't mistaken, except when she opened her eyes, all was back to normal. He'd even relaxed against the back of his chair.

"My dad and brother died in Colorado several years ago. When I was old enough to take care of myself, my mother moved back East to be closer to family. She's remarried now."

Mama looked horrified. "I'm sorry about your loss."

Nate shook his head. "Thank you. It makes it easier knowing Mother's happy again."

The lighthearted atmosphere they'd enjoyed most of the evening disappeared quicker than Andrew when he was in trouble. To Rebekah's disappointment, the conversation grew stilted with no more details about Nate's family slipping in to flavor the feast.

Nate pushed his chair back and stood. "If I'm going to find a room, I'd better get going. Perry, thanks again for the invitation. Mrs. Weaver, you're a wonderful cook. Thank you."

"You're welcome."

Daddy walked him to the door, letting in the cool night air as they said their good-byes in the opening. After shaking Nate's hand, Daddy closed the door and returned to the table. "Nice young man. I look forward to working with him in the livery."

Rebekah's ears tingled, and her heart leapt. Nate would be working in the livery. Daddy hadn't said a word until now. The evening brightened again. Humming, she ignored her mother's knowing manner as she heated water to wash the dishes.

* * * * *

Nate blew out a long breath as he retrieved his horse. He'd never get used to people asking about his family, no matter how nice the person doing the questioning. The Weaver family proved to be some of the best. Thanks to a wonderful evening, Nate had just shortened his suspect list.

He'd felt a bit underhanded, misleading them about his reason for being in town and asking about the mine trouble like he did, but he consoled himself with the fact that he hadn't lied. Not really. They'd drawn their own conclusions from the minuscule amount of information he'd offered. Once he found the culprits causing all the trouble, he could tell them the whole truth.

And speaking of the truth, his curiosity about Rebekah and her burn scars increased all through the meal. She said very little beyond defending herself against her brother's exaggerated claims of the creek incident, but she intrigued him all the more when she revealed her good sense of humor. To go through an obvious tragedy and come out smiling deserved anyone's admiration. Though the scars were difficult to look at, the person behind them left Nate impressed and wanting to know more. Did she get them from one of the mining skirmishes? Had she gotten too close? He might never find out, but it didn't keep his mind from wondering.

The silver disk she wore on her necklace added yet another question. He could see something written on the odd ornament, but in the dim lighting, the inscription was unclear. It shouldn't matter, but he wanted to know its significance. And not only that, but in a mining town, wearing something of value could put one's life in danger.

North along Jordan Street, toward the Idaho Hotel Mr. Weaver mentioned, a row of lamplights burned, their oily odor heavy on the night air. The need to lean back a bit in his saddle let Nate know he rode downhill. He couldn't wait until morning to get a better look at his new but temporary home. From what he'd seen earlier and could tell now, most of the town was built on a slant. He'd be surprised if there was a flat place in the entire town, which seemed to sprawl a good distance each direction.

Not many people wandered in this area. By the sounds drifting toward him, most of the town's night owls occupied the next street over, back toward the saloon, where the fight had taken place. If he weren't so tired, he'd join them for a while for the chance to meet more of the residents. But drinking men wearing guns were dangerous, and he'd have to be prepared for trouble. A good night's sleep was just what he needed for that type of confrontation.

Hearing a distant rumbling, he reined in his horse and glanced back, certain what he'd heard was another explosion, most likely from one of the mines. South of town, low on the ridgeline, a fiery glow dimmed the shimmer of stars. Rather than wait for the sheriff and possibly give away his identity, Nate spurred his horse past the Weavers and up the side of the mountain. He'd somehow investigate the cause, even if it meant helping to put out a fire or digging in the dirt for answers.

Chapter Five

....

Rebekah rushed through breakfast, nearly choking on her dry biscuit as she swallowed too soon. She tried to cover up with a cough while blowing her nose. Never would she admit out loud that the sooner she got to work, the sooner she'd see Nate.

Mama wiped her mouth. "If you're getting sick from your dunking yesterday, I could work for you today."

"I'm not getting sick," Rebekah said in a burst, then peeked to see if her mother had noticed.

Mama buried a smile in her napkin. Sneaky woman.

Rebekah could play the game too. She motioned around the cabin. "But if you'd like me to stay and do some cleaning while you go—"

"No, thank you. I was on my feet all day yesterday until your father sent me home. I think I'll stay home today."

Rebekah eyed her mother over the rim of her glass. She'd been looking tired lately. Saying a silent prayer for Mama's health, Rebekah stood, cleared the table, and made short work of washing the breakfast dishes. Much as she wanted to get to the store, she'd rather give Mama a rest. With Daddy leaving early instead of staying to eat a bite, she had less to clean up than usual. She wanted to ask why Daddy didn't stay for breakfast, but she had the awful feeling it had something to do with the mining troubles, and there was no need to add more worries to the load Mama already carried.

"All right, I guess I'll go open the store, unless there's something you need me to do." At Mama's nod, Rebekah gave Mama a kiss on the cheek, noting her temperature felt normal. *Thank You, Lord.*

"I'm fine, dear. I'll just do some mending before I start on lunch. Look for Andrew to bring it to you about noon."

Rebekah wrapped her shawl around her shoulders. "Sounds perfect."

Andrew had already run off outside. She headed to the barn for a fast chat with him before starting work. Mama didn't need to be chasing him around for any reason.

Opening the barn door, she spied Andrew, rope in hand, staring up at the rafters. "And just what do you plan on doing once you get that rope over the beam?"

Like a startled rabbit, Andrew jumped and hid the end behind his back. Rebekah grinned as she shuffled through the fresh straw strewn across the barn floor, knowing she'd have to pluck several stems from the hem of her skirt. "Too late. I already saw what you were doing."

His bottom lip jutted out. "I just wanted to make a swing. Daddy's been too busy."

He was right about that. Too bad Michael hadn't stayed for the summer instead of leaving for school a couple months early. He used to do just this sort of thing for Andrew. She'd do it for him if she knew how. Besides, leaving the job for Andrew would give him something harmless to work on for a while. She wrapped her arm around his shoulders. "Just be careful, all right?"

He nodded.

"I've got to get to work. Promise you'll be good so Mama doesn't have to get after you."

He batted his long lashes. "I promise."

Rascal. He knew how to get to her. She kissed the end of his nose. He pulled away and scrubbed his face with his sleeve. "Ew, Bek. Don't do that."

"Behave yourself, or I'll do it in front of everyone in town."

Eyes wide, he shook his head. "I'll be good."

She moved to give him a hug. He ducked under her arm and scooted away, his expression revealing his disgust. If she wasn't in such a hurry to get to work, she'd chase him down for the chance to pester him, like he always did her. Instead, she waved and scurried out the door.

Heart nearly fluttering at the idea of seeing Nate, Rebekah wondered why she'd reacted so strongly toward him. Thousands of men had come and gone through Silver, but none had caught her attention like Nate. Not that any man had given her more than a second glance once they saw her face. Even Nate had difficulty looking at her, but at least he tried. Over the past year, she'd come to realize the beauty inside a person was more important than outward appearances. Maybe Nate, a true gentleman, would have the ability to see beyond the surface. Only time would provide the answer.

Preoccupied with her thoughts, the walk didn't seem nearly as long as usual, yet Rebekah felt she'd never get there. A glance reminded her to mention to her father that the place could use a fresh coat of paint. Actually, most of the buildings in town needed to be brightened up a bit. Too late she realized the brass knob didn't turn in her hand and she nearly smacked her nose on the window. Odd. Daddy usually had the store open for her. Searching the bottom of her bag, she found the key, unlocked the door, and stepped inside. "Daddy?"

Instead of his usual cheerful greeting, a strange quiet met her ears, and no lamp burned to light the way to the back. Heart now hammering, Rebekah wound her way through a row of barrels filled with rice and flour to the storage room.

"Daddy, are you here?"

With the leather apron Daddy used in the livery still dangling from the peg and no coat hanging in its place, Rebekah knew her father hadn't been to the store this morning. She raced to the side door. Surely she'd find him in the livery. Maybe he'd forgotten to open the store because of helping Nate get started with his new job.

In moments, she was across the alley and inside the livery. Her father, along with Sheriff Caldwell and Mr. Gilmore, stood at the water trough at the front, plying Nate with questions while he scrubbed his face and hands, both black. Nate's clothes were in the same grubby condition.

Rebekah found her voice. "Daddy?"

He craned his neck around the group. "Rebekah?" He glanced at the sky. "I'm sorry, honey. I lost track of time. I'll open the store now."

"That's all right. I've got it." She continued to stare at Nate until her father stepped between them. His blockade didn't stop her curiosity. "What happened?"

He urged her toward the store with a hand on her back. "I'll come talk to you later."

"Daddy." She stared him square in the eyes. "I'm not a little girl anymore."

He examined her face, his own becoming contrite. "No, you're not. I apologize." He glanced behind him. "One of the mills burned down during the night. Nate saw it when he left our house and went to help."

Concern forced her to move the few steps to Nate's side. "Were you hurt?"

Nate straightened from the trough and shook the water from his hands. Rebekah untied her apron and handed it to him. He looked skeptical.

"I can get another from the store. Go ahead and use this to dry off."

He took it from her. "Thank you."

Black soot smeared the cloth as he wiped his face, neck, and hands. She'd never get it white again, but for the first time, it didn't matter. Some of the soot remained around his eyes, and a day's growth of beard darkened his face, giving him a rugged look. Not to mention it made his pale green eyes seem even lighter. Goodness, what this man did to her insides.

"I'm fine."

Rebekah blinked several times in an attempt to focus. "Pardon?"

Nate grinned, showing his even, white teeth. "You asked if I was hurt. I'm not."

"Right." *Get ahold of yourself!* "I'm glad."

"Rebekah, honey?" Daddy clasped her elbow and turned her to face him. She couldn't help but see the humor gleaming from his eyes. "Nate will need a change of clothes. Would you get a shirt and trousers from the store?"

He'd just given her a chance to escape and pull herself together. Besides, the other men were now staring. "I'll do it right away."

She nearly ran from the livery. What was wrong with her? She was acting like such a fool. The men were all probably having a good laugh at her expense right now. Stopping in the alley between the two buildings long enough to take a deep breath, Rebekah determined then and there not to lose control of her emotions again. Getting burned a year ago had taught her many things, one of them being self-discipline. She'd made it through many painful months by keeping her mind captive. Time to practice that little trick again.

Help me, Lord.

Chapter Six

....

Nate stepped from the stall while still tucking the new shirt into his new trousers. Exhaustion drained his body of strength and made his mind sluggish. He'd spent most of yesterday in the saddle, fished Rebekah and Andrew from the creek, and worked the night fighting a fire. He didn't know how he'd make it through the day. But make it he would. He had a job to do.

Still, he paused to finger the white apron draped over the stall next to his blackened clothes. The memory of Rebekah's scent as he wiped his face stayed with him, so sweet—

"Why don't you get a room at the hotel and sleep some, Nate?" Perry's narrowed eyes showed concern. "You've got to be tired."

"Thanks, Perry, but I'm still worked up. I doubt I could sleep for a while. Besides, I never got a chance to check in at a hotel."

"Good." The sheriff pushed away from the doorway. "Maybe now you can tell me what happened up there."

Nate scooped his filthy clothes from the stall, all the while wondering why the sheriff didn't go up to the mill and ask the owners and workers his questions. The lack of effort Nate had seen in the sheriff since his arrival yesterday only added to his suspicion of the man.

"Can't tell you much."

"Why?" The sheriff hooked his thumbs in his gun belt and rocked back on his heels, chest out. "Because you're involved?"

Nate fought a laugh. He'd seen too many men who acted tough behind a gun and star, only to cower or hide when those items were removed. The snort he heard from the gray-haired man at the doorway let Nate know he must have thought the same.

"He was with me since he arrived in town, Paul." Perry's glare revealed his opinion of the sheriff's accusation. "Why don't you do your job and investigate the scene?"

His bluster fleeing, Sheriff Caldwell's chest sank into his ribs. He cleared his throat. "I will. Just as soon as I get some information out of this young man." He turned toward Nate. "Well?"

Perry never called the sheriff by his title. A lack of respect maybe? Nate tucked the information into his memory. "I can't say much because they wouldn't tell me much. Said I was from the outside and couldn't be trusted."

The sheriff's smug expression irritated him. Nate debated how much more to share, but he did want a response to the next tidbit.

"I did overhear a couple men say something about Mr. Briggs getting revenge." He paused. "Is Mr. Briggs the owner of the mill?"

Perry's thick, work-roughened fingers rasped along his whiskered chin. "No, he owns one of the bigger mines farther up the mountain."

The elderly man still at the door finally joined them. "So they accepted your help but not your confidence. Not a surprise in these parts, young man." He held out his hand. "Name's Henry Gilmore, and if no one else has thanked you for your help out there, I will."

Nate shook the man's hand, impressed with his stature and proper speech. "Nate Kirkland."

Mr. Gilmore pulled a pipe and pouch from his pocket. "You helped the sheriff yesterday with those two ruffians."

"I tried, sir."

As Mr. Gilmore tamped tobacco into his pipe, Nate mulled how some men could garner respect by merely carrying themselves with distinction and authority. His father used to be like that. Others, like the sheriff, thought respect came with a badge and a gun. He made another mental note to store that information.

Once the pipe was lit, Mr. Gilmore squinted against the smoke. "You ought to hire this man, Sheriff. He's worth all your deputies put together."

The sheriff snorted, his pudgy hands waving away the comment. "I've got work to do." He stomped out of the livery.

Perry trailed close behind, nearly stepping on his heels and looking very much like he wanted to knock him to the ground. "You still have those boys in jail?"

"Nope. I turned them loose when they sobered up." The sheriff shrugged. "Their fine was paid." He pulled himself onto his horse and galloped away.

No one commented on the fact that the sheriff headed into town instead of toward the burned-down mill. Nate found that intriguing.

Perry returned, shaking his head, and perched on a barrel. "Sometimes I wonder how he manages to keep that badge."

Mr. Gilmore puffed on his pipe, staring off at nothing. "Reminds me of some cannonballs we faced in the war." He puffed once more, then used the mouthpiece to point at them. "We'd hear the explosion of one fired from a cannon, and fear would tighten our bellies. The shrapnel from those things could tear a man in half. Yet time and again the fuse wouldn't light, and the ball would roll past, doing no more damage than possibly busting the leg of a man who wasn't fast enough to jump out of the way."

Once again, he seemed to stare off at some distant memory, massaging the bowl of his pipe with his thumb. "I remember one such cannonball rolling right past me." He shook his head at the recollection. "My mouth was so dry I couldn't swallow, waiting for that thing to blow me apart. It stopped not ten feet from me and never went off." One corner of his mouth twitched. "My legs went weak, and my knees gave out." He chuckled and sucked the end of his pipe. "Those times taught me and my men a good lesson—one we all could remember."

The old man had Nate's complete attention. "What lesson is that, sir?"

Smoke billowed around Mr. Gilmore's head. "Not everything is as it appears, young man. Most times, you get exactly what you expect. But every so often, something or someone comes along that's unproductive, a useless lump. Trouble is, you have to watch out for both, just in case."

Nate could listen to this man's stories all day, especially stories about the war. Dad rarely wanted to talk about the days he fought, but the times he did talk, Nate was all ears. And now Mr. Gilmore was on his way out the door, putting an end to his storytelling.

"Time to get to work, men. I need to get my shop opened up, so I can make a dollar or two today." He hauled himself up on his horse and pointed at Nate with his pipe. "If Perry ever gives you some time off, young man, come see me. I like nothing better than a good listener." Mr. Gilmore's chuckle followed him down the street.

A grin lit Perry's face. "Gilmore could talk a dead man back to life." He shook his head. "Trouble is, I'd want to be there to hear every word. He's an interesting fellow."

"I can see that already." Curiosity about what the former war hero did to make a living made Nate ask, "What kind of shop does he run?"

"He has two. One he loves, and one to help make ends meet."

"And they are…"

Perry smiled. "He spends most of his time in his tobacco and smoke shop, usually sitting in a fog of his own making, but he also owns the bath and laundry house. If he's not busy making a sale, you'll find him sitting on the boardwalk puffing on his pipe, ready to strike up a conversation with anyone who slows long enough to hear him speak."

Before Nate could respond, an odd-looking character ambled in the back door, one he recalled seeing on the boardwalk yesterday at the scuffle. Dressed in ragged clothing, the man might reach five feet if he stood on tiptoe. But the look in his eyes alarmed Nate. Whether frantic or threatening, he couldn't tell, but even a short man could be dangerous with a weapon. Nate reached for his holster, ready in case the man brought trouble with him, but his pistol still lay in the stall where he put it when he changed his clothes. While trying to determine if he should lunge for it, Nate watched Perry turn, then jump off the barrel.

"Thomas." The two men shook hands. "Where'd you disappear to so early? I thought sure I'd catch you before you were off and running for the day."

Thomas didn't answer but eyed Nate with suspicion.

Perry stepped between them. "I'm sorry. Thomas, this is my new livery hand, Nate Kirkland. Nate, this is my all-around handyman, Thomas Beard. He calls the livery home each night." Perry motioned to the loft over their heads.

Nate held out his hand. "Nice to meet you, Thomas."

Thomas hesitated before responding. "Here, too." They shook. "You the man I heard tell about helping with the fire?"

Thomas didn't sound too educated. A man like that often grew desperate to put money in his pocket. Even though he was a friend of Perry's, Nate mentally added Thomas to his list of suspects, at least until he could check out the man and his background.

Nate shrugged. "Could be. I was there."

Still eyeing Nate, Thomas bobbed his bushy head. "Uh-huh. They said an outside man showed up, nosing around."

Nate swung between alarm and anger. He'd have to be more nonchalant with his questions or he'd blow his cover. But who did this Thomas think he was? He acted more like a sheriff than the sheriff. Maybe he was trying to protect his own backside.

Ready to throw out a few questions of his own, Nate had to bite his tongue when Perry jumped into the conversation.

"How do you know all this, Thomas? You been up there?"

Nate listened for the answer with great interest, but Thomas's response was a tight-lipped grimace. As he waited with impatience for information that might be significant, Nate spied a cat easing along the wall. Its gray color almost made the cat invisible, blending with the livery wood. If it weren't for the white splotch on its side and the tip of its flicking tail, Nate might have missed it altogether.

Crouched as if ready to pounce, the cat stared toward the stall that held Nate's dirty clothing. Nate followed the wall and spotted a mouse scurrying through the straw, stopping every so often to sniff. Maybe more tired than he realized, he couldn't look away from the scene as he tried to take in the hum of voices talking about the fire. Inch by inch, the cat crept forward, finally lunging.

Surprise rolled through Nate when the cat's head slammed

against the lowest board of the stall. It sprawled, then regained its footing before shaking its head. The mouse scampered away, unharmed. Amusement bubbled up in Nate's chest. He'd never seen anything so unusual. That mouse should have been breakfast.

"Nate?"

He glanced at Perry for only a second before returning to the cat, not wanting to miss anything. "Yes?"

"Something wrong?"

Nate grinned and aimed his thumb toward the hapless cat. "Your cat needs some hunting lessons."

The cat shook its head one more time then turned toward Nate. As the animal blinked at him, Nate did the same, wondering if he was seeing things. The cat was cross-eyed. No wonder he couldn't catch that mouse.

Thomas scooped the feline up in his arms and ruffled its ears. Both of them stared at him.

"What?" Nate asked.

Thomas shrugged, still petting the cat. "It's just that Mercy doesn't usually like anyone."

Nate chuckled. "The cat's name is Mercy?"

For the first time, Thomas managed a bit of a smile. "Got its name when Mrs. Weaver saw it and said, 'Mercy sakes.' It stuck."

Nate threw his head back and laughed. "Perfect."

Perry reached to scratch its head. "She'd starve if we didn't feed her."

"So I noticed."

Nate decided it was time to meet the feline, especially if they were going to attempt to work together in the same building. Before he could touch it, the animal leapt from Thomas's arms into Nate's.

He prepared for the claws to draw blood. Instead, the cat ran its nose against his chin and continued purring.

Perry shook his head. "Well, I'll be. If Mercy likes you, you must be all right."

After patting the cat's head, Nate placed it on the ground and wiped his chin with his sleeve. "Glad I passed inspection."

The cat began winding its way around each of Nate's legs. He didn't dare nudge it away. These two men obviously thought the world of the feline. He tried to ignore it. "So Tom, any news on how that fire started?"

By the man's expression, he'd asked the wrong question.

"The name's Thomas, and like I told Perry, the owner is still trying to find out how it started."

Nate raised his brows. "Sorry. I guess I missed hearing that."

The little man sure was prickly. In Nate's mind, that was another count against him and raised even more suspicion. Time for more digging. "How long have you been in Silver City? I take it you're not a newcomer since they'll talk to you."

By Thomas's frown and curled lip, he didn't like Nate much. "It's been awhile."

"You came for the gold?"

"I need money to live, same as anyone." Thomas crossed his arms. "What brings you here?"

The tension in the air nearly crackled. Nate wasn't sure what he'd done to make Thomas dislike him so much, but he'd keep a close eye on the man's comings and goings.

Perry clapped Thomas on the back. "Why don't you go see if there's any of my wife's biscuits and gravy left?"

Thomas cast a look over his shoulder at Nate before he wandered out the side door. Nate had no idea why his questions upset Thomas so, but they'd have to find a way to get along. At least until he finished his job.

"And you"—Perry moved right in front of him—"climb up in the loft and get some sleep. I'll wake you in a couple hours. If your mind is anywhere near as fuzzy as your eyes look, you're headed for an accident, and I know neither of us wants that."

With a grin, Nate nodded. "All right. You win. I could use a bit of rest."

He'd managed two steps up the ladder when another man entered from the back, looking dirtier than Nate had after fighting a fire all night. When Perry didn't introduce them but led the filthy man back out of the livery, Nate returned to the stall for his gun. No need to take chances. He didn't know anyone in this town well enough to trust with his life except maybe Perry. Even so, the way Perry cast that look over his shoulder at Nate while leading the stranger out stirred a bit of suspicion.

Nate shoved a wad of straw under his head for a pillow, wondering if he'd ever be able to fall asleep—or solve this case. Less than a day and he had enough suspicious people around him to keep sleep at bay until he left town.

Chapter Seven

....

Rebekah would have recognized the clomping coming down the boardwalk anywhere. Why Andrew insisted on wearing boots two sizes too big was beyond her. Drumming her fingers on the counter, she prepared to light into her little brother for disturbing Mama. Since it was nowhere near lunch time, that could be the only reason he'd come so early.

Andrew pushed through the door, his lips puckered as he practiced his shrill whistle. The moment he saw her, a wide grin replaced the pucker. "Hi, Bek."

For all she was worth, Rebekah fought to hang onto her scolding expression, because she adored the freckle-faced rascal more than she dared let him know. His smile got to her every time. She'd give him a little wiggle room to get out of trouble. But only a little.

"What brings you by so early? You bothering Mama?"

The smile disappeared. "No."

"Do I need to take you down the street and kiss you in front of everyone?"

Andrew waved his hands in front of him and took a step back. "No, Bek. I promise. I didn't do nothing. Mama just told me to come see if you needed any help and that I should go back before noon for the food."

Rebekah believed him, every word, which brought back the

worry for her mother. Something wasn't right. She could feel it. Mama had done a lot of sleeping during her pregnancy with Andrew. But with Mama's age being forty-three, she'd be too old for babies. Time would tell.

Head tilted, one eye half-closed in a squint, Andrew peered up at her. "Am I in trouble?"

She waved him over, just in time, it seemed, as two burly men entered. As usual, she prepared for their reaction to the scar on her face. She turned her head a bit, putting her left cheek toward the shadows.

"May I help you?"

One of them rattled off the list as they approached, finally setting a piece of paper on the counter. She picked it up and read everything they mentioned as well as a few they forgot. Either they worked for one of the big mine owners up War Eagle Mountain, or these were two new hopefuls who didn't want to return for supplies for a good long time.

She looked up. "I'll get right on this."

Both men stared with open mouths. Finally, the heavier of the two jabbed the other with his thumb, and they both wandered away. They needn't have. Without a doubt, they wouldn't look her in the eyes again for the duration of their stay, which was fine with her. Then she wouldn't have to pretend she didn't notice their aversion.

Many of the items they needed were in large, heavy bags, like the beans, flour, and coffee. She could handle retrieving them from the shelves in the storage room, but if Daddy caught her, she'd risk a tongue-lashing.

"Andrew, would you mind entertaining these men while I gather their supplies?"

They didn't need entertaining, but she refused to leave the store unattended for even a moment while she went in search of Daddy. More often than she cared to admit, people managed to pilfer items from right under her nose. She wasn't about to give anyone an unguarded opportunity to clean out the store.

Andrew gave her the response she expected—a wide grin just before he raced their way. The last thing she heard as she headed into the back room was her little brother asking the men if they wanted to see him make his armpit burp. As the men laughed, she stifled a giggle and went in search of her father.

"I don't know, Rube."

Rebekah stopped before reaching the back door. Her father's partner, Reuben Buckley, rarely came to town. Maybe she shouldn't interrupt.

"We shouldn't get involved," her father said. "That last dispute was rough. A man was shot and killed. If it weren't for the governor sending troops, who knows how much worse it would have gotten. You know full well I don't think that livery fire was an accident. And my little girl paid the price."

Chills raced from Rebekah's scalp all along her arms and legs. What was Daddy saying? Her burns weren't an accident? Stomach churning and knees weak, she slumped against a shelf, knocking off its contents.

Daddy raced inside, and the color drained from his face. "Rebekah? What…?" His throat worked. He grasped her arms. "You weren't meant to hear that."

She shook her head as tears scalded the rims of her eyes. She hadn't wept about her burns in months. How could she cry when she'd run out of tears? Now a fresh supply lay at the ready, just when she thought herself healed both physically and emotionally.

"Why didn't you tell me?" Daddy tried to pull her into a hug, but she pushed at his chest. "Why keep it a secret?"

"You were dealing with so much already, what with the pain." He gestured toward her cheek. "And such—" His hands fell to his sides. "I'm sorry, sweetheart. I never wanted you to be afraid to live here."

She crouched to pick up the fallen items. Her father joined her, scooping them into his arms and replacing them on the shelf. Then he helped her to her feet. She needed time to think, to run all the new information through her mind uninterrupted. But first she wanted to know more.

"Who did it?"

"I'm not sure."

She frowned. "Who do you think did it?"

His eyes sought the ground as his sigh hissed through the air, his shoulders slumping as if he'd put in a full day at the mine. He finally looked at her, his eyes filled with concern. "That fire wasn't meant for you, Rebekah."

Her heart sank. Then the fire was meant to hurt Daddy, which didn't make her feel any better. She searched his face and then his eyes. He loved her and didn't plan to tell her more; that was clear. At least not now. Wondering what, or who, he feared, she finally nodded. Maybe one day she'd know the whole truth. Today wouldn't be that day.

Reuben stepped through the doorway. He peeled off his hat and dipped his head. "H–h–howdy, M–miss B–bek."

Besides Andrew, Reuben was the only person to shorten her name. She figured his stutter had something to do with it. She didn't mind. Daddy's mining partner was a kind man. She gave him a quick hug.

"Good to see you, Reuben."

For years she'd called him Mr. Buckley, only to have him scowl. A sound scolding followed, the memory of which still burned her ears. Today she received a wide, toothless smile.

She held the list out to her father. "There's a couple men inside who need this filled. Most of the items are in bulk. If you'd ever let me—"

"I'll get this if you'll help Reuben collect his supplies." Daddy kissed her good cheek as he slipped by her on his way back to the store.

Rebekah slipped her arm through Reuben's. "I think I ended up with the better deal."

When she asked Reuben about his list, it sounded as if he didn't need many supplies, making her think the man only came to town to ask her father questions. If she thought Reuben would talk to her, she'd ask him some of her own. But past experience told her he'd be tight-lipped about anything he figured wasn't his business.

When they reached the store, Daddy eased back to her. "What's Andrew doing here already? He been pestering his mama?"

If her mother's health weren't such a concern, Rebekah might have found his question humorous. "He assured me he was good, that Mama sent him to see if I needed any help." When Daddy only nodded, she decided to ask the question she'd been pondering the last couple of days. "Has Mama been complaining of feeling sick or anything?"

Daddy frowned. "No. Why?"

She shrugged. "She seems more tired lately."

Daddy looked worried. So he hadn't noticed. Maybe she shouldn't have said anything.

He squeezed her hand and headed for the supply room at the back of the store. "I'll finish with these two men. Then if you don't mind watching the place, I aim to run home and check on her."

"That sounds like a fine idea."

Daddy could be shortsighted sometimes, probably from being too busy, but he loved Mama dearly, and for that, Rebekah could forgive him anything. She had to wonder, though, if he also had kept the secret from Mama about the fire not being an accident. That new information would probably ride Rebekah's mind for the rest of the day and beyond.

After she'd finished collecting Reuben's supplies, Rebekah dropped a handful of hard candy at the top of his canvas bag, knowing his fondness for sweets. She glanced toward the doorway where he stood and received another wide grin. For an older man—she guessed him close to sixty—many times he reminded her of a child.

She handed Reuben the bag and followed him to the livery. Doing so, she'd get to say good-bye before sending him on his way. It would also give her another chance to see if Nate liked his new job.

The moment they entered the livery, Nate rushed up to her. "These men want to rent a mule, but your father hasn't gone over anything with me yet. Does he usually rent them out?"

The poor man looked fit to be tied. It didn't help that he had straw sticking out of his hair, which also stood on end. She tried hard not to laugh.

"Give me a minute, and I'll be right with you." She turned to Reuben. "Will I see you again anytime soon?"

Reuben shrugged. "C–can't s–say."

She hugged him. "You be careful."

He ducked, nodded, then scooted out the back door.

Rebekah faced Nate. "Yes, Daddy does lease mules." She moved to the heavy table near the stalls, opened a drawer, and pulled out a ledger. She motioned to the men at the doorway. "Have you done business with my father in the past?"

The men removed their hats as they entered. "Yes, ma'am. A few months back."

Rebekah knew the moment they saw her scar. They quickly turned to Nate, who still looked helpless. Sighing, she rotated a bit to hide her burn.

"Your names?"

"Mick and Randall Shire."

She jotted them down on the first blank line. "So you know you have to pay for the animal, and when you return it, you'll get half your money back, as long as it's still in good condition."

"Yes, ma'am."

"Good. If you'll sign here, Mr. Kirkland will get you a mule."

While one man signed, the other handed her the correct amount of cash, proving they'd been there before. She stowed the money in her apron pocket.

"Nate, would you—" A loud bang made Rebekah spin around. Nate wrestled with one of the mules, which had him pinned against the stall door. She wanted to laugh. "Not that one, Nate. Get the one in the stall next to you."

Nate tied the rope in his hand to the nearest pole before retrieving the correct mule. She made a note in the journal which animal the Shire brothers borrowed, then sent them on their way.

Nate sauntered toward her. "What's wrong with that first mule I grabbed? He tried to climb on *my* back instead of the other way around."

This time Rebekah did laugh. "We're not sure why, but that mule always wanders to the left. He can't go in a straight line to save his life."

Nate turned to stare at the mule. "I've never heard of such a thing." He shook his head. "A cross-eyed cat and a mule that only turns left. Let's see. You named the cat Mercy, so I'm guessing you named the mule Lefty."

Laughter bubbled up once again. "No. Daddy named him Twister."

Nate chuckled. "Suits him. You oughta warn a body before letting them near the critter. Someone's bound to get hurt. A mangled toe, if nothing else."

"I'll let you take that up with Daddy." She moved to stroke the mule's nose. "Even though Twister is pretty much useless, Daddy can't seem to give him up. Something about him being a reminder that we're all God's creatures, despite our imperfections."

Nate joined her. "Your dad's a good man. Where is he?"

"Checking on Mama. He'll return soon, but I need to get back to the store."

She spent a few minutes filling in Nate on some of his responsibilities before leaving. He was kind and had a sense of humor, but even he couldn't look her full in the face. For the first time in many weeks, she no longer felt healed of her burns.

Chapter Eight

....

Nate left his hotel room early the next morning and rushed to the livery, hoping to catch Thomas alone before the man left for the day. Before falling asleep, Nate decided to try a different tack by being more friendly and asking fewer questions. Maybe Thomas would warm to him and be more open like he was to Perry. As things stood, Thomas was more likely than Mercy to scratch Nate's eyes out. Why there was bad blood between him and Thomas, Nate didn't know, but if he allowed it to stand, he'd likely not learn much more from or about the man.

The livery doors stood open. Someone was already up and about. Once inside, he paused to allow his eyes to adjust to the dim interior. Scattered rays of early morning light filtered through the slats in the walls. Not a sound could be heard except the munching and shuffling of the three remaining mules. Thomas couldn't be gone already. Maybe he was at the store getting breakfast from Perry. Nate headed that way, only to stop when straw trickled from overhead. In seconds, Perry's feet appeared as he started down the ladder.

"Tell me you didn't sleep up there."

"Whoa." Like a strange, overgrown crow, Perry perched on the top rung a moment before continuing his descent. "Don't scare an old man that way, Nate."

"When I see one, I'll be sure to remember that."

Now that his boots were firmly on the floor, Perry clapped him on the back and grinned. "I appreciate that, but I feel much older than I look." He brushed the straw from his clothes. "You're here early."

"I could say the same for you, except I don't know what time you usually open up. We didn't get much discussed about the job yesterday."

"True enough. Seemed unusually busy." He motioned toward the small desk. "We can take care of that right now."

They spent the next several minutes going over duties and money figures. Nate knew some because of Rebekah's help the day before. She seemed a capable young woman—one her dad could rely on. A shame she was disfigured.

"That oughta do it." Perry settled against the desk. "Any questions?"

"Don't think so. Not yet anyway." Nate glanced up at the loft. "What about Thomas? Will I be working with him?"

Perry shoved all the papers back in the drawer. "Rarely. He keeps himself busy elsewhere."

"He gone already?"

"I don't know." Perry scratched his head. "Near as I could tell, it looked like he never slept there last night. Not sure if I should be worried or not."

"Breakfast." Rebekah stood in the doorway, holding a tray.

Nate rushed to take the load from her. He hadn't realized how hungry he was until the incredible scent reached his nose and his stomach growled.

Rebekah beamed up at him. "Sounds like I arrived just in time."

"You did. The walls of my stomach nearly started a fire from rubbing together."

The second the words were out of his mouth, he could have kicked himself. What a stupid thing to say to a woman with burn scars. But her smile never wavered, so either she didn't notice or didn't care. Rebekah never stopped amazing him. Most scarred women wouldn't leave their houses, so as not to be seen. Yet here she was, out in public, facing customers on a daily basis.

He set the tray on the table Perry had just cleared. Much as he wanted to yank off the towel covering the food and dig in, manners made him wait for Perry to do the honors. Thankfully, he didn't take long, saying a short blessing before grabbing a biscuit.

"Mama in the store?" Perry mumbled through the crumbs.

"She'll be there soon. She sent me on ahead so you wouldn't have to wait." She glanced around. "Where's Thomas? We made enough for three."

Perry licked his lips. "He wasn't here. I don't think he slept here last night."

Rebekah stared at her father, as if waiting for him to say more. He didn't. "Should we be concerned?" she asked. "He's never missed a night since he got here."

"I told Nate the same thing."

The stare continued, making Nate uncomfortable and slowing his appetite, and her gaze wasn't even aimed at him. He glanced at Perry to see how he fared. Didn't seem to bother him in the least.

Rebekah's hands went to her hips. "Well, if you're not going to do anything, I will. Cora told me she'd seen Thomas headed southwest out of town. I'll start looking for him in that direction."

Now she had Perry's attention as he stood and reached for her. "Hold up, Rebekah. You shouldn't go by yourself."

"Oh, Daddy. You know it's safe in the daylight. All the trouble's been at night."

Perry shook his head. "All the same, take Andrew with you."

Sweet laughter bubbled from her. "Yes, he is a scary sort, likely to frighten off even the most stalwart of men, but he's spending the day with Martin, remember?"

Nate felt for Perry's dilemma. No doubt he wanted to know Thomas was safe, but he also wanted to make sure his daughter wasn't in danger. He almost volunteered to escort her, especially if it gave him a valid excuse to see how Thomas filled his days. Perhaps he'd even catch the man in some criminal activity. But this was also Nate's first day on the job, so he filled his mouth with another bite to keep from speaking. If Rebekah didn't have an escort by the time he swallowed—

"Nate, would you mind going with Rebekah? You'll get a chance to see more of the area, and you'll give me peace of mind by keeping my little girl safe."

He forced the half-chewed food down his throat. "Sure. I'd be happy to."

"I'm not a little girl, Daddy. Just give me a gun, and I'll be fine."

Perry choked, then started coughing. Nate thumped him on the back a few times. They grinned at each other until Rebekah growled and crossed her arms.

Perry wiped his mouth with a napkin, successfully ridding himself of his smile at the same time. "Sweetheart, I've kept a pistol under the store counter since we opened, and you have yet to touch the thing. You know you couldn't shoot anyone."

She glared. "I don't know. I'm coming pretty close right now."

Nate ducked his head to keep her from seeing his widening grin. The girl had spunk.

SILVER CITY
1869

"Aw, quit your laughing and come on if you're *escorting* me." She started for the door without waiting for him to finish breakfast or even respond. "You're a bigger shadow than I'm used to, but I guess you'll do. At least I won't have to worry about pranks." She stopped and turned. "Or will I?"

Eyebrows up, Nate shook his head. "No, ma'am."

Her eyes narrowed. "I'm not a ma'am yet." She disappeared out the back door.

Nate rose to follow, then stopped long enough to grab another tasty biscuit before racing after her, Perry's chuckle trailing behind.

Nate fell into step beside Rebekah before realizing he chose the wrong side. Every time he turned to look at her, he'd see her scar. He didn't want that to impede his time with her, yet to move to her other side would be too obvious. He'd just have to keep staring at the ground. Uncomfortable with the silence, he fished his mind for a topic.

"What trouble?"

"Huh?" Rebekah tilted her face up to his.

He slowed his step, hoping she'd do the same. He wanted plenty of time to talk before reaching their destination. "You mentioned trouble only happening at night. What did that mean?"

"Oh, that." She slowed to his pace. "I thought you said you'd heard about the fires, thefts, and killings around here?"

"I know a little about the fires and some explosions."

"That's right." She tucked some hair behind her ear as she looked up at him. "You fought one of the fires." She shrugged. "That wasn't the first. More like the third, maybe fourth since we arrived."

"So how long has your family lived here?" Perfect. This conversation would help with many of his questions. Not only would he learn more about the family, but he could continue finding out more about the trouble, the town, and its residents.

"About a year. A little longer, I guess. It's been quite an adjustment."

"I would imagine. Mining towns are always rough."

She peered up at him. "You know this by experience?"

How'd he manage to get trapped into that one? He never planned to talk to anyone about his past. "Some. My dad and brother mined gold for a while."

"Where?"

"Colorado."

"Mmm. Didn't find much?"

How did he tell her they'd found too much, which led to their deaths? "They did all right. For a while, anyway." He glanced at her before returning his gaze to the ground.

"And you decided to try your hand at it now?"

He hoped his grimace would be mistaken for a smile. "Something like that."

Rebekah stopped and peered at him, and he prepared for another tough question. Instead, she stepped around him, squatted to pick a flower, then stood and started walking again. Only this time she stayed to his left. He examined her out of the corner of his eye. Did she sense his discomfort of her scar? If so, she was very sensitive. But was it for him or for herself? How old was she? Perry called her his "little girl," but she was no child. Was it because of what she'd been through? How to find out? He didn't want to hurt her feelings even a little.

"Most women your age and as pretty as you are married and raising at least one child."

She tilted her head toward him. "Is that your way of asking my

SILVER CITY 1869

age?" She laughed softly at his obvious embarrassment. "I'm twenty-one, and I did have a suitor soon after we arrived."

"What happened?"

Her gaze dropped to her toes. "Daddy. He told Cole he couldn't call on me if he wouldn't attend church."

Nate shook his head. "Cole's mistake. I'm surprised he gave in so easily."

"I don't know that he did." The obstinate curl blew across her face again. She slipped it behind her ear once more. "Daddy told me he found Cole dead a few days after"—she cleared her throat, her hand going to her cheek—"after the fire. From a gunshot."

More violence. The town seemed to thrive on it. And this time the bloodshed had gotten awfully close to Rebekah. "I'm sorry."

She shrugged. "I didn't really know him well."

He let that pass. Death was hard, no matter how well you knew someone. "How long have you known Thomas?"

"Almost since we arrived." Her tone warmed with affection. "He was here first but kept to himself. He had built quite a protective wall. Took weeks to break it down."

"Protective of what?"

She looked at him, her expression showing her confusion. "I guess tall men wouldn't understand what an unusually short man goes through, especially when his feet are smaller than those of an average woman. The constant teasing, ridicule, belittlement. Who wouldn't want to close themselves off from the rest of the world?"

The air got colder, and it had nothing to do with the outside temperature. Nate imagined Rebekah knew all about being ridiculed, probably by the other girls in town. No wonder she befriended and championed Thomas.

"I'm sorry. I wasn't thinking." That was an understatement. Forethought and understanding had disappeared with the deaths of his father and brother, replaced by resentment and suspicion.

The easygoing atmosphere vanished, and silence returned. He almost allowed shame to sweep over him until he remembered he was only doing his job. More questions remained, but maybe he should ask someone else. In the meantime, he could turn the conversation to something lighter. At least for a while.

Thumping could be heard in the distance, like someone chopping wood. He glanced around at their surroundings. The aspens and firs responding to the breeze made him think of home. He still thought Colorado was prettier, but this place held a close second. Or maybe his heart still remained back where he grew up. Surely that would change someday. It had to. He never intended to return unless it would bring him closer to his dad and brother's killers.

The slow but steady incline made their trek more difficult. Yet Rebekah's breathing wasn't any more labored than his, right up until she stumbled. He grasped her arm and held her until she regained her balance. He took the opportunity to examine her more closely. The first time he'd seen her, she was drenched, making her hair look much darker. Today, dry and full of waves, the color was more a light brown. But where the sun touched her tresses, a hint of red could be seen. Rebekah was a very attractive woman....

What was he thinking? Time to get his mind back on track. He released her arm. "Where are we?"

"Southwest of town." She pointed to her left. "Over there is where you fished us out of the stream."

Nate fought a smile. Women were so literal. Did she really think him lost? Females were usually the ones who didn't know directions.

"Let me try that question again. Where exactly are we headed?" Her answering laugh reminded him of the beautiful tinkle of his mother's expensive bells in the wind. "What's so funny?"

"Typical."

"What's typical?"

Her smirk pulled slightly to the left. "Men. They'd never admit to being lost."

"But I'm not lost."

The smirk still on her face, she shook her head. "Of course not." She pointed up ahead. "Not too much farther is an old homestead with a new family. I thought we'd check there first."

He stared in surprise. "How do you know that? You seem to know everyone in town."

Her expression revealed her amusement. "No. Regardless of the large number of people in town, word still gets around rather fast. Especially if you have a friend who makes it a point to know everything about everyone."

"Let me guess—your friend Cora."

Rebekah's sweet laugh made him want to keep her in high spirits at all times.

Just then the tinkling laugh was replaced by a gunshot. The bullet hit the tree next to him, showering them with shards of bark.

Chapter Nine

....

Rebekah ducked her head, only to be tackled to the ground by Nate, knocking the wind from her lungs. He pushed away from her.

"Stay down."

Right. As if she'd get up when she couldn't breathe. Her chest burned like fire before the air decided it would let her live and rushed to fill her lungs. She gasped twice just to make sure she still had the ability.

Blinking away the stars dancing in her eyes, she spotted Nate hunkered behind a large tree, pistol in hand. The rattling she heard in her ears came from either the wind blowing the aspen leaves behind them or the clattering of her teeth. Maybe both. Pounding in the distance pulsated at half the speed of her throbbing heart. She hadn't been this scared since her skirt caught fire almost a year ago.

"Who shot at us?" She cringed when the question came out louder than intended.

"Don't know." He pressed a finger to his lips before pointing down the path and peeking around the tree.

She rolled onto her stomach and peered through the trees. As if she didn't know to be quiet. His gruff whisper reminded her of her father's tone when she went hunting for deer with him once back in Kansas. She never intended to do that again. Too bloody. And the blast of the gunshot was just as loud and scary then as it was now. By the look of things, today could wind up being even worse than that hunting trip.

Who would want to kill Nate, and why? He was new to town. Not many people knew him yet. Or did they want her dead? After learning the fire that burned her wasn't an accident, she was ready to believe most anyone could be the culprit. But why? She hadn't done anything to earn anyone's wrath.

Disbelief changed to annoyance, then to outrage. Rebekah gritted her teeth. Of all the nerve. She had just as much right to live in Silver as anyone. Her outrage grew until she could no longer fight her aggravation and curiosity. She pushed to her knees for a better look.

Nate turned, mouth open and brows nearly touching. He placed his hand on her head and shoved her back to the ground. "Have you lost your mind? Stay down before you get your head blown off."

Before she could respond, he held up his hand and stood noiselessly. If she didn't know better, she'd think he'd done this before.

A man came in sight mere feet from where they hid. Nate reached out and placed the barrel of his pistol against the shooter's temple. "Drop your gun."

The man froze. "Hold up. I was just—"

"I said, drop the rifle."

The gun barrel lowered. Nate reached out with his free hand and grabbed the rifle, then threw it to the ground near Rebekah. "Keep your hands where I can see them."

Irritation formed on the man's face, though it was difficult to see through the bushy eyebrows and scruffy beard. "Now looky here, you young pup. I was after that big buck over yon till you up and scared it off. Gimme back my gun, so's I can chase it down. That giant will feed my brood for weeks."

The man took a step toward his rifle. Nate pulled back the hammer, the click louder than a snapping branch. Rebekah held her breath, praying Nate didn't get hurt. Or hurt the hunter. He looked so angry.

"Don't move, mister. I didn't see any deer. I think you tried to kill us."

The man's mouth dropped open. "No, sir. Like I said, I was after that buck."

Nate's face turned red. "We just came from back there. No deer would have stayed around while we wandered through those trees."

"You don't hear good, do ya, boy? I done said you spooked it off. I was trying to get him 'fore he disappeared completely."

For the first time, uncertainty flashed across Nate's face. "What's your name?"

"Watch out!" A voice in the distance ricocheted through the air.

Both Nate and Rebekah jerked at the loud warning. Several cracking sounds ripped from the tree line. Nate pushed the man at the same time he jumped back. A tree crashed to the ground, its top branches landing on Nate's boot tips.

Seconds later, Thomas appeared. "You all right, Nate?" He bent over, resting his hands on his knees as he gasped for air. "I couldn't believe it when I saw you two dawdling around over here." He shook his head and took a deep breath before standing upright again. "You done scared the liver clean out of me, son."

The perspiration running down Thomas's face alarmed Rebekah. She stood and rushed to his side, clutching his elbow. "You feeling all right, Thomas?"

He spun around. Hands over his heart, he gasped. "Oh goodness, Rebekah. Your daddy's gonna have a fit when he finds out how close you came to getting squashed."

He wrapped her in a hug, and she felt him tremble. "I'm fine, Thomas. It wasn't close to me at all. Nate, on the other hand…" They turned toward Nate. His chalky white face unnerved her. "Nate?"

He held up his hand. "I'm good." Nate holstered his pistol. "What about you, mister?"

But the hunter no longer stood with Nate. In fact, he was nowhere to be seen. The scoundrel had slipped away in all the uproar.

Nate turned a full circle. "Where'd he go?" He looked at Thomas. "Did you see him? Do you know who he is?"

"Not a clue. I was so concerned about you, I didn't pay much attention." He turned to Rebekah. "I need to get you home."

Nate grabbed Thomas's arm and spun him back around. "Wait a minute. Why are you out here?"

Thomas's top lip curled. He hesitated as if he didn't want to answer. Then he glanced at Rebekah. "I was chopping down this tree."

Taking a moment to eye the length of the tree, Nate gazed intently at Thomas. "I won't ask why yet, but this I have to ask. You saw us standing over here. Did you hear the gunshot?"

Thomas frowned. "What gunshot?"

Now Nate looked fit to be tied again. "You were standing not fifty yards from here, and you didn't hear the gunshot?"

Thomas crossed his arms. Rebekah got the feeling it was so he wouldn't take a swing at Nate. "That's what I'm saying."

These two men didn't like each other much at all, but why? They hadn't been together enough to have something go wrong between them. What had happened to create so much tension? Nate's lips tightened and his jaw clenched. Rebekah knew she needed to keep them from coming to blows. She hooked her arm through one of Thomas's and started walking along the fallen tree, easily one of the tallest she'd ever seen.

"You didn't stay at the livery last night, Thomas?"

As if coming out of a trance, Thomas blinked as he walked alongside. "Ah, no, I didn't."

She waited, hoping he'd continue without prompting. He fell silent and only stared. Impatience crept through her like the fog that swept down the mountains to fill their town. She took a breath. "Well?"

Thomas stopped and faced her, his eyes softening. "You sounded just like my mama did when she demanded an explanation for something I done wrong."

Fighting a grin, Rebekah decided to let that comment pass, though she could have really lit into him for comparing her to his mother. She was nowhere near that age. Some men had no tact, but then some men didn't have much experience when it came to women and relationships. Just where did Nate fall in that matter? A glance at him let her know he still wasn't over his grouch.

She returned her attention to Thomas and continued walking. "You didn't sleep out in the cold night air, did you?"

He put his hand up as if taking an oath, his expression as earnest as a preacher speaking on the perils of sin. "No, Mama. I promise I didn't. At least no more than I usually do."

That did it. Rebekah swatted at his arm before shaking her finger at him. "I'm not anywhere near old enough to be your mama, Thomas, so you better watch your tongue." She paused. "Or I'll send you to your room without your supper."

They collapsed against each other in laughter, but she hadn't finished with him yet. "Seriously, Thomas, you slept in a warm, safe place, right?"

He grinned and nodded. "Warm and safe as they come. I give you my word."

By that time, they'd walked far enough to see a corner of a house. A few steps later, the residence came more fully into view. A monstrous dog rose from the porch, gave a deep growl and bark, then came bounding toward them.

Rebekah wanted to scream, but extreme fear froze the cry in her throat. She stepped behind Thomas, more than willing to let him deal with the dog. But Nate had already pulled his pistol and stood with feet apart, aiming at the beast.

Thomas took a step forward and shoved his hands in front of Nate's gun. "Whoa, hold up there." He turned, squatted, and called, "Tiny!"

The dog skidded to a stop, looked at Thomas, then wagged its huge tail hard enough to make its entire body sway. Its mouth dropped open in a pant that looked much like a smile, reminding Rebekah of a youngster thrilled to see his daddy come home after a long day.

Thomas patted his chest. "Come 'ere, boy."

The humongous animal bounced across the yard, swiftly closing the distance, and leapt into Thomas's arms. The two sprawled and rolled. Thomas, laughing, got to his feet and ruffled the dog's ears.

Recovering her senses, Rebekah clamped her mouth shut. She'd never seen such an animal. Another foot taller and the dog would be able to look Thomas in the eyes. Nate must have thought the same.

Head shaking, he stepped forward to pet the dog.

But evidently Tiny hadn't forgotten that, only moments ago, Nate had intended to shoot him. He growled low in his throat.

Nate pulled his hand back. "Tiny? Don't tell me—he was the runt of the litter."

Thomas chuckled. "Not from what I was told. He was the biggest; that's why they took him. Thought he'd be good protection for the trip here."

Nate jammed his hands into his pockets. "They could have used him as a pack mule." He turned to Rebekah. "You could rent him out as such. Make good money." He shook his head again. "A cross-eyed cat, a mule that only goes to the left, and a monstrous dog. Are there any normal animals in Silver City?"

Rebekah couldn't help but laugh. He certainly had a point. She rested her hand on Thomas's arm. "So I take it by Tiny's reaction you slept here last night?"

"Yep." He pointed toward the house. "Right up there on the porch. They put out a straw mattress, and Tiny nearly slept on top of me. I was warm and had the best protection in the mountains." He scratched the dog's ears. "Ain't that right, boy?" Tiny immediately agreed with a lick to Thomas's face. "Come on and meet these fine folks."

Rebekah and Nate followed Thomas to the house. The door opened before they reached the porch. A gun barrel poked through the opening.

"You all right, Thomas, or do I need to peel some hide off of them two?"

"You can trust them, Pearl. They're good people." Thomas waited for the woman to show herself, then motioned to Rebekah. "This here's Rebekah Weaver, and that's Nathaniel Kirkland."

The woman nodded, then took a couple steps farther onto the porch, allowing three children to join her. They all could have used a good scrubbing. Grime smeared their faces and their hair was slick with grease, but otherwise they looked healthy enough. Their eyes sparkled with curiosity, but none of the three spoke a word. Quite a contrast to Andrew, who would have been spewing questions the minute he spotted them.

"Howdy. Name's Pearl Loomis," the woman said, then gestured toward her children. "This is Libby, Helen, and Micah."

By the bulge under her apron, another child was on the way. "I'm pleased to meet all of you," Rebekah said kindly to the children. "I've got a little brother who'd just love to get to know you three." She smiled.

The smiles she received back were sweeter than honeycomb. Oh, but she'd love to get her hands on these children.

"That's quite a dog you have." Nate reached to pet him and received another growl. He returned his hand to his pocket, probably to keep his fingers intact.

"He was," Pearl said and jabbed her thumb toward Thomas. "Till that old man got a hold of him. Now he's spurled."

Nate looked confused. "Spurled?"

"Yeah. Something fierce. Used to get some work out of him, but Thomas has him rotten to the core."

"Oh, you mean spoiled," Nate said.

Pearl's scowl ran so deep, the crease between her brows could have held water. "That's what I done gone and said, ain't it?"

Nate ducked his head. "Yes, ma'am."

Needing to hide her amusement, Rebekah suddenly found the

big rock by her toe very interesting. Poor Nate. She'd never heard that word before either, but he'd been the one to take the brunt of Pearl's disapproval.

Pearl pulled her young son against her side. "Yeah, well, I ain't letting that old man near my young'uns, or they ain't no telling what they'll turn out like."

Her words were tempered with a teasing tone, and Thomas howled with laughter as he slapped his thigh. "Too late."

Nate bent and picked up a rock, examining it in the sunlight. He took a step and handed it to Micah, who did his best to imitate Nate's action. Then a grin washed over his face as he tucked it in his pocket. Nate returned the smile before looking up at the boy's mother.

"Your husband around, Mrs. Loomis?"

Pearl examined him from the corners of her eyes. "Nope. Lit out early this morning. Won't see him again till after dark. Boss man works him too hard." She poked her thumb toward Thomas again. "Weren't for him, we'd likely go hungry."

Nate nodded. "By your accent, you're not from around these parts."

"Nope."

Nate and Pearl shared a stare-down. Nate licked his bottom lip, as if he were struggling with asking another question. He glanced the direction they'd come, then turned back. "Been here long?"

As if she'd been smacked with a branch from that falling tree, Rebekah suddenly realized Nate's thoughts. He wondered if Pearl's husband was the man who shot at them. In an instant, she also wanted to know the answers to Nate's questions.

Pearl squinted a bit. "Depends on who you ask. Eugene thinks we haven't been here long enough. I think we're long past due to leave."

The woman had a knack for avoiding proper answers. Thomas swung around in front of Nate. With the two men standing so close, their difference in height was nearly comical. If Nate were to lift his arm, Thomas would have been able to walk under it and get his almost bald head buffed by the sleeve. But the humor of the sight disappeared the moment Thomas jabbed Nate in the chest.

"I know what you're thinking, and you're dead wrong. Eugene's a good man. Now you get yourself outta here 'fore I drag you out."

Before anyone could react, a toddler waddled onto the porch, banging into each side of the door frame in the process, nearly losing his balance. Drool dangled from the fingers jammed in the small boy's mouth as he grinned and gurgled at them. The oldest girl, Libby, scooped him up in her arms, glaring at Nate the whole time.

Nate's gaze went from Thomas to the kids, then to Pearl. He touched the rim of his hat. "My apologies, ma'am." The sincerity in his voice echoed the contrition on his face. "If there's anything I can do to help, you can send word through Thomas." He nodded to the entire group. "Good day."

Rebekah waved at the children before racing after Nate. They were halfway back to town before she worked up the nerve to ask her question. "You think her husband is the man who shot at us?"

Nate slowed his stride. He shrugged, still looking regretful. "I don't know. Maybe." He shrugged again, his struggle evident. "But Mrs. Loomis had nothing to do with it either way. She's got her hands full right there at the house. I had no right to saddle her with more problems."

That very moment Rebekah's estimation of Nate rose high enough to burst a hole in the sky. And her heart followed close behind.

Chapter Ten

....

Nate pulled the metal from the fire, placed it on the anvil, and hammered as though it deserved to die. When he first accepted the job from Perry, he thought it would be an ideal situation, a place he could meet many of the residents and ask questions. But three days had passed since the stranger took a shot at him. He'd been so busy, not a question had yet been asked as part of his investigation. Not only that, but all the men who'd come by needing work done hadn't hung around. They stated their instructions and disappeared out the door as fast as their legs could carry them. Most returned inebriated, revealing the reason for their rush.

"Whoa there, young man. You trying to shape that metal—or kill it?"

Henry Gilmore stood an arm's length away, eyebrows raised and a smirk on his face. If Nate didn't like him so much, he'd have been tempted to throw the hammer at him. Mr. Gilmore put up his hands in a defensive posture, making Nate warm to him.

"So"—Mr. Gilmore took a step closer and clapped Nate on the back—"you hating your job already?"

Giving the metal one last pound, Nate shoved it back into the fire before glancing at the elderly gentleman from the corner of his eye. "You ever made a decision you regretted?"

Chuckling, Mr. Gilmore rocked back on his heels. "At one point or another, all mankind has stubbed their toe on that very rock. Some many times over from lack of thought or learning." He dropped onto a nearby bench. "What has your big toe throbbing?"

The old man's humor lightened Nate's mood. He perched on a barrel, trying to determine just how much to tell Mr. Gilmore. The man had tons of experience in life, much coming from the War Between the States. He'd probably be a good man for advice. Or just to chat with for entertainment. If he led the conversation right, Nate just might get another war story out of him.

Nate crossed his arms and got comfortable, though he knew he should finish his task. "Much as I like Perry and appreciate him offering me a job, I'd planned on spending a lot more time up in the hills with colors other than"—he motioned to the forge—"orange and black."

Gilmore cackled and slapped his knee. "I like you, boy. You remind me of myself many years ago."

He fished inside his pocket and pulled out a pipe and pouch. Nate welcomed the action. It meant he'd likely get another story. Not only had Perry warned him of that, but he'd witnessed it for himself. Nate examined Mr. Gilmore as the man tamped tobacco into the bowl of his pipe. If his hair was a bit more gray and his beard a mite longer, Gilmore could almost pass as General Lee. Nate didn't dare mention that fact. He had yet to learn which side Mr. Gilmore had fought on.

Smoke billowed as the man puffed on his pipe and gazed off at some distant scene in his memory. A full minute ticked by before he pulled the pipe from his mouth and pointed the mouthpiece in the direction he stared.

"I've known many a man who felt as you. That war," he said with a shake of his head, "awful thing. I can only hope every man who fought felt some kind of regret, cuz then I'll know there's still hope." He placed the pipe's stem against his bottom lip. "Hope that mankind still has a heart that can feel love."

He finally inhaled, his eyes looking as though he relived yet another battle. Nate felt for the man. Dad had had just as much trouble thinking and talking about his experiences. Empathy for the similarities made Nate want to open up and mention his father's own turmoil.

"My dad was in that war. He could hardly talk about the things that happened."

Mr. Gilmore nodded. "Not a day goes by that I don't think of the men who fought under my command. Painful memories." He slouched as though experiencing the agony all over again. "The men fought for what they thought was right and lost their lives, legs, or arms for their beliefs." As he shook his head, he pointed the pipe stem at Nate. "But I'd do it all over again for the chance to battle alongside men of such fine courage and honor. Did they regret going to war and taking lives? No doubt. But they fought with pride and character, and I respect every one of them for that. "

Nate understood exactly what Mr. Gilmore was trying to get across. No matter what a man did, whether he liked his task or not, respecting himself in the morning meant doing it to the best of his ability and with pride and dignity. Nate felt certain his father took pride in his position in the war. The memories of lost friends were what haunted him.

"Dad said he almost froze and starved to death one year."

"Mmm." He inhaled from the pipe and blew the smoke out in a long, slow breath. "I think most men suffered those difficulties." His eyes glistened with moisture. "I lost a company of men outside of Hancock." He finally met Nate's eyes. "And it was the first time I came close to hating someone. Actually did for a while, I reckon. Truth be told, it still eats on me some when I dwell on it."

Mr. Gilmore pulled out a handkerchief, wiped his eyes, then blew his nose. Nate wished he could make it easier for the poor man in some way.

"I'm a good listener if you think it would help to talk."

Mr. Gilmore eyed him for a spell, then nodded. "Yes, sir, it just might. I've only spoken of it one other time, and that was with some men who'd been through the war. A set of young, caring ears might be just what I need."

Nate waited with much patience, wishing his dad were still alive and could have met Mr. Gilmore. Maybe they could have helped each other through the rough memories.

"I'd already lost two men from cold and hunger. More hunger than anything." He shook his head. "Awful way to go. Wasting away until there's no strength left." He sucked air between his teeth, showing his dismay. "I managed to urge my men to move west, promising I'd find food. In the middle of a small prairie, they gave out and fell to the ground. The grass was the color of honey, it was so dry from all the frosty nights. But it was tall enough to hide them, so I told them to stay put and I'd bring food to them."

His face turned sad with a trace of anger. "I was just about to rope a cow when I heard someone talking. I backed behind a small cluster of bushes to get a look." He motioned with his hand, as though seeing it all happen again in front of him. "A line of uniforms stood at the edge of the prairie, too many for me to take without getting killed myself, so I stayed hunkered down. And that's when I saw it."

The old man's lips trembled as he wiped fresh tears from his eyes. Nate didn't figure he'd hear the end of the story. Mr. Gilmore didn't look as though he could go on. Then he cleared his throat.

"Smoke. Lots of it, headed right toward us. In no time, flames licked at the air." His body quaked. "Those dirty varmints lit the dry grass on fire and waited at the edge for my men to run out so they could shoot them." His nostrils flared. "Those that didn't want to get shot ended up burning to death. Worst day of my life." He shook his head again. "I was a coward and didn't do a thing but watch."

"That wasn't cowardice, Mr. Gilmore."

"It was." His eyes flared, daring Nate to disagree again. "I'm not denying it." He took one last puff on his pipe before standing and tapping the tobacco from the bowl. "I never led another regiment again. Couldn't. Thankfully, the war ended not too many more months after that."

Nate stood to follow Mr. Gilmore from the livery and nearly ran into him when he abruptly stopped. He followed the man's gaze and found Rebekah standing in the doorway.

Her expression was horrified.

Mr. Gilmore headed toward her. "I'm so sorry, my dear. I never meant for you to hear that story." He didn't get a chance to say more as Rebekah fled into the store, and he gave a woeful shake of his head. "I wish I'd known she was there. I wouldn't have told that dreaded tale. Poor girl. She's been through enough, what with getting burned herself. She didn't need to hear such horror." He looked up at Nate. "What were you saying about regretting a decision?" Though his lips curved, there wasn't an ounce of humor in them.

Nate rubbed Mr. Gilmore's back, feeling his pain. "I'll check on her—see if she needs to talk."

Although he had wanted to help by listening, Nate doubted he'd helped a tiny bit. Some memories refused to go away or fade even a little. And some men couldn't forgive themselves for decisions made, even when they weren't at fault. Nate figured this particular memory ate at Mr. Gilmore every day.

They were almost out of the livery when Nate spotted an odd item near the doorway that hadn't been there earlier. "Hold up." He pointed. "What's that?"

This time, Mr. Gilmore's smile was sincere. "That, my boy, is the reason I came in the first place. Forgot about it in all your frenzied racket." He chuckled. "You looked so angry, I was afraid to ask if you had time to fix my chair, so I left it here to see what fanned your flame."

Nate laughed. "I wasn't that bad." He took in Mr. Gilmore's raised brows and laughed again. "All right, so I was a bit out of sorts, but that's over now. What can I do for you?"

Mr. Gilmore explained how his favorite chair broke and that he'd love to have it fixed rather than find a replacement. Nate silently vowed to have it repaired by the end of the day. Anything to make life more pleasant for the tortured man.

"I'll get to it as soon as I can, Mr. Gilmore. You have my word."

Gilmore stuck out his hand. "Thank you, young man. And call me Henry. I believe we've crossed the line of formality today, thanks to your kind heart."

Nate shook the offered hand and clapped him on the back, feeling much affection for the old man. "Any time, Henry. You'll find my door and ears open to you."

After watching him climb onto his buggy and ride away, Nate turned and eyed the doorway leading to the store, wondering if he'd get fired for not finishing his work on time. But if Rebekah needed him, he'd take that chance. With a deep breath, he headed next door to see what he'd find, though this wasn't exactly the kind of investigation for which he'd been hired.

Chapter Eleven

....

Rebekah returned to the store more shaken than she cared to admit. That story Mr. Gilmore told about burning men made her relive her own painful memory. So much for thinking she'd healed inside as well as out. If such a tale could disturb her so deeply, then she wasn't over the horror at all.

Her mother's concerned stare made Rebekah struggle to hide her emotional upset. But her attempt didn't work. Her mother approached, a question creasing her forehead.

"You brought back the piece of pie. Wasn't Nate working in the livery?"

Rebekah eyed the dessert in her hand, then set it on the counter. She'd forgotten the very reason she'd gone next door. Much as she didn't want to respond, her mother wouldn't leave her alone until she received an answer, though the question she'd asked probably wasn't the one on her mind.

"Yes, Mama, he was in there. But Mr. Gilmore was telling him a story. I didn't want to interrupt."

Her answer was the truth, just not all of it. Her mother didn't need more to worry about, and Rebekah didn't want to try to explain her feelings right now. Better to distract her somehow, letting her own troubles go for a while.

Loud murmuring from several customers in the store managed

to snag her attention. Heads together, they looked rather excited. Or was it closer to anxiety?

She nodded toward the group. "What's happening, Mama?"

Mama turned to look, then whispered, "They said something about a note being found on a house. Nailed to the porch post, so they say."

Rebekah continued to watch, hoping to read the lips of some. "Whose house?"

"I didn't catch that part." She peeked back at the group. "As curious as I was, I figured I was dancing on the edge of gossip, so I stepped away."

Peering at her mother's face, Rebekah spied a bit of a smile lurking. She nudged her. "Mama! I'm shocked."

Mama pulled her into a hug, a chuckle shaking her shoulders. "Oh, go on with you. You're just as curious, and you know it."

Rebekah grinned as she pulled away. "I am, and I'll be sure to find out and let you know all about it when I get home tonight." She turned her mother and gently pushed her toward the door. "Now go home and get some rest. Don't let Andrew wear you out. In fact, he can stay here this afternoon when he brings the lunches."

"Just for your sass, young lady," Mama whispered over her shoulder, "I'll take you up on that offer."

Rebekah placed a kiss on Mama's cheek before she stepped out the door. Once she'd disappeared down the boardwalk, Rebekah turned back to her customers. None of them even attempted to appear to be shopping but continued to stand in a cluster, talking in low tones.

Ignoring the urge to join them, she scooted past Nate, who leaned against the frame of the side door, and grabbed the rag to wipe down the counter. The reason for his visit was obvious, but she didn't want to talk to him about it any more than she did her mother. She needed time alone to think about her reaction before she could speak with any kind of sense or logic.

Nate cleared his throat. "Everything all right?"

"Fine." She could feel him examining her and scrubbed all the harder at the already clean wood.

Rather than leave, Nate wandered closer, finally sliding onto the stool for a better view of her face. "Convince me."

Rebekah nearly melted, not only because of his obvious concern but because he no longer tried to avoid looking at her. Very few people managed to look her in the eyes like Nate did right now. She gave up the pretense of tidying the place and returned his gaze. Seeing his worry, she would have kissed his cheek, had it not been inappropriate. The action would really give the customers something to whisper about, and she had no intention of being the subject of their gossip again.

She edged a hip against the counter so she could watch the patrons and still be able to see Nate's face. "All right, I'll admit it. Hearing about those men burning to death upset me. That story was awful enough to bother anyone."

"I agree. But you have more reason than anyone to be disturbed by it." He dipped his head to make her look at him. "Anything I can do to help?"

"I'm fine." Didn't he have some work to do? Or couldn't he at least find something more pleasant to discuss?

"So you said. Which means your new definition of 'fine' is sad eyes and tight lips."

The man certainly had an abundant supply of charm. Rebekah found herself fighting a reaction to his wit, which he must have seen because he cocked his head and winked.

"Well, that's better. At least you're getting closer to the old definition."

She threw the rag at him as she grinned. "You've given a whole new meaning to 'nosey.'"

He peeled the rag from the top of his head and pointed his finger at her. "I think—"

The front door slammed open. "Look what I got, Rebekah!"

Cora Peters waved a slip of paper in the air as she raced across the floor. Nate had to step out of the way in order to avoid being tackled. Rebekah had never seen Cora quite so excited, yet she didn't want to ignore Nate either. He'd been so sweet. As Rebekah endured an enthusiastic hug from Cora, Nate said softly, "We'll continue our chat later. Your hands look a little"—he motioned to Cora, his eyebrows high— "full." He headed out the door, stopped, and pointed at the pie on the counter. "Was this for me, or were you just trying to torture me?"

Rebekah smiled. "It's for you. Go ahead and take it."

He scooped it up. "If it means getting a pie, I'll come check on you anytime."

She grinned but didn't get to respond. Cora grabbed her by the shoulders.

"I need your help." The slip of paper flashed before Rebekah's eyes again. "This was nailed to our porch this morning."

Rebekah's mouth dropped open. Cora had received the note? What in the world took her friend so long to come tell her? She glanced at the customers, who had stopped whispering and were shuffling their way toward the counter, acting as though they were looking at the goods along the way. Cora tried to continue talking about her note, but Rebekah held her finger to her lips, then pointed at the patrons.

She made a face only Cora could see. "Let me help these people, then we can talk." She turned to the customers. "Has everyone found what they're looking for, or do you need some assistance?"

Most understood they'd get no more information, at least not while inside the store, and made their way outside. Once alone, Rebekah grabbed Cora's hands. "*You're* the one who received the note?"

Cora's head nearly wobbled from her shoulders, she nodded so hard. "And just wait till you see what it says. Maybe you can help me understand what it means."

She laid it on the counter but kept her finger on the paper as though afraid it might somehow fly away or get snatched from her. Rebekah huddled close, anxious to read the words.

> *Sometimes the thing so desperately sought,*
> *Cannot be stolen, made, or bought.*
> *It could be close, across the street.*
> *To dally could be bittersweet.*

Rebekah read the rhyme again. Her heart wanted to believe the meaning was good, positive. But with all the trouble that had been going on in and around town lately, caution fought for her attention. By the excitement beaming from Cora's face, Rebekah needed to be careful not to stomp all over her high hopes.

"Now you look like my parents." Cora's bottom lip jutted. "They warned me this might be something bad instead of beneficial, that I needed to be more suspicious than happy."

Alarm rattled through Rebekah's head. She had to ask. "So they think this was meant for you and not one of them?"

Cora flipped the note over. "See." She pointed to her initials. "It's for me." She clasped the paper to her heart. "And I haven't done anything to make someone want to do me harm. So it has to be good, right?"

Rebekah wanted to be as thrilled as Cora. "Let me read it again."

Cora laid it on the counter in a way that let Rebekah know how precious it was to her. They read it aloud together. Again, Rebekah thought the saying could go either way, but Cora's energy moved her toward the positive. She looked her friend in the eyes.

"Have you been seeking something? Something you lost, maybe?"

"No. That's what's so strange about it. I can't figure out what it means."

Rebekah moved to the third line. "All right, so what's across the street? Let's think."

She'd just started picturing the street across from their boardinghouse in her mind when Cora began reeling off the stores.

"There's the general store, the saddle and leather goods place, as well as the butcher shop. The barber shop, hotel, and also the saloon are along there." She made a face. "Not much to choose from, huh?"

"Oh, I don't know. Most of those are owned or run by very nice people."

That hopeful look returned to Cora's face. "So you think this note means a person? A suitor, perhaps?"

Rebekah laughed. "I didn't say that, but it certainly doesn't hurt to think along those lines at first, don't you think? We have to start somewhere."

"Right." Cora tapped her chin while she thought, then pointed at Rebekah. "All but the saloon owner has sons. Most are older than me."

"Which ones have spent a lot of time trying to get your attention?"

Cora's eyebrows winged upward. "Don't you think I'd know if one of them was interested in me?"

Rebekah fought a smile and lost. "Well, I'm not sure, Cora. You're so busy trying to know everyone in town, I figured you might have overlooked something like that."

Cora's mouth dropped open as she took a swing at Rebekah's arm and missed. "I can't believe you said that. I'm not nosey."

"I didn't say you were."

"That's what you meant." The two stared at each other for several moments before they collapsed with laughter. "All right, so maybe I do like to make everyone feel welcome and special."

That made Rebekah laugh harder. "You make them any more special, and they'll feel adopted."

"Stop that."

Rebekah sobered. "All right, if you haven't noticed any out-of-the-ordinary attention, then we'll have to take measures to figure out who it might be. And it would be nice to know who managed to learn of this interest before you noticed and why he or she wants to make sure you find out about it."

That last question latched onto Rebekah's mind like a miner to a gold nugget. If their hopeful assumption was correct, then who had been so watchful to notice Cora had a secret admirer?

Cora's hand fastened onto Rebekah's arm. "It sure wasn't my parents. Their reaction to this note proves that." She made a face. "It's a little creepy to think someone's been watching me so intensely, don't you think?"

Yes! But Rebekah hid her concern so as not to scare her friend. "Unless the person who wrote the note is the same person who wants your attention."

Cora's brows furrowed with bewilderment. "All right, so how do we learn who's been admiring me?"

Rebekah racked her brain for some way they could discover the author or the admirer, or both, and finally came up with a possible solution. "The town picnic tomorrow. Everyone from miles around will be there."

"But we only want the ones from across the street."

"That's right, but with so many people milling around, we'll be able to look for those watching you, instead of all the events."

Cora squeezed her arm, a grin stretching across her face. "Ooo, I'm glad you're my friend. You're so smart."

The side door opened, interrupting what Cora planned to say next. Nate walked in with blood dripping from his hand.

"I need some help."

Cora's hand went to her throat. "Oh my." Her eyes closed. "I need to sit."

Heart pounding with alarm, Rebekah managed to slide a stool under Cora before she collapsed. Then she rushed to Nate, peeling her apron from around her waist to use as a temporary bandage. While wrapping it around his hand, she led him to a chair.

He stood next to it as if unwilling to sit. "It's not as bad as it looks."

She peered up at him, pasting on the same stern expression she used on Andrew when he balked at her commands. "Sit."

A smile inching across his lips, he obeyed. "I can tell you have a young brother."

"Yes, well, don't make me have to apply any more of my techniques I use on him. He wears me out enough."

Nate's low chuckle seemed to make her heart vibrate. Fighting the reaction, she shook her finger at him, hoping the motion would keep him in place, and scooted over to the shelf where they kept the first aid products.

Cora nearly toppled from the stool as she raced to follow. She grabbed Rebekah's arm and pulled her close. "I've got to leave before you start to work on his wound. You know I can't stand the sight of blood."

Rebekah patted her hand. "It's all right. You go ahead and leave. I'll find you tomorrow at the picnic, and we'll put our plan in motion."

Without a word, Cora nodded and hurried from the store. Before she shut the door, she stuck her head back inside. "Make sure you invite your friend to the celebration." With a wink, she was gone.

Nate eyed Rebekah as she returned to his side. "What was that all about?"

"What?" Rebekah feigned innocence as she laid out the items on the small table next to them.

"That wink. Why'd she do that? And what celebration?"

The last question was something she could answer. She unwrapped Nate's hand. "I think we're celebrating the fact that Timmy managed to catch a frog in his pocket while it was in mid hop."

Nate was obviously confused. "What?"

She finally started to laugh as she wiped the blood from his hand for a better look at the wound. "You know miners. They'll use any reason, sane or not, to have some kind of festivity. Helps them get rid of some of the stress and worries from the work they do, I think. I honestly have no idea what we're celebrating tomorrow. I just show up for the fun. And now you can come too."

Nate's brows rose as if he liked the idea, only to follow with a shake of his head. "I doubt I can go. Your dad probably needs me to watch the livery."

"That's where you're wrong." She held the soiled apron below his hand and prepared to pour iodine on the wound. "This will sting a little."

The liquid hit the gash, and Nate reared his head back. Then he hissed as he sucked in air. "Sting a little? That felt like an entire nest of hornets on a rampage."

Rebekah chuckled as his head moved over the wound as if to see if the mentioned hornets were still inside. She studied the back of his head, thinking him incredibly good-looking and wondering what it would feel like if she ran her fingers though his hair. She sucked in a roomful of air herself as she tried to rein in her thoughts. Better to get her mind on something else.

"So, how'd you get cut?" Perfect. He'd never know where her thoughts had brought her with a question like that.

He gave a rueful shake of his head. "Well, you see, it was like this. Twister and I had a bit of a discussion." His lips turned up. "I lost."

Rebekah broke into laughter again. She loved his humor. "And what, pray tell, were you discussing?"

"His inability to walk straight. I told him he could do it if he set his mind to it." He shrugged. "He responded by shoving my hand into a latch with a nail sticking out." He held the cloth while Rebekah wrapped a binding strip around his hand. "I've got to learn to lead him from the left instead of the right, like I'm used to doing. Then maybe we'll get along."

With an extra tug to make sure the knot was tight, Rebekah sat back. "Done." She patted his arm, then moved to put some distance between them. "I think you'll live." His nearness did things to her she'd never experienced before, like somehow removing all the vital air, leaving her breathless.

"Uh-huh. Till my next go-round with that dunderhead." He stood. "Thank you, Rebekah."

"You're welcome." He needed to leave so she could sort through her jumbled feelings.

"About that picnic." Nate leaned on the counter like he had all the time in the world. "You said I was wrong about having to stay at the livery to work?"

"That's right. Every business in town closes for the day, us included." She started cleaning up the mess she'd made. "So just show up to have a good time. And plan on eating with us. We'll have plenty."

"All right. Sounds great." He eyed her as if he had more questions. Finally, he thanked her again and returned to the livery.

Rebekah dropped onto the chair Nate had vacated and, hand on her chest, paced her breathing so her heart would slow its thundering pace. He had to wonder why she'd been acting strange lately.

Rebekah's heart refused to slow. He'd never learn from her how close he came to getting kissed while being doctored.

Chapter Twelve

Nate descended the hotel steps with more excitement than he'd felt since he'd been awarded the assignment of finding and arresting the troublemakers in town. Today would be his first chance to meet many of the residents since he'd arrived. Perry kept him so busy at the livery, he'd met only a handful of the miners needing repair work done. Though Rebekah had invited him to join the family, he planned to spend as much time as possible roaming the streets and observing the revelers. He'd look for the Weavers at noon, unwilling to miss another chance to enjoy their tasty food.

The clamor of voices raised in merriment met him long before he opened the door, the volume increasing to almost a roar once he stepped outside. As he made his way along an avenue to get to Washington Street, he wondered where all the people came from. He'd been told Silver City had grown in the last four years since it had been established, but he hadn't seen so many residents before. They seemed to have popped up out of nowhere, like weeds after a summer rain.

As he wove his way along the boardwalk, he examined the many faces, recognizing a few here and there and nodding his greetings. He finally arrived at the opposite end of the street and guessed it had taken at least half an hour. By the excited chatter all along the way, everyone sounded ready for a good time.

"Nate! Here!"

Nate turned and found Henry Gilmore waving him over. Careful not to knock over a couple of youngsters playing a game that seemed to require them bouncing off people's legs, Nate picked his way through the throng and dropped onto the chair next to Henry.

"This is madness." He hoped his grin tempered the comment, though there was truth to the statement.

"Yes, but isn't it grand to see so many smiling faces?"

"It is. I hope they're still smiling when the day is over."

Henry studied him, his brows puckering. "You thinking something bad will happen, boy? Or are you knowing it?"

"Nope. Just hoping for the best." At Henry's obvious puzzlement, Nate tried to clarify. "I've heard about the trouble in and around town, as well as the mines. Even experienced a fire myself, if you recall. With all these people milling around, they make for easy targets, especially when preoccupied with fun and food."

Lips pulled to the side, Henry shook his head. "Ain't you a gloomy thing."

Laughing, Nate relaxed against the back of his chair. "Not at all. I'm just starting to care about this place and its residents and want the best for them."

Henry peered into Nate's face. "I don't suppose a certain young lady has anything to do with your new feelings."

"What?" Nate's mind scrambled to figure out who Henry meant. Rebekah's face came to mind, but surely he didn't mean her. He couldn't remember giving any kind of indication he was interested. At least he hoped not. He didn't plan to be in town long and didn't want to mislead anyone, especially Rebekah. He'd have to be more careful.

"I guess not. My mistake." Henry leaned back. "Forget I mentioned it."

Not an easy task. If he were at liberty to explain why he'd come to town... Nate inhaled deeply. No sense thinking on the impossible. He scrambled for a change of topic. "So, what am I in store for today? This will be my first celebration, if that's what you call this. I hadn't heard of anything special happening that would warrant a festival."

Henry chuckled. "Don't need much to happen to get these folks looking for merriment."

"That's what Rebek—ah—" He briefly closed his eyes. How did she manage to keep coming up in conversation? He ignored the grin on Henry's face. "Why the need for so many festivals?"

"It's a release for many of the miners. Their families too, if I give it some thought." He tilted back on the chair's legs, the very chair Nate had repaired mere days ago. "Mining is a tough life. Long hours of back-breaking work. It's a risk to life and limb, and that stress rubs off on the wife and children."

Nate remembered all too well. Dad and Simon would go off to work their mine, and the moment the door closed, Mother would drop to her knees in prayer for their safety. Worry lines would make miniature tracks across her cheeks and forehead, adding to those already started from when Dad was at war. In no time, her dark hair made way for streaks of gray. He never told her about his churning stomach, which kept him from eating the lunches she sent with him to his blacksmithing job. No need to add to her worries. The thought of celebrating to alleviate the pain had never crossed their minds.

"Makes perfect sense. My dad and brother worked in a mine. What it did to my mother..." He shook his head.

"Then you know what I'm talking about."

"Yes, sir." He could honestly say he was glad the town found a way to find release. "I know there will be good eating." His mouth watered at the thought. "What about games and such?"

"Oh, goodness." The old man chuckled. "The day is filled with them. Some for kids and some for men."

"That's right." Perry bounded up the two steps and stopped in front of them. "In fact, that's why I've been looking everywhere for you, Nate."

Nate stood and motioned for Perry to take his seat. "Oh, no. Do I dare ask?"

"Probably not." Perry laughed and dropped onto the chair Nate had vacated. "What if I guarantee you'll have a good time?"

Nate propped himself against the nearby pole. "You have my interest, but not my agreement."

Perry bumped Henry with his elbow and motioned toward Nate. "Reckon I should have him hit or hold?"

Henry rubbed his whiskered chin. "That's a tough call. Did you see the cut on his hand?" He shook his head. "Not sure how to advise you, my friend. Have you ever seen him swing a hammer?"

"No, I haven't. Not the big one, anyway." Perry lifted his hat and scratched the top of his head, then snugged the cap down tight again. "Might be safest to have him hold."

Nate had fought a laugh as long as he could before letting it loose. "All right, you two. Spill it."

They joined him in laughter. Then Perry leaned forward, his elbows on his knees. "We always have rock-drilling contests. Single-jack and double-jack. Whoever drills the deepest wins the purse. I usually enter the double-jack. Since Rube doesn't plan to be here, I'll need a partner."

"Rube?"

"Yep. He's my partner in the mine we own and work up in the Florida Mountain range off to the west of town."

Nate's mind scrambled back a few days to the scruffy man who entered the livery, only to have Perry lead him back out. He'd have to make it a point to meet the man, or at the very least, ask questions about him. At the moment, most everyone in town was suspect.

"So, whadaya say, Nate? You gonna partner up with me and show these other ruffians who's boss?"

Nate grinned. "Now, how can I turn down a chance like that? But you realize you're taking a risk. I don't know much about how this contest works and I haven't swung a hammer like that in years. Set a log down, and I can chop it up any way you'd like it. Not sure about hitting a small spike."

Perry bumped Henry again, pointing his thumb at Nate. "The boy thinks I'm going to trust him with the hammer." The two men slapped their knees as they displayed their amusement. Perry stood and put his arm around Nate's shoulders. "See ya later, Henry. I gotta show Nate his role in the contest."

"Good luck to you both. I'll see you there."

Perry led him down the steps. "Let's head to the livery to practice. There's good money in this contest and I'd like to win it just once. Rube is good, but he's old and doesn't have the strength required for winning." He gripped Nate's bicep. "Yep, just what I thought. I might actually stand a chance today."

Nate strode next to Perry, trying to keep up while wondering what he'd gotten himself into. Half an hour later, he knew exactly what could happen and doubted his good sense. If Perry missed the mark just once, Nate might never hold a gun again. Or even a fork, for that matter.

The two young men Nate helped arrest his first day in town strolled past, their heads together, looking very much like they were scheming. Nate fought the urge to turn and follow them to see what they were up to.

Perry, who hadn't stopped talking since Nate agreed to help him with the competition, grabbed him by the arm and pulled him along the street, his eight-pound hammer resting on his other shoulder.

"Quit your dawdling, young man, or you'll make us late."

Nate gripped the drills tighter in his hand. "Yes, sir." Without a doubt, it was a good thing the competition came before lunch. The way his stomach was churning, he might have lost all he ate. He'd much rather be pursuing suspects with the chance of making an arrest, or even getting shot at, than pursuing the winnings of a silly competition with the chance of losing the use of his hands.

Once they'd arrived at the designated site, Nate wondered if Perry had lost his mind. One look at the arms of their opposition and Nate knew they didn't stand a chance. Some of the men looked like they could lift their mule with one arm and not break a sweat. But Perry strode up to the table, plopped down a roll of money, and signed their names on the list without hesitation.

Perry turned to him. "Ready?"

Nate forced his enthusiasm. "Sure. Lead the way."

For the first time since his dad and brother were killed, Nate felt the need to pray, but the words wouldn't form. Instead, he took several deep breaths and knelt next to the rock Perry chose. Were they serious about drilling a hole in granite? He couldn't picture them getting more than a few chips knocked from the rock.

"Got yourself a new victim, do ya, Weaver?" The massive man

wore a grin that told Nate the man wasn't being cruel but tossing a friendly taunt his way. "You know that's why Rube stutters, don't ya?"

Perry laughed at the jest. "I'll make you eat them words, Jack."

Jack grinned. "I'll settle for some of your wife's great cooking."

He nodded off to the left. Nate followed the direction he motioned and found Mrs. Weaver, Rebekah, and Andrew waving and clapping. Cora stood next to them. Then Rebekah folded her hands and lifted her head, her eyes closed. The way the sun glinted off her hair, she could have passed for an angel, and the good Lord knew he needed a guardian angel right now. Nate hoped she remembered him in her prayer.

Taking a quick look around, Nate noticed that some of the men who would be holding the drills were sweating, making him feel better about his own ruffled nerves. Most of the men with the hammers were all smiles and very relaxed. Small wonder. Nate gripped the drills tighter. If he found the troublemakers in the next week or two, he couldn't be roped into this insanity again.

"All right, men, take your positions." The sheriff stood on a platform with his chest puffed out, looking for all the world like he owned the town. He pulled his pistol from the holster and held it in the air. "On the count of three, I'll fire the gun, and you can start."

All the men with hammers hefted them to their shoulders while those holding the drills placed the points on the rocks. Trying to keep his hands from shaking, Nate dropped the longer drills next to him and put the point of his shortest steel spike on the mark Perry had made. He stared at the head of his drill, determined not to look away but to hold it steady as Perry had instructed. Sweat ran down his back as more beaded on his forehead.

Nate didn't hear the sheriff's count of three, but the gunshot was unmistakable. Barely a second later, the first strike from Perry landed on the spike. He turned the drill and prepared for the next hit. Each time Perry hit the spike, Nate would give it a slight turn. This went on for several minutes until Nate hardly had room to hold the metal, then Perry shouted for the next drill. Nate tossed the short tool away and grabbed the next longest one from the ground. He placed the tip of it in the hole, his hands still feeling the vibration as though the hitting hadn't stopped. He had no doubt the ringing in his ears would last a lifetime.

Forearms starting to ache, Nate held tight while the slamming of the hammer continued. Perry called for the next drill. Nate had just placed the new bit into the deep hole when Perry brought the sledge down again. The hammer skimmed his knuckles, raking away the skin. Nate closed his eyes against the throbbing, instantly opening them in fear of getting hit again.

"Sorry," Perry shouted as he prepared for the next blow.

Pain radiating through his entire hand, Nate gritted his teeth and forced himself to hold the drill steady, wishing he were any-where but here. An eternity later, after changing the bit one more time, the gunshot sounded, ending the competition and Nate's tor-ture. He stood and moved next to Perry to await the results as blood oozed from his stinging knuckles. At least his fingers still worked. Without a doubt, he had a newfound respect for miners.

Cheers and whistling filled the air until the sheriff called for quiet. The judges moved in to measure the depth of the hole in each rock. The man who'd teased Perry earlier eased up to them and looked at Nate's hand.

"Let me hear you talk."

Nate shrugged. "Huh?"

The man burst into laughter. "Oh, no. Perry's bad aim's got you babbling, too. Guess I shoulda warned ya better."

Perry only grinned and shook his head in response, never taking his eyes from the judges. In minutes, the judges approached Sheriff Caldwell with the results. He glanced over them, then raised his hand to get everyone's attention.

"We have a winner!"

The cheering resumed. The sheriff let it go on a bit before he grinned and waved his hand again. "Quiet. Quiet down, everyone." He waited for silence before continuing. "We have a new champion."

Nate could feel Perry tense up. The man wanted badly to win this contest, but Nate had his doubts that today he'd get his wish.

"At a depth of thirty-two and a half inches"—the sheriff stopped and took his time looking around the crowd, drawing out the strain of anticipation—"the winner is…" Again he paused, and everyone looked like they wanted to take the hammer and drill to his head. "The winner is Jack 'The Hammer' Demmer and his partner, George Eason."

The sledge in Jack's hand dropped to the ground, along with his bottom jaw. "I won?"

George whooped and raced up to the podium to collect the prize.

Perry clapped Jack on the back and then shoved him to join his partner, George.

Perry's shoulders then slumped in defeat. "If it couldn't be us, I'm glad it was Jack." He grabbed the wrist of Nate's injured hand. "Maybe next time. Now, let's get this taken care of."

They collected their tools and headed toward the Weaver family, though Nate was ready to go his own way. He'd had enough of all this togetherness. It was time to separate and get some investigation done.

Before he could decline the help and make his escape, Rebekah grabbed his arm and nearly dragged him away from the crowd. Nate gave an inward groan. Now what did the Weavers want from him? He'd already bled for them. He didn't have anything else to give.

He looked in Rebekah's eyes. Or did he?

Chapter Thirteen
. . . .

Rebecca tugged Nate along behind her, wishing he'd move faster. There wasn't much time before the eating began, and she needed to retrieve their food from the house and get it to the picnic grounds without being gone too long. So far, she and Cora hadn't noticed extra attention from any of the men, but she didn't want to take the chance of missing a clue. And now she also had to tend to Nate's hand.

"How are the knuckles?"

Nate pulled her to a stop. "Where are we going?"

"To the house." She tugged at his arm again, getting his feet moving, though not nearly fast enough. In fact, she got the impression he was fighting her efforts. "I need to bandage your hand, and then I need your help getting our food and such back in time for the picnic."

He plodded behind, moving slower, even leaning back a bit like the crazy mule. "You don't seem surprised my hand got hurt."

At that comment, Rebekah had to stop. She turned to face him. "Ah, well, no, not really."

Eyebrows winging upward, he crossed his arms. "So that begs the need to ask." He tilted his face toward hers. "Why didn't you warn me?"

Stunned, Rebekah could hardly speak. She felt her jaw drop open and forced it closed. "I didn't know Daddy planned to ask you to partner with him until this morning, and I didn't see you until you were already at the contest."

That sounded weak even to her. But it was true. And truth be told, she doubted anyone could have changed her father's mind once it was set. Hadn't Nate learned that yet? If not, that certainly wasn't her fault.

"Rebekah!"

She looked for the person calling her name and saw Cora, arms spread in a position that screamed, "What do you think you're doing?"

"I'm hurrying, Cora." Rebekah latched onto Nate's arm once again and nearly dragged him behind her. His boots clomped along. He wasn't exactly trying to keep up.

"What's the rush? And what does Cora want?"

Grinding her teeth in frustration, Rebekah turned to face him. "I'll tell you if you'll try harder to walk faster." She caught the twitching of his lips. Knowing he found her amusing, she growled her annoyance. "Never mind."

She started on her way again, only to have Nate tug her to a stop. Irritated, she pulled her arm free. "I've got to hurry."

Nate rushed to her side, a grin stretching across his face as he easily kept pace. "You've got me intrigued. Tell me."

She cast a glance his way, and her exasperation melted away at his good looks. Why did he have to be so handsome? She decided then and there not to look at him again for the duration of their time together. Doing so would keep her mind from whirling off in the wrong direction.

What were they talking about? Oh, that's right. "It's about the note Cora got yesterday."

"A note?"

Stunned, she looked at him, only to turn away quickly. "You haven't heard? You must be the only one in town who doesn't know."

"So, enlighten me."

Hastening her steps even more, Rebekah filled him in on how Cora received the note and what it said. Then she told him of their plan to find out not only who the note spoke of, but who the writer might be. "And that's why I'm in a hurry to get back. I don't want to take a chance of missing clues."

Even as she said the words, she thought they sounded a bit childish, and worse, Nate might think the same. A brief glance at his face told her his mind treated Cora's note with suspicion just as hers had when she first read it. She decided it might be wise to ask for his input.

"You look concerned." She climbed the steps of their porch and unlocked the door. "What are you thinking?" She didn't wait for his answer but headed for the kitchen and the cabinet, where they kept the bandages.

Nate trailed behind and sat at the table, placing his wounded hand on top, as if she'd already instructed him to do so. His action made her wonder if he felt at home—or if he'd been injured enough times to know what to do. After she dampened a scrap of cloth, she sat next to him and started to clean his wound. He still sat mute.

She could no longer stand the silence. "Enlighten me."

Nate looked her in the eyes and chuckled. She'd repeated the very words he'd used on her earlier.

"All right, since you ask." He cleared his throat, his expression abruptly turning grim. "You act as though that note had good news, a possible suitor, but have you considered the fact that the verse might be more of a threat? Maybe a warning of danger?"

So his first reaction was the same as hers. The very real possibility of trouble sent a chill down her spine. "Yes, I'd thought of that. But I allowed Cora to convince me that it was good news."

She finished cleaning the scrape and started wrapping a strip of cloth around his hand. The act—not to mention the calluses on his palm—was very familiar since she'd done almost the same the day before. He had a very strong hand. She enjoyed holding it in hers.

Stop it! Taking a deep breath, she licked her suddenly dry lips. "You can help us."

What was she thinking? She needed to get away from this man so she could think clearly. How to get out of this?

"I'd be glad to."

Oh, goodness. Now what to do? "Great."

That meant he'd be spending most of the day with her. The thought made her heart give a little leap. She rushed from the chair before he could see the blood rushing to her face and started placing the food, plates, napkins, and utensils in a box.

He moved next to her, hefted the crate into his arms, and motioned for her to precede him. "Tell me what you two have planned, so I'll know how I can help."

Once he'd stepped through the doorway, Rebekah closed and locked the door. "There's not much of a plan, really. We were going to keep an eye out for anyone who spent a great deal of time staring or staying close to Cora." She peeked at his face. "Pretty weak, isn't it?"

He chuckled. "Not really, since you don't know for sure what to look for. With me helping, we might have a better chance of seeing something out of the ordinary. Trouble is, I don't know many people here, so I won't know what's strange and what isn't." He paused a few seconds. "Especially when I have a cross-eyed cat and a mule that can't walk straight to compare to."

Rebekah burst into laughter. Nate could make her laugh at the most inappropriate times. "The people in town aren't *that* bad." She laughed again as his brows raised in skepticism. "All right, maybe some are, but most have good hearts."

"I look forward to finding out for myself." He readjusted the box, making her wonder if his hand hurt, but he seemed to carry it easily enough. Before she could ask, he nodded. "You'll point out all the men who live or work across from Cora for me, won't you?"

"Absolutely." And thankfully the distraction would keep her from spending too much time thinking about the man at her side.

Cora chose that moment to rush up to them. "What took you so long? I can't watch all these men by myself."

Rebekah slipped her arm around her friend's shoulders. "And here I thought you'd relish the idea."

Cora elbowed her in the ribs. "Stop that." She turned to Nate. "We've not been properly introduced. I'm Cora Peters."

Nate couldn't release the box to greet her with a handshake. He simply nodded. "Nice to meet you, Cora. I'm—"

"Nathaniel Kirkland. I know. I saw you in the store the other day. Rebekah's told me all about you."

Shock and embarrassment started at the top of Rebekah's head and quickly radiated down to her toes. How could Cora say that to Nate? What would he think? She would have shoved her elbow into Cora's ribs like she'd received moments ago except she was afraid Nate would see, compounding her humiliation. She glanced up at him and found him smiling at her. Mortified, she looked away.

"And what all has Rebekah said about me?"

Rebekah wasn't about to let Cora answer, though she'd opened her mouth to do just that, and took the opportunity to fill Cora in on Nate's offer to help. Thankfully by the time they'd finished talking about the note and their plan to uncover the writer and Cora's possible suitor, they'd arrived at the picnic grounds.

Cora rushed off to help her mother lay out the food while Rebekah showed Nate where to put their dishes. As usual, there was more food than could possibly be eaten, even by the multitude of people in attendance.

Nate gave a low whistle. "Where does one start?"

Rebekah opened her mouth to answer, but Cora swooped by and scooped her arm through Nate's. "Right over here." She pointed as she led Nate away. "With the dish *I* made."

Speechless, Rebekah could only watch them walk off together. She'd never seen Cora quite so bold, but maybe the note caused the change, getting her hopes up to where she didn't even try to control her actions. Unless—surely she didn't think Nate was the author—

"Everyone!" The sheriff shouted to be heard. "Please quiet down so the pastor can say the blessing."

Rebekah heard very little of the pastor's prayer. Once he'd finished, the group converged on the tables laden with food. From a distance, Rebekah watched Nate fill a plate and wander off toward one of the shade trees while Cora remained next to her mother. Having learned who the better cooks of the residents were, Rebekah was selective about the dishes she chose to sample, then moved in the direction she'd last seen Nate.

Carefully picking her way through the crowd, trying very hard not to get bumped and spill her plate, Rebekah maneuvered to a position where she could see Nate while keeping an eye out for anyone watching or talking to Cora. But when she arrived at her chosen location, Nate was nowhere to be found. Rebekah scanned the area but still didn't spot him among the different clusters of people now sitting on the blankets they'd placed on the ground.

Deciding to start where she'd last seen him, Rebekah moved to the tree. That's when she spotted him, leaning behind the farthest tree from the picnic area, looking very much like he was sick to his stomach. Alarmed, she rushed toward him, praying he was all right.

Chapter Fourteen

....

If Nate didn't know better, he'd swear Cora was trying to poison him. He heaved one last time before spitting out the remnants and wiping his sleeve across his lips. That was the nastiest stuff he'd ever placed in his mouth. With no qualms whatsoever, he scraped the rest of her questionable cuisine from his plate. Surely she didn't allow anyone else to—

"Are you all right?"

Nate turned to find Rebekah staring from a short distance away, concern written on her face. "I think so." He wiped his mouth one more time to be sure nothing remained. "But if I die in the next few minutes, you'd better ask Cora a few questions about her food."

When Rebekah smiled, then started to laugh, Nate wondered if the two women were working on some sort of conspiracy. If so, was it just for him or for all the men? Were they trying to kill all the males in town or just make them wish they were dead?

"What's so funny?"

Rebekah fought to control her mirth. She took a deep breath. "I should have warned you about Cora's cooking. I think she's the only one in town who believes her dishes are tasty."

He stared, running what he'd heard through his mind again. "So, she's not trying to kill me?"

Rebekah covered her giggle with her hand. "Actually, I think she was trying to impress you."

"Yes, well, the reaction of my stomach meeting her food was quite impressive."

Rebekah doubled over with laughter, and Nate grinned at the pleasant sound. She sure was easy to amuse.

He shook his head and motioned toward the tables. "Come on. I need something to drink to wash away this taste in my mouth." Several pitchers crowded one table. He asked Rebekah quietly, so no one else would hear, "Did Cora make any of these?"

He could have been tickling Rebekah, so great was her hilarity. She finally managed a shake of her head. They both poured a cup of lemonade and returned to the nearby shade tree, positioning themselves so they could observe Cora while they ate, most likely for two different reasons.

Nate didn't want to destroy the girls' dream of an unknown admirer seeking Cora's attention, which is why he kept his opinion to himself. But he felt fairly certain the note was a threat, not an announcement of a suitor. So instead, he'd be alert for anyone who might be looking to harm the unsuspecting young lady.

While Rebekah kept an eye on Cora, Nate couldn't help but watch the poor soul wandering around the tables of food after everyone had filled their plates. For whatever reason, the young man managed to wander past all the good food and stop at Cora's dish. He scooped a heap of something that resembled watery potatoes onto his plate. Nate felt the urge to run up to the man and warn him, yet in no way did he want to hurt or embarrass Cora, so he kept his seat and continued to watch for the results of the man's poor choice.

Nate nearly choked when he saw the young man approach the area where Cora sat with an older couple, probably her parents, then sat near them. The poor man would be so humiliated when he gagged on the food Cora made. Nate felt for him and told himself not to watch, yet he couldn't look away as he waited for the horrific scene to unfold. He bumped Rebekah and motioned toward Cora and the young man.

"That man just took some of Cora's food and is now sitting next to her. This isn't going to be pretty."

Rebekah gasped. "Oh, no. That's Will Bradford. He's the most shy man I've ever met. If he gets sick from Cora's food, I don't know that he'll ever recover from the shame."

"What can we do?"

Rebekah made a face. "Nothing, I'm afraid. Anything we try to do to stop him will only make matters worse."

The whole situation seemed odd to Nate. If most everyone knew of Cora's cooking, why would the young man take the food and move to sit with her? Dismay formed in Nate's mind and quickly moved to his gut. Was this the man planning to do Cora harm? Why else would he do such a thing? But surely he wouldn't try anything with Cora's parents sitting with them.

Fully alert, Nate cringed as he watched Will take his first bite, remembering quite clearly the mutiny declared by his mouth. Stalling in his chewing for a brief moment and his face turning red, Will swallowed hard. Nate could only imagine that the poor man wanted that ghastly taste out of his mouth as soon as possible. But what in the world could be happening inside his stomach? Nate's own stomach tightened at the thought.

Then Will took another bite. While Nate's jaw dropped open at Will's bravery, Rebekah's hand went over her mouth. "Oh my goodness."

Nate stared, waiting for her to continue. She didn't. "What?"

She never looked away from the dreadful scene. "He's the one."

Nate's tension intensified. Now was not the time for a woman to decide not to babble. "The one what?"

Rebekah finally looked at him. "Cora's admirer. Who else would force himself to eat that food, if not the man trying to win her heart?"

Nate peered back at Cora and Will and couldn't argue with Rebekah's reasoning. Only a lovesick heart could overrule an upset stomach. As he relaxed, he laughed and shook his head.

"What?"

He could see the curiosity in Rebekah's eyes and decided to speak his mind. "To be honest, I thought you girls were silly thinking that note was about an admirer. I thought someone planned to harm Cora."

Rebekah's mouth dropped open. "Silly girls? I think I moved beyond silly years ago. Or, at the very least, a year ago."

He knew she must be referring to getting burned. Other than what little Henry told him, Nate knew next to nothing about what had happened. Maybe she'd tell him more. "I apologize. I never meant to imply you were childish." She'd never given him that impression. In fact, everything about her was just the opposite.

An explosion cut off Nate's next comment. He could feel the vibration through the ground. Dropping his plate, he leapt to his feet. "Stay with Cora."

He only got two steps away before Rebekah yelled, "Wait!"

He took a second to turn and shout over his shoulder, "Just stay here."

As he raced to keep up with all the other men, Nate refused to miss out on a chance to learn anything he could about the latest bit of trouble. He had a job to do and, up to now, he'd been completely unsuccessful. No way would he let an outlaw best him.

Chapter Fifteen

....

By the time Nate had climbed the hill south of town—what seemed like halfway up War Eagle Mountain—he was out of breath and wishing he'd stopped to saddle his horse. Many men were on foot, though, with only a few on horseback or wagon, leaving most gasping for air.

Smoke billowed from another mill, this one an ore-extracting mill instead of a lumber mill. Listening to all the chatter and murmurings, Nate discovered the name was Zimmer's Stamp Mill. Now he had to find out who Zimmer was and why his place was targeted. He'd met enough men in the time he'd worked for Perry that learning information shouldn't be as difficult this time as it was at the fire he'd helped put out.

Perry huffed up beside him, bending over to rest his hands on his knees and suck in great breaths. "I ain't—as young—as I used to be."

"You all right?"

Perry nodded. "Just—give me a minute."

Impatience ate at Nate. He needed to find out what had happened. Just as he'd decided to try to gain entry into the mill to see if he could help, a few men came out, more smoke trailing after them through the doorway. Suspicion snaked through Nate's thoughts until it took over his entire mind. They'd all raced up the hill from the picnic together. So how did these men get into the mill before everyone else?

The lead man put his hands up, quieting the crowd. "There wasn't much of a fire. It's already out. Everything's under control."

The crowd clustered around the men. The sheriff, almost the last to arrive, pushed his way to the front. "What happened, Mr. Zimmer?"

So this was the owner? Nate moved closer to make sure he heard everything said. Perry was right on his heels.

"The crusher's been blown up, along with all the mechanisms that make it work properly. It'll take months to get it back in working order." The owner shook his head, his hands lifting and dropping in a helpless gesture. "If it's even worth the trouble."

The last was said so quietly, Nate was sure the man didn't mean for anyone to hear it. Someone bumped his arm. He looked down and found Henry at his side.

"What was the explosion, Grant?"

Mr. Zimmer's gaze was steady. "Only thing it could have been was dynamite or something similar."

"You saying someone wanted to put you out of business?" Henry seemed to want to make certain there were no doubts in anyone's minds as to the intent.

"That's exactly what I'm saying, Henry." Now that the shock was over, Mr. Zimmer's anger began to show. "And if I get my hands on the person—"

The sheriff grabbed Mr. Zimmer's arm and tried to turn him around. "Take me to the damage, Grant. I want to look at it. Maybe I can see something you missed."

Nate stepped forward. "I'd like to go too."

The sheriff waved him away. "I don't think so."

"I think you should consider it, Grant." Perry moved between Nate and the sheriff as if to ward off any kind of disagreement that might arise. "Nate's been working for me in the livery, and he's pretty handy with metal works. I'd trust him with even the most difficult task."

Sheriff Caldwell shook his head. "Be that as it may, I don't think—"

"Actually, I think Perry's right." Mr. Zimmer reached out his hand. "I'm Grant Zimmer."

Nate shook his hand. "Nathaniel Kirkland. I'll help in any way I can." And he meant every word. His help just might not be what everyone expected.

The sheriff cut Nate a venomous look before Mr. Zimmer led the way through the door, across a room, and up a set of stairs. A wide platform ran along a chute. A thin ribbon of smoke still rose from the site of the blast. Several pieces of metal lay twisted and torn, ripped apart from whatever explosive was used to do a great deal of damage to the area that seemed most important to the mill's operation. From his experience with metal, Nate knew it would take weeks of work to repair the destruction. If only he had as much experience with explosives.

"So, what do you think, young Nate? Any hope for getting this thing up and running any time soon?" Mr. Zimmer's eyes looked hopeful.

Nate hated to snuff that hope, but he had to be honest. "I wish I could say yes, Mr. Zimmer, but this is a mess. Even working nonstop, it'd take weeks to patch up all this. Some pieces are beyond repair." He scanned the area. "You'd need to order more, or let me cut and form new pieces." But doing that, he'd have no time to investigate.

Looking down, Mr. Zimmer nodded. "That's what I thought.

Thank you, Nate, for your honesty." He released a long, slow breath as he descended the steps. "I should have paid."

Nate frowned. "What?"

The sheriff placed his hand on Nate's back. "Could you help me with this? I'd like to look under this sheet of metal. See if there's anything that'll tell me what was used and who might have put it there."

As much as Nate wanted to follow Mr. Zimmer and ask what he meant about paying, he also wanted the chance to investigate, and the sheriff just gave him the chance. He'd look up the owner and ask his questions later.

At least half an hour later, Nate knew no more than when he'd walked in the door. Whoever blew up the mill managed to do so without leaving any traces to disclose who they were. It was as if these people had been doing this type of work long enough to know exactly how to keep from being discovered. How else could such damage be done without leaving a hint of evidence behind? And from what his superiors told him, this had been going on for months.

Perry was the only one who'd waited for him. All the other men had returned to town. Doing his best to answer Perry's questions as they descended the mountain, Nate's mind was on one thing only. He had to find Mr. Zimmer and ask what he meant by paying. Paying whom? And how much? But most of all, for what? This was the first indication blackmail might be involved. Up to now, Nate and his superiors had thought all the crime was due to mischief or attempts to slow other miners from finding ore.

They arrived in town with the celebration back up and running, the noise level high again now that the meal was finished and the games had started. With all the frenzy of people milling around, finding Mr. Zimmer would be like trying to find daylight at the bottom of a shaft.

Perry tapped his arm. "Looks like the single-jack contest is over. I'm going to see if I can find my family. Want to join me?"

Much as Nate liked the Weaver family, this might be the only day he had plenty of time to look around and ask questions, not to mention meet more of the residents. "Maybe later. I'm going to wander around for a while, watch more games, and meet more people."

"All right. Have fun."

Seconds later, Perry was out of sight, enveloped by the crowd. Nate glanced down both sides of the street. Where might he find Mr. Zimmer? The sheriff's office might be a good place to start. He made his way north, jumping off the boardwalk when it became too busy.

Commotion to his right grabbed his attention. One of the two young men he had helped arrest his first day in town had fallen, probably off the boardwalk because of his obvious drunken state. His friend remained on the boardwalk pointing and laughing while hanging onto a post in front of the same saloon where Nate had last seen them inebriated.

Disgusted, he continued down the street, only to stop after a few steps and turn back. He'd been told all businesses closed on celebration days, yet the saloon was open. Whether or not that was usual, Nate didn't care. But was Mr. Zimmer inside? The possibility of losing a business would drive many a man to drink. It would take but a minute to venture inside for a look.

Nate pushed through the swinging doors and waited for his eyes to adjust to the dark interior, while a bitter stench assaulted his nostrils. Once he could see clearly, he noticed several men occupied the tables, most with decks of cards strewn across their surfaces.

Off to his left, the long bar also supported the elbows of a few men, including those of Henry and Mr. Zimmer, the latter with his head sagging close to the polished wood and the glass of whiskey dangling precariously from his fingertips. No glass or mug sat in front of Henry. Only the local paper occupied his hands.

Sliding onto the stool next to Henry, Nate motioned toward Mr. Zimmer. "I guess he came directly here after leaving the mill to be in that condition already."

"Yes, sir." Henry folded the paper and dropped it on the bar. "He looked mighty upset so I trailed him here. Thought maybe I'd keep an eye on him. Make sure he didn't run into any trouble."

"Couldn't keep him from drinking, though, huh?"

"Nope. He seemed dead set on finding solace at the bottom of a glass."

Nate nodded. "That's what I figured. I planned to look for him at the sheriff's office but thought a quick check in here might be in order." He crossed his arms and rested them on the bar. "I thought all businesses closed for these celebrations."

Henry chuckled. "You really think a saloon will stay closed with all these men in town, especially if most of the men are miners?" He clapped Nate on the back. "A day like this is a barkeep's own gold mine." He hunched over the bar like Nate. "So, did the sheriff find anything at the mine that will help locate the men who blew it up?"

"Not a trace." Nate shook his head. "If there hadn't been so much damage, you'd almost think it exploded all by itself, which is really strange. There should be some hint of the explosive used."

Henry bumped him. "Don't fret on it too much. That job belongs to the sheriff. The only thing you need to worry about is having too much fun today.... Speaking of fun, what in the world are you doing in here instead of kicking up your heels out there with a pretty girl?"

"Same as you, I guess. Wanted to make sure Mr. Zimmer would be all right." He shrugged. "Thought maybe if I found him, I could ask a question or two."

"Well, I doubt asking questions will work at the moment." Henry stood and placed his hand on Mr. Zimmer's shoulder. "But how about you help me get this man home safe, then we both can start enjoying what's left of the day?"

Nate rose. "I like the sound of that."

He hooked his arm under one of Mr. Zimmer's while Henry took the other side. Together they lifted the large mill owner from the stool, Nate taking most of the weight, and headed for the door.

Henry nodded the direction they needed to go; then a hint of trouble flickered across his face. "What questions?"

Nate grunted. Mr. Zimmer was a lot heavier than he looked. But then, he wasn't giving them a lick of help in taking on some of the weight by walking. They nearly had to drag the man.

"He made a comment about how he should have paid."

"Paid? What's that mean?" Henry's question came out like a growl, probably from the strain of their burden.

"That's what I wanted to ask him."

Henry choked on his laugh. "Right."

"Hold up there."

At the command, both Nate and Henry stopped. Sheriff Caldwell swung around in front of them. "What's going on here?"

Henry muttered something Nate couldn't understand, then cast a sneer toward the sheriff. "Look, Paul, either help—or get out of the way. The man's falling down drunk, and we aim to get him home."

The sheriff shoved Nate away and took his place holding up Mr. Zimmer. "I'll take over here. I think Perry's been looking for this young man." He motioned toward Nate, then gave Henry a nod. "Let's get moving. I got work to do."

Determined to locate Mr. Zimmer in the next day or two to get answers to his questions, Nate watched them stumble off for only a minute or two before heading to find Perry. Following all the shouts of laughter, Nate found Perry and his family, along with most of the other residents, crowded around a small pen. He moved next to Perry, only to be grabbed by the arm and pulled close.

"You have to see this, Nate. The funniest thing you'll see today."

As far as Nate was concerned, that wasn't much of a challenge. Not many humorous things had taken place so far. "What's happening?"

"One at a time, the kids are turned loose inside the pen along with a chicken. Whoever catches one the fastest wins a prize. You made it just in time. Andrew's next." In the next second, Perry deafened Nate as he yelled for his young son. Then he turned back to Nate. "Guaranteed there will be a shortage of eggs tomorrow after these kids are finished scaring these chickens half to death."

He hooted with laughter at his own joke, drawing a smile from Nate. Shaking off the remainder of his tension, Nate decided the rest of the day would be reserved for fun. He glanced around at all the faces, taking in the festive atmosphere. Even Mrs. Weaver had more color to her cheeks than he'd seen since they'd met. He spied Rebekah standing on the other side of her mother just as she looked up at him. The sparkle in her eyes nearly matched that of when she caught him choking on Cora's food. Rebekah had never looked prettier.

Before he could move to her side and ask her about finding Cora's possible admirer, someone gave a shrill whistle. In the blink of an eye, a chicken was tossed into the pen and Andrew burst toward it from the side. Tongue peeking from the side of his mouth, Andrew gave chase for several seconds, then leapt a good four feet and grabbed a leg of the chicken. Both of them rolled in the dirt, feathers and feet flying. Giving a shout, Andrew stood, grinning, the chicken's leg still grasped in his hand. More than a little unhappy, the chicken squawked and flapped its wings, beating Andrew on both sides of the head. With a peck at the boy's arm for good measure, the fowl was suddenly free as Andrew clasped his hand over the wound.

The crowd howled with laughter as they clapped and shouted. Looking a bit dejected, Andrew made his way toward the gate. The man who whistled—Nate assumed he was the judge of the game—grabbed Andrew's arm and raised it high, nearly lifting the boy from the ground.

"The winner!"

As soon as Andrew claimed his prize of a ribbon and a small bag of candy, he raced toward his parents.

Rebekah groaned. "All that sugar will make him excited enough to leap to the roof of the house."

With feathers still stuck in his hair and a good layer of dirt—not to mention chicken excrement—attached to his clothes, Andrew wrapped his arms around his mother's waist. He pulled away from her embrace and held up his prize, his wild eyes flashing between his father and Nate.

"Did ya see? Did ya see me get that chicken?" He swung his arms as though grabbing for the fowl once again. "That bird didn't stand a chance."

Perry tilted back his head and laughed before ruffling his son's hair. "You did great, son."

Nate squatted to be able to look Andrew in the eyes. "You were so fast, no one else had a chance."

Andrew's grin did the impossible of stretching even wider, making his freckles nearly disappear.

Nate patted his arm, then stood and moved next to Rebekah. "Did you and Cora find out if she has an admirer?" he murmured.

She turned to fully face him. "Are you poking fun at us?"

As much as he wanted to burst into laughter, he fought it. He placed his hand on his chest and let his jaw drop, hoping to look completely innocent. "Me? Of course not."

She swatted his arm and shook her finger in his face, showing him she didn't believe a thing he said, though her lips gave away her amusement. "I'll have you know we were right. Mr. Will Bradford is completely taken with Cora and has already asked her to dine with him after church."

Chuckling, Nate grabbed her finger and held on. "Well, I'll have you know that I'm happy the two of you were right."

Rebekah, head cocked to one side, examined his face. "Thank you."

Perry moved between them, making Nate release Rebekah's finger. "Don't want to interrupt whatever you two are arguing about, but, Nate, we've decided that today has been so much fun, we're having another picnic after church tomorrow, just the family this time. I think we'll plan to have as many of these as possible each summer since we have warm weather for such a short amount of time. How about you join us?"

Just the family? That sounded a bit too—intimate.

Andrew grabbed his hand and shook it. "Come on, Nate. You can help me catch fish."

Nate squatted again and closed one eye while squinting the other one. "Does that mean I have to jump in the stream again? Or do I get to use a pole?"

Andrew's face grew serious. "I didn't jump in. I fell in."

"Oh, that's right. I guess that means your sister doesn't plan on getting in either."

Andrew laughed. "Or maybe you can teach her to swim."

Eyebrows raised, Nate turned to see red washing up her neck and into her face. He cleared his throat and put his arm around Andrew's shoulders. "I don't think there's even the smallest chance of that happening."

Grinning, Perry embraced his daughter in a way that looked consoling. "Does that mean you'll join us, Nate?"

He stood and nodded. "I believe I will."

More than anything, he needed to get busy with his job as deputy marshal. But there was something special about this family, and he looked forward to another afternoon with them, even if that meant enduring a Sunday morning sermon. Investigating lawbreakers would have to wait another day. And besides, he couldn't think of a better way to spend an afternoon than seeing how many times he could get Rebekah's face to change color.

Chapter Sixteen

....

Rebekah moved only her eyes this time. If she turned in her pew once more to check if Nate had arrived, she'd strain her neck and have to deal with sore muscles. Where was he? Did he decide not to attend or did something happen after he left them yesterday? Neither option sat well, making her stomach nearly as painful as her neck.

A peek at her friend sitting to her right told her she wouldn't get to chat with Cora today. Will sat next to her, and the two only had eyes for each other. But, oh, did she want to talk to her friend. Rumors abounded about yet another note—this one received by their very own piano player, Mrs. Phipps.

The widowed woman, perched on the piano bench up front, wore a dreamy expression, far from the hopeless and futile one they were used to seeing. Her apathy was the very reason they allowed her to continue playing the piano. The dear woman had to be tone deaf, so awful and ear-bending were the notes flowing from the instrument. But playing every Sunday morning was all she had left, the only thing that made her happy since her husband died in the mines. No one had the heart to ask her to stop.

Rebekah sighed. She should've been a better friend to the woman. She'd dearly love to see that note. The only other person she could talk to about the new missive was Nate, and he had yet to show himself. She fought the urge to turn around—and lost. A scan of the entire room still didn't reveal the man she sought. Where was he?

At the first chords from the piano, Rebekah grimaced as they clashed in such a way as to make her teeth ache. Then she huffed and faced front. If Nate didn't want to attend church services, it was his loss, though she prayed for him to show up. It was bad enough Andrew squirmed next to her. Why he didn't sit with their parents, she didn't know. Regardless, she needed to be a good example to him and sit still.

The pastor motioned for them to rise for the first hymn. Standing also gave her the chance to glance around without becoming too conspicuous. She spotted the new family Thomas had introduced to her and Nate. Loomis, was it? They looked like they'd taken time to clean up a little. She welcomed them with a nod and smile. But by the time the hymn was finished, Nate still hadn't arrived. She tried to force herself to think about the words and meaning of the second hymn but to no avail. With a quick prayer for help to focus, Rebekah sat with the rest of the parishioners and found the passage the pastor referenced.

In an effort to concentrate, Rebekah centered her attention on the open Bible in her lap. The words blurred when Andrew's elbow bumped her side for the third time. She turned to tell him to sit still, but the sight of a frog's nose and eyes peeking out from the boy's shirt pocket froze the words in her throat. Memories of her little brother tormenting her with all manner of revolting creatures sent a tremor through her. In one motion, Rebekah clapped one hand over Andrew's shirt pocket, grabbed him by the arm with the other, and made him stand with her so they could leave.

"Excuse us," Rebekah mumbled to Cora and Will as she slid past and pulled Andrew with her into the aisle.

Rebekah marched toward the back of the church with Andrew in tow in hopes of making it to the entry door before her trembling legs gave out. She could feel everyone watching, but she kept her eyes focused on the door so she wouldn't have to meet the gaze of anyone. As the murmurs and laughter reached her ears, she prayed for a quick escape. But Andrew wasn't making that feat very easy. He tugged to get away while pushing at her hand covering his pocket.

"You're squishing it, Bekah," Andrew said in loud protest.

Rebekah slowed her steps and loosened her pressure on the frog. Another mistake. The nasty critter took the opportunity to scoot all the way out of Andrew's pocket. Just as it hopped away, Rebekah caught it in midair. She regretted the action the moment she felt moisture squirt down her palm.

In disgust, Rebekah held the vile creature long enough to get outside, then flung it away from her, only to see it land on Nate's chest. Though she was glad to see he'd finally arrived, she hadn't the time to be concerned about him right now. She had some kind of amphibian discharge dripping off her hand. Rebekah froze in shock, wondering if her skin would ever be the same.

Nate's snicker drew her attention.

He's enjoying this!

A second later, her thoughts moved to what he had done with the frog. No doubt it was in the hand he held at her back. She stepped away from him, her own hand still sticking out in midair. Then Nate released the frog under the bushes near the steps. Brushing his hands against his pants, he said, "I think we've probably seen the last of that poor little critter for a while."

Rebekah stared at him. "Poor little critter? *Poor little critter?*"

She took a deep breath in an effort to calm down. "Look what that nasty frog did to my hand."

Nate grasped her outstretched arm by the wrist and pulled her closer for a quick examination. He grimaced and narrowed his eyes. "Oh, my." He shook his head. "The skin's a mess. In fact, I think you might lose your hand."

"*What?*" Rebekah jerked her hand away from him to see for herself. Her fingers looked normal—no blisters or wounds that she could see. She looked up and found Nate shaking with quiet laughter. Then he burst into loud guffaws, bringing on Andrew's giggles. She stared at the two of them and felt her tension melt away.

Their mirth tugged at the corners of her mouth but she fought it back. "It's not *that* funny."

Nate snickered further. "Oh yeah, it is." He squatted down and bumped Andrew with his elbow. "Isn't it?"

Her brother peered up at her, mischief dancing across his face.

Rebekah tried to frown but couldn't quite pull it off. "Oh, all right, but that doesn't excuse the fact that those"—she shivered and motioned toward the bush—"those tiny beasts have no place in a church service."

Nate managed a more serious expression. "Your sister's right. You need to save those critters for the picnic later."

Rebekah's mouth dropped open. Nate was actually conspiring against her. In fact, when he looked up at her, he was downright smug. She gave him a glare that she hoped let him know he was in trouble. In the meantime, church was still in session.

"We need to get back inside." She made a face. "Not that I want to after the scene we made."

"*You* made, you mean." By the amusement on Nate's face, he obviously enjoyed her predicament.

She'd have to come up with a way to get him back—later. She held out her hand. In no way did she want that frog scum to remain on her any longer.

"What about my hand? It still has frog stuff on it."

Nate smirked before he could hide it behind his hand, along with a forced cough. "We'd better take care of the lady first, don't you think, Andrew?" Nate started past her. "Toad."

What? "I beg your pardon!" Why would he call her that?

"It was a *toad*, not a frog." Nate aimed a wink in her direction before he lifted the canteen from his saddle and pulled out his handkerchief. He poured water onto the cloth, all the while keeping his gaze on her face as he bobbed his eyebrows up and down. It was too much for Rebekah, and she finally burst into laughter.

Nate took her outstretched hand in his. The sensation of his touch crawled up Rebekah's arm and stifled her laughter, not to mention her breathing, right up until he hesitated washing away the slime to examine the scarring on her hand. When he glanced at her, she saw the regret in his eyes. With a slight twitch of his lips and tender squeeze on her wrist, Nate wiped her fingers with slow, almost intimate movements. She should pull away, clean her own hand, but she was helpless to stop him.

"There," Nate said with one final swipe. "Is that better?"

Rebekah's dry mouth refused to let her answer. Drowning in the depths of his pale green eyes, she managed a nod.

Nate turned, stuffed his kerchief into his saddlebag, and cleared his throat. Staring at the church door like he thought it might attack, he pointed with his thumb. "Should we get inside?"

He motioned for her to lead the way, and she obeyed. Rebekah sank onto the back pew. No one but the pastor seemed to be aware of their return. She tried to concentrate on the pastor's words, to no avail. Nate didn't help matters when he put his arm along the back of the pew, his fingers resting near her shoulder. If she leaned just a fraction, he'd be touching her. Rebekah closed her eyes.

Stop it. Just stop it, Rebekah.

The sound of rustling forced her to open her eyes. Everyone was standing. Rebekah jumped to her feet. Once the song started, she wanted to sneak out the door, but Nate blocked the aisle and continued to do so once the song was over. When he finally stepped aside, she made her way toward the pastor.

"I'm so sorry for all the disruptions. If I had known—"

The pastor enveloped her hand in both of his. "Don't apologize, Rebekah. How could you have known?" He grinned and winked at Andrew. "He livened up the morning a little, though I don't know that I'd want that done on a regular basis." He reached to shake Andrew's hand. "What do ya say we let God's critters have their own service outside?"

One side of Andrew's mouth lifted. "Yes, sir."

Daddy approached and placed his hand on the back of Andrew's neck. "I can assure you it won't happen again. Isn't that right, son?"

Andrew peered up at him, a hint of fear in his eyes, and nodded. Daddy shook the pastor's hand and then propelled Andrew out the door and down the steps. Then he crouched down to eye level.

"I won't discipline you this time, Andrew, but if you do anything like that again, you and I will be doing more than talk. Understand?"

Biting on his lips, Andrew nodded once again. Daddy ruffled his hair before he stood and shook Nate's hand.

"Good to see you made it. I started to wonder." Without waiting for an explanation, he turned to Rebekah. "You three can either ride with us to get the food, or you can walk to our spot near the river and wait for your mama and me."

Rebekah glanced up at Nate, willing to do whatever made him comfortable.

He gave a quick shrug. "I think I'd like to walk. How about you?"

At the moment, she couldn't think of anything better she'd like to do. Some time alone with Nate would be—

"That sounds great!"

Andrew's voice rose high with excitement, bringing Rebekah's dream crashing down. How could she have forgotten Andrew?

Daddy held out his hand. "I'll take your Bible home." Once he had it in his possession, he waved, then helped Mama board the buggy and pointed the horses toward home. "See you in a little bit."

Rebekah stared after them. Would the day ever come when she'd be held by her husband in just the same way?

"Which direction?"

Nate's voice so close to her ear made shivers go down her back and arms. She couldn't decide if she wanted her reaction to him to stop or happen more often. Unable to speak at the moment, she pointed southeast. Andrew took over leading the way, his nonstop chatter about everything that moved in their path keeping Nate from speaking and Rebekah from thinking. He managed to catch a butterfly and brought it to them for inspection. Nate made all the expected exclamations before suggesting it be turned loose so it would still be able to fly. Andrew flung it into the air and raced off for his next adventure.

Several minutes later, Nate slowed his pace, so Rebekah did the same. Andrew continued at his same rate, darting after grasshoppers and other loathsome creatures, putting him farther away from them. Even his discourse on the benefit of bugs became nothing more than a quiet buzz carried away on the warm breeze.

Nate gave a soft chuckle. "Do you think he'll notice we're no longer listening?"

Smiling, Rebekah shrugged. "He will at some point. It'll depend on when he runs out of critters to chase. Then we'll get a sound scolding for not keeping up. He may even start all over with whatever he said, not wanting us to miss out on his wisdom. It's times like this I miss Michael. He was better at keeping up with and entertaining Andrew."

As her words tapered off in the midst of Nate's laughter, she suddenly felt tongue-tied. She'd been waiting for the chance to get to know more about him, but now, with the opportunity right in front of her, she couldn't figure out how to get the conversation going. Just blurting out the questions didn't seem right.

"Speaking of listening…" Nate glanced at her, then looked away. "Doesn't anyone else in your church know how to play a piano?"

Knowing exactly where his question was leading, she tried to smother her smile with her hand, hoping to come across as thoughtful. "Yes. Why?" As he struggled with his next sentence, she decided to help him out, but only a little. "You didn't like the way Mrs. Phipps played this morning?"

He stopped and looked her in the eyes. "You knew what I was going to say?" At her nod, he shook his head and motioned for them to continue walking. "Why does the pastor allow her to keep playing when she's so bad at it?"

She tilted her head. "Her, ah, technique does leave a little to be desired."

"To put it mildly."

She chuckled, then became serious. "It's all she has left—the only thing that seems to make her happy. No one wants to take that away from her."

"What do you mean, all she has left?"

She stared at the tree line along the river. "Her husband died in one of the mine explosions about ten months ago. I think a part of her died with him." She recalled the soft look on Mrs. Phipps's face earlier. "Until today, anyway."

Nate groaned. "You keep talking in riddles." He grinned and bumped her lightly with his elbow. "Why was today different?"

She wondered if he would give her a bad time about the second note, but she'd been waiting for the chance to tell him. "Remember the note Cora received?"

"How could I forget? My association with her was nearly the death of me. She should be arrested for trying to poison people with her cooking."

Rebekah laughed and swatted at him. "Stop."

He waggled his eyebrows up and down. "What about the note?"

"Mrs. Phipps got one this morning."

He opened his mouth, closed it, then shook his head. "What did this one say?"

"I don't know. I'm not sure anyone has seen it. All I've heard is that she found one tacked to her front door, and whatever it said made her very happy."

Swiping his hand from the top of his head down to his neck,

he snorted. "First a woman who can't cook gets help finding an admirer. Now a tone-deaf woman is receiving the same help. Do I dare ask who's next?"

Rebekah hadn't thought about it that way, but he was right. She knew he hadn't meant to point out their flaws in a mean way, but she couldn't help but think of the scars on her face and side. Would she be the next pitied woman?

Nate's hand flashed in front of her face. "What is that?"

She frowned up at him. "What?"

He motioned again, pointing at her throat. "That little ornament you have attached to your chain. I've noticed several times that you like to hold it. I've never seen anything like it."

Rebekah released it, not even aware she'd reached for it. "Daddy made it for me. He gave it to me a couple months after I was burned."

Heart thundering in the silence that followed, she waited for him to change the subject. Everyone else grew uncomfortable talking about the accident. Only now she knew it wasn't an accident.

His steps slowed even more. "Do you trust me enough to tell me what happened?"

The question so surprised her, she had to make a conscious effort to keep her mouth closed and not stare. Very few people had asked her about that day. But was she ready to tell Nate? She had no reason not to trust him.

"I guess I don't mind telling you."

He shoved his hands inside his pockets. "I'm glad. I hoped you'd come to know you could rely on me."

She tilted her head to peer up at him. She decided to let his comment go for now and answer his question.

"Not long after we moved to Silver City, Daddy met Reuben Buckley. I'm not sure how it all came about, but they became partners in a mine on Florida Mountain west of town."

His brows puckered. "They hadn't met before you moved here?"

"No, but it was as if they'd known each other forever. They became instant friends." She waited for him to comment, but he only nodded. "Anyway, while they were first trying to get the mine to produce, Daddy would go up into the mountain first thing every morning and spend a couple hours helping Reuben dig tunnels and build the braces."

She had yet to get up there and see the mine. Daddy kept putting her off, saying there wasn't anything to see yet.

"To help out, I'd go to the livery and stoke up the fire in the forge, just so nothing would slow him down with his work. He always came home so tired, I wanted to do what I could for him."

"I'm sure he appreciated it."

The familiar ache returned to her chest in remembering the anguish of what was to come. "He did, right up until that day." She took a deep breath to calm her racing heart. "I went into the livery as usual to get the fire going; only this time, the fire was completely out. I thought that odd because Daddy always kept hot coals inside the forge. But because he'd been so weary, I figured he'd forgotten to add wood. I tossed in a couple logs just to get the fire going before adding the charcoal. When I struck the match..."

The memory of the blast from the forge was so vivid, she could almost see the flames and feel the heat all over again.

Nate touched her elbow, drawing her to a stop. "It exploded?"

His voice was soft, tender. She couldn't look at him but responded with a nod. Tears inched toward her eyes, and she fought them as her chin quivered. It had been a year ago. Why did she relive it like it was yesterday?

The next thing she knew, Nate had pulled her into his arms. He held her so light and gentle, she wanted to lean against him. She wasn't sure if the tremble that raced through her was because of her emotions from the fire or from being held. Before she could decide, Nate pulled away, though he kept his hands on her shoulders.

"You all right?"

She nodded, then looked up at him. He was so handsome, so sweet. "Thank you." She shrugged. "I don't know why I let it get to me. It happened long ago."

"Actually, I think you've handled it quite well. Better than most people I know, myself included."

His voice and expression revealed his sincerity. She'd never wanted to kiss someone as much as she did—

"Hey, you two." Andrew had stopped on a hill looking down on them. "You coming?"

Giving a nervous laugh, Rebekah continued their walk, picking up the pace. Nate easily kept up.

"The necklace your father made you, it helped?"

Drawn like a magnet, her hand went to the silver disk. "It did. When he made it, he engraved the reference to a verse on its front. Through all the pain, recovery, and difficulties, I held the ornament and recited the verse."

"What's the reference?" he asked.

"Isaiah 48:10." She closed her eyes as she prepared to say the verse. "'Behold, I have refined thee, but not with silver; I have—'"

"'Chosen thee in the furnace of affliction.'"

Stunned, Rebekah stared up at Nate. "You memorize Scripture?"

He grinned. "Why is that so shocking?" He didn't wait for her response. "Mother used to help my brother and I memorize verses when we were growing up. That was one of her many favorites."

She smiled. "It's one of mine now too." She took a breath and nearly trembled. "If God chose to strengthen me by putting me through this affliction, then He must have a plan in mind, something important for me to do."

The thought both excited and frightened her. Would she be able to live up to the expectation? God wouldn't have selected her if He wouldn't help her make it through. The thought was suddenly overtaken by a new one. No matter what happened the rest of the day, nothing would dim the joy bubbling up inside. Nate was raised by a believer, and by all the evidence she'd witnessed, he was one too.

Chapter Seventeen

....

Full and refreshed, Nate took his leave from the Weaver family, still lounging next to the river, with a standing invitation to join their picnic every Sunday. Though the words hadn't been said, he felt fairly certain he'd only be welcome if he also attended the church service.

The idea didn't bother him as much as it might have mere weeks earlier. Not only were the Weavers a great family, their faith, especially Rebekah's, gave him hope that God wasn't the wrathful, vengeful being that Nate once thought. She'd gone through an awful experience and still managed to praise God. He'd have to do a bit more thinking on the matter. But that would have to wait. For now, he had a job to do, and if he wanted to keep it, he'd better get some investigating done so he could send information to his bosses.

As he walked toward town, he ran his list of suspects through his mind. He'd only considered Perry for a brief amount of time. Now that he knew him and his family well, there was no way Perry could be involved with fires and explosions. His partner, Reuben Buckley, still needed a bit more consideration. Though Reuben was an older fellow, Nate wasn't quite ready to rule him out completely.

First and foremost, he needed to find Grant Zimmer and learn what he meant by paying someone. Nate had a feeling the answer to that question would explain a great deal of what had been happening in and around the town. Since Mr. Zimmer was in the saloon the last time Nate sought him, that would be the best place to start looking.

Finally arriving in town and wishing he'd thought to bring his horse, Nate cut through one alley and crossed Jordan Street. With the sun dipping low in the sky, the shadows in the next alley taking him to Washington Street were long and dark. Once on the boardwalk he turned to his right, and in a matter of minutes pushed through the swinging doors of the saloon. If the thick smoke clouding the room was any indication, Henry Gilmore was doing a booming business at his tobacco shop.

Nate scanned the room. Many of the same men from the day before occupied the chairs around the tables. The boys he'd helped arrest his first day in town were involved in a poker game, a bottle of whiskey sitting between them. Two saloon girls nearby drew leering smiles from them as the ladies cheered them on.

Nate gave them little attention as he spotted the man he sought. Sitting at the table against the far wall, Mr. Zimmer nursed a glass of whiskey. Nate wound his way around the tables, then motioned to the chair next to Mr. Zimmer. The man nodded his welcome, recognition filtering through his bloodshot eyes.

"Buy me another drink, and I'll let you have a seat, especially if you've got good news for me."

His words slurred, letting Nate know he'd been there a good while and didn't need any more alcohol. Hopefully he was lucid enough to answer questions. Then again, drunken men rarely could hold their tongues. Nate hesitated. He wasn't sure he wanted to add to the man's inebriated state, but he also knew he'd do just that if it meant keeping the townspeople and their businesses safe. Nate motioned for the barkeeper to bring another drink as he took a seat.

"You ain't drinking?" Mr. Zimmer wagged his head. "Don't know that I can abide your company if you don't join me."

Hiding a shudder, Nate signaled for a second, knowing full well the liquid would never enter his mouth. He waited for the drinks to be delivered and slid a couple coins across the table.

Once they were alone, Nate leaned back in his chair until only the hind legs touched the floor, giving the casual appearance he desired. "Not sure what good news you were hoping for. Nothing's changed since we talked yesterday."

Nodding, Mr. Zimmer took a large gulp from his glass. Wincing from the burn as he swallowed, he set his drink down, yet grasped the glass like it might try to escape. "I figured. So that brings the next question."

"What's that?"

Mr. Zimmer turned his head just enough to look Nate in the eyes. "What can you do to help me?"

What did Mr. Zimmer think he could do? Nate plunged ahead, hoping to somehow comfort him in his loss. "Other than mending or replacing the metal like I mentioned yesterday, I'm not sure what else I can do." An idea struck. "Have you thought about contacting other mill owners? Maybe they've shut down or know of someone who'd sell you the parts you need."

Eyes flashing at the notion of a possible quick and simple solution, Mr. Zimmer's face brightened. He shook his finger at Nate. "You're a bright young man. How'd you like to come work for me?"

Grinning, Nate shook his head. "I already have a job. You know that."

"Can't blame a man for trying." Mr. Zimmer took another drink. "I'll start checking around first thing in the morning for mills that have gone out of business. Something tells me your idea will work out in a big way for me."

"Why's that?"

Pulling out a pouch of tobacco, Mr. Zimmer began rolling a smoke. "I've heard word that some of the stamp mills have shut down for lack of enough metal to keep them going." He shrugged. "Surely one of them would be willing to sell to me."

Nate remained silent, allowing Mr. Zimmer to enjoy his smoke and drink. When he saw his companion had relaxed, he started his investigation, reminding himself to be nonchalant, if that were possible, while he pried at the truth. "Can I ask you something?"

"Young man," Mr. Zimmer said and clapped him on the back, his good spirits evident, "right now you can ask me anything. Go ahead."

With that kind of positive reception, Nate thumped the front legs of his chair onto the floor and rested his forearms on the table. "What did you mean yesterday," he whispered, "when you said you should have paid?" He glanced around. "Paid what to whom?"

So much for being nonchalant. That was as straightforward as it got. The urge to pray hit Nate again. That seemed to happen often since he'd arrived. This time, he gave in.

Lord, grant me favor. Simple, but it was the best he could do in this situation, especially since Mr. Zimmer sat staring at him.

The man scratched at his unshaven face. "I actually said that?"

Nate's pounding heart calmed. "Yes, sir."

Shaking his head, Mr. Zimmer put his face in his hands. "If he finds out I said something to someone, I could lose even more."

"What do you mean?"

Mr. Zimmer looked him in the eyes. "That's what his note said. I was to pay five hundred dollars, and he'd leave me alone if I kept my mouth shut. If I went to the authorities or told anyone about the note, I'd lose everything."

Several thoughts tumbled over each other, all wanting answers. Nate made himself land on one. The rest would have to wait.

"Who wrote the note? Who were you supposed to pay?"

Blowing out a long, slow breath, Mr. Zimmer slumped. "I don't know. The note wasn't signed. It just told me where to take the money." He flopped his hands on the table in a helpless gesture. "As you know, I didn't pay. Look where it got me."

"Where?"

"Huh?"

Nate tried to slow down. His mind was darting all over the place and he had to keep his questions from doing the same. "Where were you to take the money?" He said the words slow and quiet, hoping to keep the appearance of indifference.

Mr. Zimmer waved one hand in the air. "Someplace east of town." He snatched up his glass and gulped down the remainder of his drink. "I didn't pay a whole lot of attention since I didn't plan to give the man any money."

"Did you keep the note?"

"Nope." He motioned for another drink, his hand trembling, then peeked at Nate from the corner of his eye. "You won't tell anyone what I said, right?" He let out a shaky breath. "I can't lose anything else."

Nate patted the man's back. "You've got my word. Look, Mr. Zimmer—"

"Call me Grant."

Nate nodded. "Grant, did the note say why they wanted money from you?"

Mr. Zimmer rubbed his hand along his whiskered cheek. "Protection."

What? Nate ran the answer through his mind several times. It made no sense. "Protection from what?"

The response he received was a shrug. Then Zimmer shook his head. "To keep from what just happened from happening, I suppose."

Everything started falling into place. If he'd guessed right, all the mishaps occurred when someone refused to pay. The only way to know for certain was to contact some of the others who'd endured fires and explosions. Doing so would be risky, but it was a chance he had to take.

He reached to shake Mr. Zimmer's hand. "I've got to go, but if you get another note, will you let me know? I'd like to help you if I can."

Grant held his hand an extra moment. "Thank you, Nate."

"You're welcome." He slid his untouched drink in front of the man. "Be careful."

Grant raised his glass to Nate. "I will."

Nate strode out of the saloon, his mind already miles ahead of him. He needed to find the owner of the sawmill that burned down the night he'd arrived. If he'd been thinking, he'd have asked Mr. Zimmer for the name of the owner. Then again, the poor man might have panicked at the thought of Nate talking to someone, anyone, about receiving notes. Much as he hated wasting time, he'd have to wait and ask Perry in the morning. Until then, he'd have to try to learn as much as he could about any of the others who'd gone through loss. Maybe the hotel owner would be open to some evening company and conversation.

Deciding to again take the shortest route, Nate cut through the same alley as earlier. Halfway, shuffling sounds met his ears. Nate stopped and turned. Something hard slammed into the side of his left temple. Sharp pain sent flashes of light through his eyes.

Swinging his fists in defense, Nate dropped to his knees. A kick to his side threw him to the ground. Gasping for air, he rose to his elbow and peered up to get a look at his attacker. A fist caught him on the chin, sending him backward. More fists than he could count slammed into him. His face and torso took the brunt of the blows, which came faster than he could ward off.

As quick as the attack began, it ended. Much as he struggled to see who assaulted him, he couldn't get his eyes to open. While one set of hands grasped his coat front, another seized fistfuls of hair, lifting his shoulders from the ground.

"Leave." Whiskey-laden breath blasted in his face. "Get out of town if you don't want this to happen again."

"Next time, you might not get to walk away."

Through the painful haze, Nate made note of the two different voices. There was no doubt in his mind they belonged to the men he'd helped arrest. Then one last smash to his face sent him into blackness.

Chapter Eighteen

....

Glad she talked her mother into exchanging days, Rebekah donned her apron, unlocked the safe, and pulled out the cashbox. The look on Mama's face told her she hadn't fooled anyone about her excuse. Since when had she ever enjoyed or even wanted to organize the shelves in the store? But it didn't matter she'd been found out. She was here now and might get the chance to visit with Nate again. She didn't get much time to quiz him about his beliefs. Today she would succeed, even if it meant working late.

The cashbox safely behind the counter, Rebekah unlocked the front door, ready for customers. She stepped away just in time to keep it from smacking her on the face. Cora rushed in and grabbed her by the arms.

"Another note. We got another note, Rebekah. But this one sounds threatening." She released Rebekah and started pacing, her hand on her forehead. "You don't think we were mistaken about the first note, do you? I really thought it was telling me of an admirer. Especially when Will showed me so much attention Saturday and yesterday and told me he'd liked me for a long time." She stopped in front of Rebekah. "What do we do?"

All the while Cora talked and paced, Rebekah's heart rate increased, hammering almost as fast as Cora's words were spoken. "Where's the note?" She had to see it. Maybe then she could help.

"Daddy has it. He's a mess. Panicked. We don't have that kind of money."

"What?" This time it was Rebekah's mind that raced. "What money?"

Cora slapped both her hands over her mouth.

What was wrong with this girl? Rebekah wondered. She grasped Cora's wrists and pulled her hands down. "What money, Cora?"

"I wasn't supposed to say anything about that. Both the note and Daddy told me not to tell a soul."

"Why?"

"I don't know. It just said not to tell anyone." She pulled Rebekah into a hug. "I'm so scared." She pulled an arm's length away. "What are we going to do, Rebekah? You helped with the other note. You've got to help with this one."

What did she expect her to do? "Who wrote the note?"

"It's unsigned, just like the other one."

That's what she figured. "What did the note say?"

"Oh, no." Cora glanced around. "How long have I been here?" She pulled a scrap of paper from her dress pocket. "Daddy told me to get all the food on this list and hurry back."

Rebekah held out her hand. "Give me the list. I'll fill it while you tell me what that note said."

Cora trailed her around like they were roped together, her hands flapping in the air like she was trying to fly. "The note said we needed to pay if we wanted protection for our business. That if we didn't pay, something bad could happen."

Pausing only long enough to look in Cora's eyes and see terror, Rebekah scrambled for the last items on the list. "Bad like what? Did it say?"

"No, and I don't want to find out." She grabbed Rebekah's hand. "I'm so scared. When I read my note again after seeing this new one, the first one sounded like a warning—just a nicer one is all."

Rebekah had been thinking the same but held her tongue so as not to add to Cora's fear. "What else did it say?"

"That we weren't to tell anyone, or the bad things could still happen."

Placing the last of the items in a basket, Rebekah wondered if anyone else had received such a note, especially those who'd suffered the loss of their businesses. "How much did they want?"

"Two hundred dollars." Cora gulped back a sob. "We don't have that kind of money, Rebekah."

She raised her brows. "No one does." Handing the basket to Cora, she held on to make sure she had her attention. "Write what the note says on another piece of paper and get it to me as soon as you can. I'd like to see how it's worded."

Cora nodded faster than a bird eyeing a scrambling bug. "I will." She pulled the basket from the counter and raced out of the store.

Rebekah stared at the empty doorway. Cora's parents were well-liked in town. If someone could threaten them, then no one in town was safe, not even her own parents. Alarm raced through her. From what Cora said, no one should know about the note in order to keep them safe, yet Rebekah felt the need to warn her parents. What should she do?

"Rebekah!"

Daddy's shout scared her so much, her heart nearly lurched through her chest. "Yes, Daddy."

"I need you in the livery."

"But no one's here to watch the store."

"Then lock up." Daddy's voice almost sounded angry. "I've got water. Bring some bandages."

Bandages? She flipped the lock on the door and ran to the storage room. *Oh, Lord, please let Daddy not be hurt.*

Grabbing everything she thought she might need, Rebekah raced across the alley and into the livery. Expecting to find her father on the ground, or at the very least standing in his own blood, she almost tripped when she stopped cold at the sight of her father leaning over someone lying in the bed of a wagon. Taking cautious steps forward, she recognized Nate's shirt. Gasping, she hurried to his side.

"Oh, goodness." The sight of Nate's bloody and swollen face made her choke on a sob. "What happened?"

The question was so softly spoken, she doubted anyone heard. Without waiting for an answer, Rebekah went to work washing the dried blood from his face and neck, trying to be as gentle as possible. Who would do this and why? She couldn't believe Nate had done anything to encourage such a brutal beating. And where was the doctor?

Eyes closed, Nate never moved. Rebekah had to look at his chest to make sure he was still breathing. Tears blurred her vision as she wiped the moisture from his face.

Daddy put his arm around her and gave her a gentle hug. "Make sure you wash the blood from his hair. I'm going to get a new shirt from the store. I'll be right back."

She nodded and soaked her rag once more. Squeezing out the water over his scalp, she repeated the process until his hair was completely wet. Lathering up her hands, she rubbed the soap through his thick, dark mane, pausing to examine his beaten face. His eyes suddenly opened. Startled, she pulled away.

"Don't stop," he whispered, voice hoarse. "It feels wonderful."

She made a face. "Have you been awake this entire time?"

He chuckled, then simultaneously winced and groaned. "Don't make me laugh."

Instantly contrite, she leaned over him. "I'm sorry."

He winked. "I'm sure I look worse than I feel."

"Well, you must feel pretty bad because you look downright awful."

His attempt to laugh made him cringe. "Thanks a lot."

Her heart ached to see him in such pain. "You lie still and let me finish."

"Yes, ma'am."

Daddy returned with the shirt just as she finished toweling dry his hair. "Remove that shirt, Nate. I'm not sure we can save it. All that blood…" He shook his head. "You sure you don't want the doc to take a look?"

"I'm sure." He struggled to pull his arms from the shirt. "I just need a day or two to recover."

Rebekah turned away at the sight of his chest but not before she saw all the bruises. Again, the question rose in her mind, *Who would do this to him?* He hadn't made any enemies since he arrived, had he?

"All right, then." Daddy helped him with the new shirt. "You can either go back to the hotel to rest, or you can work with Rebekah in the store. No lifting, of course, but I'm sure she could find something easy for you to do. I'd prefer you're not left alone. There's a bed in the back if you get tired."

Rebekah's heart skipped a beat as she waited for his answer. Nate at her side all day? As exciting as that sounded, she wasn't sure her heart or nerves could take his undivided attention and company. She looked at him just in time to see him staring at her.

His lips twitched. "I don't think I could handle lying around in a hotel room all day. Working at the store is a fine alternative."

She examined his face as she wondered if he had any idea what his presence did to her. If so, this would be a very long day—probably not for him but certainly for her.

Chapter Nineteen
....

Nate hobbled over to the Weavers' store and slid onto the first stool he found. What was he thinking, spending the day with Rebekah? He needed to lie down. His head was already spinning just from the walk over here. Catching her anxious gaze, he took a breath as deep as his sore ribs would allow and tried to sit up straight.

She returned from unlocking the front door. "You sure you don't want to go to the back and sleep? Your face is so white, you look like you're about to pass out."

Two customers entered, forcing him to lower his voice and shade his bruised face with his hat. "Maybe after a bit. I'll visit with you for a while first."

Eyeing him a moment longer, she motioned to the patrons. "All right, let me check on them first; then I'll be right back."

He'd have to try harder to convince her he was fine. It would help if he could prove that to himself. Just limping from the alley to the livery this morning made him feel like each bone in his body had separated from every muscle. And that was after he'd spent the night trying to rest and let his strength return. The plan didn't work after he shivered most of the night in the cool mountain air.

She hurried back to his side and occupied the other stool. "If you're going to be silly enough to try to sit here all day, then you can tell me what happened to you. Who did this and why?"

He smiled at the intensity in her voice. She was worried about him. That much was obvious. "I thought only women were silly."

She narrowed her eyes. "Well, you've just proven that theory wrong."

His answering chuckle was impossible to contain, making him flinch at the pain that followed. "I told you not to make me laugh." He held up his hand to stay her oncoming response. "There's not much to tell."

"Tell me anyway."

Nate noticed Rebekah's eyes became darker whenever she was passionate about something or someone, which was often. First about Thomas, then Cora, and now him. He liked her enthusiasm. He'd have to remember to keep her that way.

"I'd run into Mr. Zimmer, owner of the stamp mill that exploded the other day." No need to tell her he went looking for him, or where he'd found him. "After we talked for a while, I cut through an alley on my way to the hotel. A couple men stopped me with their fists."

She winced as if feeling the pain. "What men?"

"I don't know. They hit my temple with something hard before I could turn and see them." He touched the area where they first hit him, still very tender.

"Why did they beat you?"

"I wish I knew. I wouldn't do it again." He was trying to lighten the mood, but Rebekah didn't accept the change.

"They didn't take your money or anything?"

Nate wagged his head.

A frown wrinkled her brows. "That's very odd."

"I agree." It was past time to change the subject. Hopefully she'd learned enough to let him do so. "How's Cora doing with her new beau?"

Rebekah's frown deepened, as did the color of her eyes. What had happened since yesterday to cause such an expression of alarm?

"Is she all right? That man didn't hurt her, did he?" He didn't know Cora much at all, but because she was Rebekah's friend, he'd do what he could to help or protect her.

"No. From what I can tell, the two of them are well on their way toward the altar."

He ran that information through his mind twice. "But they just met."

"No, they met months ago. Now that there's known interest, the relationship is moving quite fast."

"To say the least." Women. They must dream of marriage from birth. "So why the concern?"

She turned her head away. "I didn't say I was concerned."

"You didn't have to. I could see it on your face and in your eyes."

Her head swiveled to look at him, her expression now one of surprise.

He tugged at a stray lock of hair. "Hey, I thought you trusted me."

"I do." As if saying those words uncorked the very air that held her up, Rebekah slumped onto the counter, bringing her that much closer to him.

The fresh scent of her hair wafted toward him. She always smelled so good....

He cleared his throat to get his thoughts back in order. "So tell me what has you so upset."

Before she could answer, one of the lady customers approached.

Nate turned away, trying to hide his bruises. He didn't want to be the cause or source of town gossip.

"Rebekah, do you have any other fabric in the back somewhere? I'm getting ready for the cold weather that's coming by having warm clothes already sewn. All you have out is the bright summer fabric."

"It's wise to plan ahead," Rebekah said. "Give me a minute to check. Go ahead and continue looking around. I'll let you know what I find."

Rebekah sounded so sweet and patient, but Nate would give his last dollar to prove she'd rather throw the patrons out and lock the door so they could talk. He trailed behind her.

"Need some help?"

She cast a glance over her shoulder. "You can keep me company, but you're not to lift a thing."

"I'm not in that bad of shape."

"You will be if Daddy sees you carrying anything."

He grinned, reminding himself how much laughter would hurt. Rebekah had a good sense of humor. He'd have to be careful around her today. She lifted three rolls of material from a shelf and headed back to the store. When he reached for them, she shifted them to her other side, avoiding him completely—and easily, much as it bothered him to admit that fact.

He waited until the women finished their business. After the customer left, Nate joined Rebekah at the counter and occupied the same stool. "All right, back to the original question. What upset you earlier?"

"You don't forget easily, do you?"

"Not the important things."

She eyed him for a bit. "I'm not sure I'm supposed to tell anyone."

Brows raised, he tilted toward her. "Now I'm intrigued."

A sweet smile curved her lips. "Men. And they say women are the nosey ones."

He grinned. "They are. You just have a tendency to rub off on us." He held up his hand when the expected rebuttal started. "I'll take it back if you tell me what you're not supposed to tell me." That brought on the laughter he anticipated. "So, what happened?"

The way Rebekah sobered almost instantly, her body growing tense again, Nate prepared to hear the worst.

She took a deep breath. "Another note. Only this one was to the Peters family, not just Cora."

There was no excitement with the announcement, not like the other day when they plotted to find Cora's admirer. That meant this note probably carried the same kind of threat Mr. Zimmer received.

"Tell me about it."

Rebekah crossed her arms, giving him the impression she desired some kind of shield or protection. "This note demanded money."

Dread washed through him. The Peters family was the next target for whoever was blackmailing the owners of local mines and businesses. They'd either have to pay or lose their boardinghouse, of that he was certain. Unless he could stop the blackmailers first. If almost a dozen businesses had either burned or been blown up, how many people had paid to keep from risking danger?

"How much?"

"Two hundred dollars."

Though not as much as they'd asked of Mr. Zimmer, that was still a lot of money. But what struck him most was that whoever demanded the money knew the people in and around town enough to know the maximum amount they could get.

Rebekah propped her chin on her palm, her stare boring right through him. "You don't seem surprised."

Did he ever need to learn how to act.... Evidently, from last night, someone had figured out he'd been asking questions, and now Rebekah had noticed his lack of shock. Being undercover, he couldn't let her know his real reason for his presence in town. But because she knew the people in town so much better than he did, he wanted her help. He had but one safe answer for now.

"I've heard a rumor about notes. And I don't mean notes like what Cora received."

Rebekah's spine straightened. "What have you heard?"

He'd gotten himself into this, and now that he had, he might as well tell more. "I think if we were to put our heads together, we might be able to discover who is threatening these individuals for money. But if we're going to do this, I need your word this won't go any farther than you and me. Not even Cora can know about any of this." He stared into her expressive eyes. "Agreed?"

She nodded. "What did you hear?"

He almost laughed. In many ways, Rebekah was the typical female. It was the ways she wasn't typical that interested him. "It's not so much what I've heard as what I think I might have figured out."

"And what would that be?"

At the moment, she reminded him of an inquisitive child. "First of all, I learned that the reason Mr. Zimmer's mill blew up was because he'd received a note demanding money, and he decided not to pay."

Rebekah's face paled. "Oh, no."

"Yes, and he was also warned not to tell anyone, just like the Peters family."

Rebekah's throat worked as fear washed over her face. "We need to tell the sheriff."

"No!" At her look of surprise, he reached and briefly touched her forearm. "Think of it this way, Rebekah. The notes have told Mr. Zimmer and the Peters family not to say anything to anyone. If we tell the sheriff, word will get out all over town. You know it will. That being the case, there's no telling what this blackmailer will do to them, or others for that matter."

Indecision raced across her face. He could tell she wanted to help but felt helpless. He knew the feeling all too well. He touched her hand again to get her full attention.

"Here's what I've been thinking. Let's try to figure out who's doing this. If we can narrow it down to one or two people, then maybe we can take the information to the sheriff."

This time, she looked a bit more relieved. "That's a great idea. Where do we start? Have you already thought of a few possible suspects?"

He recognized the all-too-familiar problem of thoughts tumbling over one another because they came much too fast to organize. He'd been in that same predicament last night. Maybe with the two of them working together, they'd be able to keep each other focused.

"Well, we can start with the obvious person." Again, he could almost see the names of every resident flashing through her mind. He'd make it easy for her. "First and foremost is the man who shot at us while looking for Thomas last week. We don't know who he is yet, but we can keep searching until we find out."

She nodded. "I can see why you put him first. I don't know how we'll ever find him again, but I hope we do. Who else?"

He scratched at a spot over his ear, stalling for time. He didn't want to reveal the names of the other suspects, but he was already in too deep. "The two young men I helped the sheriff arrest the day I arrived here."

She thoughtfully rested her elbows on the counter, as if trying hard to understand. "You think those boys are smart enough to think up and accomplish a scheme like this?"

Nate sat up a bit straighter. She certainly had a point. They didn't seem to have the intelligence to come up with something so bold and make it work well. But still...

"I think they were the men who beat me in the alley last night. They saw me talking to Mr. Zimmer, and there were definitely two of them doing the beating. The voices were young." He paused. "And they told me to leave town. I'm assuming they don't want me helping the sheriff again, and if they're the ones doing the blackmailing, they have good reason not to want me talking to Mr. Zimmer."

He'd have to spend more time thinking about who might be the conspirator using the two young men to do the dirty work. It sure made a lot more sense than the boys doing the scheming all on their own. Rebekah was an astute woman. She never ceased to amaze him.

Planning to praise her intelligence, he swallowed the words when he saw her expression. "What?"

"You've got to tell the sheriff. If they've warned you to get out of town and you don't, they'll try to hurt you again. Or worse."

Good thing he didn't tell her they'd threatened just that.

She lifted a hand, forestalling his response. "If you go to the sheriff now, you could keep them from doing harm to anyone else like—"

Her mouth bobbed open and closed before the tears appeared. He stepped close, putting his hands on her shoulders. Tremors shook her entire frame.

"What is it, Rebekah? What has you so upset?"

Still trembling, she peered up at him with dazed yet frightened eyes. "I heard Daddy say last week that he didn't think my getting burned was an accident." She grasped his forearms. "You don't think Daddy was getting blackmailed like the others, do you? That he refused to pay and this"—she touched her cheek—"is what happened?"

Fear and anger ripped into his heart as he pulled her close. If what she said was true, not only would he need to increase his efforts to find this beast of a person, but he'd have to try to protect the Weaver family at the same time. If the blackmailer threatened the family once, more than likely he'd be back.

Hearing voices and footsteps, Nate pulled away from Rebekah just as the door opened. She spun away from the customers long enough to dab at her eyes, then turned back and called, "Go ahead and look around for a bit. I'll be right with you."

Once they'd moved to the back of the store, Rebekah swung toward him. "Does this mean they'll come back? Do you think they'll try to hurt Daddy again?"

Nate needed to calm her so they could both think clearly. He dropped onto his stool, feeling suddenly weary, and took a deep, slow breath. "Did your father receive a note before that fire?"

She shook her head. "I don't remember either one of my parents mentioning a note. That's not to say they didn't."

He'd rather not ask the next question and risk upsetting her, but he had to cover everything. "Did your father have any enemies, anyone who was angry with him?"

Again she shook her head. "Not that I can recall. Everyone seems to like him."

"Yeah, I noticed that too."

One of the customers harrumphed, pointedly staring at them.

Rebekah jabbed her finger just inches from his nose. "Keep thinking. I'll be right back."

While she helped the patrons, Nate once again ran those he'd met through his mind, crossing most off his mental list of suspects. His thoughts continually returned to one person—Thomas. Though he couldn't pin down a specific reason for his suspicions, he couldn't shake his distrust of the man, either.

After ringing up the purchases of her patrons, Rebekah waved and bid them a cheery good-bye. When she turned to him, her nostrils flared as sparks nearly leapt from her eyes. He hoped she wasn't upset with him. He was in no condition to fend her off, though she was so cute in this state, he wouldn't mind trying.

"I was scared earlier, but now I'm downright angry." She began to pace. "I want to get these people, mainly so they won't have the chance to hurt anyone else. But most of all, I want to see them get what's coming to them." She spun, planted her hands on the countertop, and blurted, "Why are you smiling?"

Doing his best to wipe off his grin, Nate shrugged. "I've just never seen you quite like this." In an instant, his mistake in stating his thoughts became clear. He raised both hands in surrender, though he wanted to laugh. "I'm sorry. I'm really not trying to make light of this. I know it's a serious matter."

She squinted as if considering his apology. "Good. Then you'll help me tomorrow?"

He was immediately on the alert. "Help with what?"

"Finding this man." Her tone was incredulous, and she waved her hand through the air. "What else have we been talking about?" She lowered her voice. "Oh, yes," she murmured. "Mama's working the store tomorrow. That gives me part of the morning and all afternoon to do some scouting."

Every hair and nerve stood on end with her announcement. "Now wait a minute, Rebekah. You can't go off exploring possible suspects by yourself. It's much too dangerous."

Hands clasped in front of her, she rocked from her heels onto her toes. "Which is why you need to go with me."

Why, the devious little imp. She knew full well he wouldn't let her go off by herself. He pointed an accusing finger in her face. "You spent that entire time helping those ladies, plotting how you'd get me to go investigating with you tomorrow, didn't you?"

Brows high, she batted her eyes in a failed attempt to appear innocent. "Of course not. It only took me half that amount of time."

Never before had he wanted to kiss a woman like he did Rebekah at that moment. She was a delight in so many ways. And yes, he'd look for any opportunity to spend time with her, but he'd never let her know. He couldn't let her realize the power she held over him.

"And if your father needs my help in the livery?"

"I'm almost certain I can convince him you need an extra day to recover."

She didn't even hesitate with her answer, which meant she'd already thought of that. He wouldn't argue the point. Having tomorrow off would give him the chance to do the job he'd been sent here to do, and he'd get to investigate while in the company of an amazing woman. Not only that, but he'd be able to keep an eye on her, hopefully protect her from any further harm by staying close. He'd do whatever was necessary to keep her from ever getting hurt again.

Chapter Twenty

....

Rebekah struggled to keep up with Nate's long strides as they followed the same path they took what seemed a lifetime ago while looking for Thomas. Nate acted even more determined to find the blackmailer today than he was yesterday. And he seemed adamant about staying ahead of her.

He'd already mentioned the chance of getting shot at again, probably the very reason he'd positioned himself in front. If he'd had his way she'd be home, baking another cake, instead of trailing him around. She'd already fixed one cake and a loaf of bread with the intent of giving them to the Loomis family, hoping to gain a new friendship. It was the right thing to do, and it might get the woman to talk about the man who'd shot at them. Pearl might not be the cleanest woman, but she knew a great deal of what went on around her.

After tripping for the third time, Rebekah reached forward and grabbed the back of Nate's shirt, giving a jerk to make him stop. "You walk any faster and we'll be running."

"Sorry." He glanced around, looking more skittish than a rabbit under attack. He gripped the handle of the basket containing the cake and bread as if someone planned on stealing their food.

"What's got your knuckles in a knot?"

His brows nearly touched. "What?"

She waved a hand at him. "Well, look at yourself. You're so tense, I half expect you to explode into tiny pieces."

He shook his head. "I'm such a fool. I should never have allowed you to come out here again. How can I protect you out in the middle of nowhere?" He spread his arms. "Any one of these trees could be hiding the same man who shot at us the last time. Or any criminal for that matter." Shifting the basket from in between them, he peered into her eyes. "I don't suppose I can talk you into returning to town—maybe get a horse and buggy for the trip out here."

She shook her head. "If we let this man scare us into doing nothing and going nowhere, we'll never stop him." She squinted up at him. "Besides, if we go back to town, I'm guessing you'll try to make me stay behind, or, at the very least, you'll sneak off without me."

When he raised his brows and tilted his head, she shoved her finger under his nose. "I knew it. You were going to do at least one of them, weren't you?"

He remained silent.

She propped her hands on her hips. "Well, I'm going, and you can't stop me."

Nate took a deep breath and let it blast from his nostrils. "That's what I was afraid of." Placing his hand on her back, he gently pushed her forward. "Let's keep moving."

Very few words were spoken as they continued on their trip. Rebekah was too out of breath to speak, and Nate seemed too preoccupied with his thoughts. He kept her and the basket to his left while his right hand hovered near his sidearm. His obvious anxiety increased her own until she found herself glancing around like a nervous cat. She nearly jumped onto Nate's back when she saw someone moving through the trees. She grabbed his arm and pointed just as that person charged toward them.

Nate swept her behind him as he pulled his pistol and cocked it in one smooth move. Rebekah peeked around him.

Thomas stood at the edge of the tree line with his hands raised. "Whoa, there. Don't shoot."

When Nate didn't lower his pistol, Rebekah shifted around front and shoved his gun hand away. "He's not going to shoot." She peered up at Nate's face. "Are you?"

The muscle in Nate's jaw worked. What was wrong with him? He knew Thomas.

She scooted toward her dear friend. "What are you doing out here, especially nearly scaring us to death?"

Grinning, he swept off his hat and opened his arms. She stepped into his hug. It had taken months to get used to the top of his head only coming to her nose. The days he hadn't bathed, she regretted the embrace. Today was one of those days. She held him at arm's length.

"Where have you been? I'm used to seeing you almost every day. I haven't seen you in several."

He lifted a shoulder. "Trying to make a living, my dear, just like usual."

She frowned. "But you used to come home every night."

Just as the words were out of her mouth, she wished she could yank them back inside. What if he had a woman friend and spent the nights with her? Rebekah didn't want to know or hear anything about that kind of information. Time to change the subject.

"Back to the original question. Why are you here?"

Thomas crossed his arms. "Why is it you're the only woman who manages to make me feel like a young lad in trouble?" He waved away her response and winked. "Just picking at you, sweetheart.

Actually, I was on my way to check on the Loomis family, to see if Pearl needed help with anything before I got busy elsewhere. With her husband working so hard, I thought I'd try to lend a hand." His brows puckered. "Why are you two out here?"

Rebekah glanced at Nate, who was just now holstering his pistol. "We're headed there too. I made some bread and cake." She hooked her arm through Thomas's and started walking. "We can all go together."

"I know Pearl will appreciate it. That's quite a brood she has to feed."

With another on the way. Rebekah didn't say the words but figured Thomas was thinking the very same. Another peek at Nate let her know he wasn't the least bit thrilled with the turn of events. If his eyes could hold bullets, they'd be firing nonstop right now, and all pointed at Thomas. She'd have to ask one of them about the obvious dislike between them. When did it start and why? In the meantime, no need stirring up a rattler's nest with only her to intervene if it turned ugly.

Nate trailed behind for the first time since they'd left the store, though his hand still hovered near his gun. His tension should have diminished now that another man had joined them, but instead his eyes seemed more intense. The scowl never left his face, making the hope of light and animated conversation all but disappear. Thankfully, they arrived at the Loomis home in a short amount of time.

The humongous dog, Tiny, raced out to greet them like the first time they'd visited, lathering Thomas with a tongue almost the size of the loaf of bread Rebekah had made. Just to feed the beast, Mr. Loomis would have to shoot a deer every day—two if he wanted to feed his family.

One by one, the children darted from the house, dashing across the yard and into Thomas's waiting arms. Rebekah's heart warmed at the sight. The children adored Thomas, and he obviously returned the feeling. When the door slammed, Rebekah looked up to find Pearl settled against the porch post and smiling at the sight.

Rebekah moved to join her. "The children don't care too much for Thomas, do they?"

Pearl cackled her amusement. "They treat him like a second family pet, climbing all over him like they do Tiny." She cocked an eyebrow at Rebekah, then examined Nate from head to toe as he strolled toward them. "What brings you two all the way out here? Didn't figure on seeing you again, what with all the displeasure from the last time."

"Don't be silly. I was glad to meet you and even more delighted to see you in church Sunday."

A grin spread across Pearl's face. "That young man sure gave you fits, didn't he?"

"Andrew." Rebekah nodded. "My little brother. He can be a handful at times."

Pearl waved at the group headed their way. "I reckon I can understand that. I might have to show up again for the next sermon just to see what Andrew does next."

Rebekah's mouth dropped open. "Oh, don't even think such a thought, or it might come true."

The two women shared a laugh as the children piled onto the porch, the youngest wrapping one arm around Pearl's leg while the dirty thumb on the other found its way to his mouth. Rebekah tried not to let her shudder show. Andrew had done the same thing when he was little. That alone should have shown her how many times he'd make her skin crawl. No telling what all had been squished through his fingers before they hit his mouth. Her stomach quivered at the thought. Best not to think about it.

Spotting the basket, the toddler's fingers popped from his mouth as he pointed. Rebekah reached to take the goodies from Nate. She held it out to Pearl.

"I made a cake and a loaf of bread, hoping maybe we could try once more to start a friendship."

Pearl looked her square in the eyes as if to determine her sincerity. She finally gave a nod and motioned to the door. "Much appreciated. Bring it on inside. We can sit a spell."

The inside was dark with only the sun coming through the dusty windows to light the room. The children raced to the chairs around the battered table, only to be scolded by their mother to let the guests use them. As Rebekah placed the basket on the table and took a seat, she noticed very few adornments on the windows or walls. A long curtain separated a room from the rest of the house, probably where the parents slept. Several blankets were rolled up and stacked near the fireplace. Rebekah guessed the children slept there. Much as her heart went out to this family, she also realized how happy they seemed, saying a great deal about the parents' love for their children.

Seconds after Nate sat, the toddler climbed onto his lap. Rebekah stifled a laugh at his look of shock. To her surprise, he pulled a small top from his pocket and handed it to the boy. Little Micah tilted his head toward the top, then peered up at Nate. He retrieved it from the boy, set it on the table, and gave it a spin. The boy's eyes widened as he reached to snatch the toy from the table, probably to keep his siblings from grabbing it first.

Though interested in the top, Micah's focus shifted to the basket. Chin propped on the table, Micah stared several moments before casting a longing glance at Pearl. "Mama?" The quiet voice dripped with sweet yearning.

Pearl reached to ruffle the top of his head. Then she turned to her oldest daughter. "Get a knife, Libby. We'll save the bread for tonight, but I can't imagine a bit of cake right now will hurt anything."

She caught Rebekah's eye and mouthed a thank-you. Rebekah's heart ached for this family. She should have done more—brought a more filling and nutritious meal. Next time she'd know better.

As the children dug into their cake with gusto, Nate and Rebekah waved away the offer to have their own piece, though Nate pretended to try to steal bites from them, sending the kids into squeals and giggles as they protected their food.

Rebekah sat back, enjoying the relaxed atmosphere, far removed from the earlier tension. Even Nate seemed to enjoy himself. And she hadn't heard Thomas laugh so hard in a long time.

An explosion brought the fun to an end. What sounded only a mile away had the children running to their mother as Nate, Thomas, and Rebekah leapt from their chairs.

Nate raced to the door and paused long enough to look first at Rebekah, then at Thomas. He pointed to Thomas. "Make sure Rebekah gets home safe."

Then he was gone.

Chapter Twenty-one

....

Nate raced toward town and promised himself never to leave without his horse again. He was almost near town but spotted smoke to the south. As he veered that direction, it didn't take long to figure out the smoke came from Mr. Zimmer's stamp mill. His heart sank as he arrived to find men hauling Grant Zimmer out on a long piece of lumber, the ends of the wood still smoldering.

Praying the man was still alive, Nate ran to his side. Cuts and burns covered Grant's face and body. "Is he dead?"

Grant's one good eye opened. He grabbed Nate's hand, tugging until Nate dropped to his knees. Up close, he couldn't believe Grant had lived through the blast. His entire right side was shredded. The poor man had to be in incredible pain. If he were honest, Nate didn't figure he'd survive the night.

"Put me down."

Grant's raspy order was obeyed. The four men hovered until Grant waved them away. They only moved as far as the building, their anxious eyes fixed on their boss. Grant motioned for Nate to move closer.

Nate leaned down, and Grant rose a few inches and grasped his forearm. "Stupid of me," he choked out, then fell back on the board, gasping for air.

Nate's mind scrambled. What was stupid? Why was he in the

building? None of this made sense. He had to find out what Grant meant.

"What was stupid of you?"

"What?" Grant winced. "I can't hear you, boy. You gotta speak up."

Nate shifted toward Grant's left ear, figuring the right one to be injured. "Why are you saying you were stupid?"

Grant closed his eyes. "I shouldn't have been here. I was warned."

Nate wished Grant wouldn't speak so loud. He didn't know who all they could trust. Not even the men Grant had hired or any of those standing nearby could be trusted. He leaned close again. "Warned by whom?"

Swallowing hard, Grant gripped his arm harder. "You've gotta help me."

"I will. Just tell me what happened."

Several men were racing up the hill toward them. Grant had to hurry, or the rest of their conversation would have to wait, if they finished it at all. The man was breathing harder all the time.

Grant yanked on his arm again. "I was making a list—of what I needed—to fix the place." He released Nate's sleeve and closed his eyes. "I saw it."

Nate waited for him to continue. How much longer would Grant be able to talk? "Saw what?"

Grant took a shaky breath. "Dynamite." He took a gulp of air. "It flew through the door. I tried to run but tripped." He panted as if reliving the moment. "It went off soon as I got up." A tear rolled from Grant's left eye. "What did I do to—?" The broken man turned away, his face masked in defeat.

The men from town arrived and all but shoved Nate away. He wandered into the building to take a look. Anger boiled in his belly before raging through his body. This was too close to what had happened to his dad and brother. He refused to let it happen again.

Fists clenched, he paced, running every man he'd met through his mind to find the one most suspicious. Thomas returned over and over. True, he was with Nate and Rebekah at the time of the explosion, but without a doubt, he could be the brains behind the scheme and have used the two young men to carry out his evil deeds.

Nate reined in his thoughts. He'd be a fool to focus on only one man, which could allow another to continue working his plots right under his nose. Who else? The few other men who raced through Nate's mind he scratched off right away. He didn't know enough people in town yet to draw a conclusion.

Stepping out of the building, he eyed the men milling around Grant. As they hefted him on a canvas litter, Nate followed everyone back to town, staying close enough to hear the conversations. If finding the right man meant quitting the livery job, he'd do just that in order to learn of the culprit and end the blackmailing for good. In the meantime, he'd start by following the two young men who beat him up. Sooner or later, they'd lead him to the leader of the scheme. Only this time, he'd have his gun at the ready.

* * * * *

The sight of a man being carried down the street brought Rebekah to a stop. Relief washed through her when she saw Nate trailing a short distance behind the group. She'd prayed for his safety from the moment he raced out of the Loomis house. But his expression made the worry return.

Thomas stepped to her side. "Wonder who got hurt."

"Not Nate."

Though spoken in a whisper, Rebekah wished she could take the words back the moment they left her mouth, especially when Thomas snorted.

"You spend too much time thinking about him, Rebekah." He started back down the boardwalk toward the livery. "And you spend too much time *with* him."

She stared at his back for several seconds before hurrying after him, her frustration rising. Finally catching up, she clasped his arm and tugged him to a stop. "What is it between you two? Why the anger and distrust? What happened?"

Thomas crossed his arms, making him look burly. She'd be scared if she didn't know he was a very sweet man. She wasn't about to take his silence, or his grumpy expression, for an answer. Hands on hips, she planned to wait him out. His groan let her know he'd surrendered.

"I don't know what it is about the man, but you're right. I don't trust him."

She trusted Nate with her whole heart—could she be wrong? "Why?"

He groaned again, muttering something about why he never got married. "I told you, I don't know why." He kicked at a crumpled piece of paper. "Look, Rebekah, there's just something strange about the man. He's—secretive, too guarded. In my experience, men like that have something to hide, and trust me, that's not a good quality."

She considered his words, her stomach twisting in knots. "I thought all men were like that."

Jaw dropping, Thomas raised his arms only to let them fall back to his sides. "Women." He took a step, stopped to pick up the piece of paper, shoved it into his pocket, then started toward home again. He paused when he noticed Rebekah didn't follow. He made a sweeping motion with his arm. "Shall we, madam? I believe I'm to see you safely home."

Rebekah narrowed her eyes at him, knowing he was talking about Nate's request. She groaned in imitation of him earlier. "Men."

She stomped past him, but not before she saw a grin spread across his whiskered face and heard his quiet chuckle. At least he was in a better mood.

* * * * *

Grant was deposited at a building that looked more like a shanty than the doctor's office. Since none of the men stayed, Nate went inside to check on Grant's condition and ended up sitting with him until the doctor had finished doing, as he called it, "all the good he could do." Now the rest was up to Grant. The doctor said he had a long fight ahead of him.

His anger reignited, Nate left Grant in the doctor's somewhat questionable hands and went in search of the two young men. He needed to learn their names so he'd know who to ask for next time. Perry could help him with that in the morning. For now, he'd start at the saloon they seemed to enjoy.

With the sun in bed for the night and the moon only a sliver, Nate would have a much easier time stalking his prey without being seen. He only hoped he wouldn't lose sight of them in the inky darkness.

Deciding to avoid the alley, Nate took the long way to the saloon. He'd hoped to be able to peek through the window, but if he had to guess, the glass hadn't been cleaned since the building went up. He moved to the doorway and took his time looking at all the faces, but the two men he sought weren't inside. Pray God they weren't up to more mischief. Nate ducked into the shadows and continued his search by heading to the next saloon. If they weren't busy somewhere in the mountains obeying their leader's orders, they were more than likely busy getting as drunk as they could before passing out. It seemed to be their favorite form of entertainment.

After checking the second saloon and coming up empty, Nate stepped into the alley to get out of the glow of the street's gaslights. Skittish from his last beating, he took a moment to listen for anyone who might have joined him in the narrow passageway. Hearing nothing more than a chorus of crickets, he concentrated on where he should look next. He didn't want to go back to the hotel room without some kind of information that would lead him in the right direction.

Frustration rode him hard as he decided to return to the first saloon and wait across the street to see if the men showed. Before he took two steps, he saw Thomas dash along the boardwalk on the opposite side and duck into the alley. Changing his target, Nate scooted farther down his side of the street before racing across to the other side. He poked his head into the alley and listened. Hearing nothing for several seconds, he took a breath, pulled his gun from the holster, and crept into the shadows.

Reaching the end without meeting anyone, Nate peeked out, looking both ways. Thomas was just rounding another corner when Nate finally spied him. He only managed two steps before a gun was cocked behind him, the barrel scuffing the back of his head.

Chapter Twenty-two

....

"I'll take that shooter, boy."

Nate had heard that voice before but couldn't place where or when. Arms in the air, he tried to hand the man the gun over his shoulder. The man's barrel jammed harder against his skull.

"Slow and easy, just drop it on the ground."

Finally recognizing the voice, Nate turned, only to have the gun jab him in the back. "Don't move. Next time, you die."

Lifting his hands back in the air, Nate tried again. "Sheriff Caldwell?" Not getting a response, he wondered if maybe he was mistaken. "Sheriff?"

"Take three steps forward but don't turn around."

"Sir—"

"Do it!"

Nate obeyed. From the corner of his eye, he saw the sheriff bend down to pick up the pistol, then shove it into his belt.

"Look, Sheriff—"

"Shut your mouth and start walking."

Nate gave up trying to reason with him and headed toward the sheriff's office. He'd talk to him there, at least try to explain his actions.

The sheriff poked him in the back. "Where you going?"

Anger flickered, but Nate tamped it down. "To your office."

"Not there." Sheriff Caldwell gave him a shove the opposite direction. "That way."

Nate slowed his steps. "Where?"

"Just walk. I'll tell you where to go. And keep your hands where I can see them."

For the first time, Nate's nerves clanged with alarm. He'd come here knowing to keep an eye on the sheriff, to treat him with suspicion. In a short amount of time, he'd disregarded the information in order to set his sights on someone else. Calling himself every kind of fool, he shuffled the direction the sheriff ordered.

"Just where are you taking our young Nate, Sheriff—and why do you have a gun in his back?"

Nate stopped and looked in the direction of the voice, relief making him sag. Plumes of smoke billowed from the corner of a building before Henry Gilmore eased into view, his ever-present cigar in one hand, the fingers of the other tucked into his coat pocket. He took another puff and blew out a long stream. "Well?"

The sheriff stepped next to Nate, his gun still aimed at his chest. "I caught him sneaking around. I was bringing him in for questioning."

Henry strolled closer, the street lamp casting his shadow in a long, wavering silhouette. He motioned to the north with his cigar. "If I'm not mistaken, your office is the other way."

Sheriff Caldwell shuffled his feet. "Yes, well, I—was just gonna, uh, finish up an errand first."

"I see." Henry drew himself up tall by taking a deep breath.

To Nate, he looked every bit the military leader he used to be, his bearing bordering on regal. He certainly wouldn't want to be confronted by Henry at the moment. By the sheriff's jumpy movements, he felt the same, especially when Henry cleared his throat.

"How about I help you question young Nate so this foolishness can be over and you both can be on your way?" He nodded at the sheriff's gun. "And I don't think that's necessary any longer, do you? Nate doesn't look like he's going to run or fight." He paused a few seconds. "Isn't that right, Nate?"

"That's right." Nate lowered his arms, thankful for Henry's friendship. The sheriff holstered his pistol. "This ain't the proper way of doing things, Henry, and you know it."

"Yes, well, proper or not, let's get off the street." He motioned with his head. "My shop is right there. What do you say we move inside?"

Nate could almost feel the anger and tension radiating off the sheriff as he tried to decide if he wanted to let Henry tell him what to do. He finally nodded and gave Nate a shove in that direction.

"Let's get this over with. I got work to do."

Henry unlocked the door to his shop, then stepped back to let Nate and the sheriff enter. In moments, he had the lamp burning bright, making the shadows retreat and the cigar and tobacco tins glow like he'd lit them too. He blew out the match and dropped it in a small bowl on the lamp stand, each movement slow and meticulous. Nate got the feeling Henry's actions were meant to irritate the sheriff much more than to keep up a calm appearance. He wanted to smile but figured it would only get him into deeper trouble.

Shoving his free hand into his pocket, Henry turned and eyed Nate through the smoke curling from the end of his cigar. He moved closer to study Nate's face, then shook his head. "So, young Nate, what had you wandering in the dark instead of resting in your hotel room?"

He wished Henry would stop adding the word *young* before his name. Made him sound and feel like a boy no older than Andrew. "I was on my way back from sitting with Mr. Zimmer when I saw someone sneaking around the street and alleys."

The sheriff snorted. "You sure it wasn't your own shadow?"

Nate ignored the dumb remark. "I decided to follow him and see if he was up to something wrong. With all the fires and explosions lately, I thought it best to check on him."

Henry nodded. "Sounds reasonable."

"Really? Then why did he have a gun in his hand?" Sheriff Caldwell dropped onto a chair like the night had taken everything out of him.

Henry turned from the sheriff to him. "Nate? Care to explain that?"

"Sure." He looked right at the sheriff and motioned to the bruises on his face. "I was beat up a couple nights ago. I didn't want to take the chance of being caught off-guard again."

The sheriff's smile looked more like a snarl. "And yet I got the drop on you anyway."

"Those bruises didn't come from a straight-on fight but from someone jumping you?"

The question and concern that should have come from the sheriff came from Henry instead. In Nate's eyes, that put yet another mark against the lawman. The man had the perfect cover for a blackmailing scheme. Who would suspect a sheriff of such a plot? Granted, he did arrest the two young men the day Nate arrived, but he could have done it to cover his trail, or even to keep his assistants out of trouble.

"Nate?"

He looked up at Henry. "Yes?"

"I asked about you getting beat up."

"Right." He had to get a handle on his thoughts. "Two men beat me up in an alley a couple nights ago."

Henry frowned. "Why?"

With a shrug, Nate shook his head. "You'll have to ask them. And if you happen to find them, I'd like to talk to them myself."

"I'll bet." Henry rested his hip against a table and brushed something from his pant leg. "You satisfied with his explanation, Sheriff?"

Nostrils flaring and top lip curled under, the sheriff spouted, "Not really." He turned to Nate. "You shoulda told me about the beating."

Again, Nate shrugged. "Sorry. But you didn't give me a chance."

Sheriff Caldwell glared at him for several long moments. "All right. I'll let you go." He rapped his knuckles on the table a few times before pointing his pudgy finger at Nate. "Just know I'll be watching you, boy. I catch you sneaking around again, and you'll spend some time behind my bars."

Nate choked on his next words. "Thank you, Sheriff. Now, may I have my gun back?"

The lawman rose, handed him the pistol, and stomped from the store, slamming the door behind him. Nate turned to look at Henry, who was smiling.

"For such a personable young man, Nate, you sure seem to make people angry."

Nate laughed. "It's a gift."

Henry chuckled as he moved to take the seat the sheriff vacated. "Not many mind getting Paul mad. It's almost become a game. He doesn't deserve the badge, but no one else wants it." He puffed several times on his cigar. "Tell me about the beating, Nate."

He really didn't want to discuss it. He'd make the story as short and meaningless as possible. "I left the saloon and cut through an alley to get to my hotel. Two men jumped me."

"Why do you think that happened?"

He sat back in his chair and ran a hand over his face, suddenly weary. "That, I can't answer. Like I said earlier, you'd have to ask them."

Henry eyed him through a curl of smoke. "All right, I'll let it go. But if I get my hands on those two fools…"

Nate nodded his thanks. "How long has the sheriff worn the badge?"

Blowing out a breath filled with disdain, Henry peered up at the ceiling for the answer. "Let's see. I've been here over a year and he accepted the position not long after that." He looked back at Nate again. "Why? You looking for a new job? Because I'd be first in line to speak on your behalf."

With a short burst of laughter, Nate shook his head. "Not a chance."

Henry slumped against the back of his chair. "Which is why Paul still wears that badge. No one wants to take his place."

"It's quite a responsibility."

Henry cocked an eyebrow. "If you do it correctly, yes, it is."

Nodding his agreement, Nate had to appreciate Henry's decency. A thought quickly followed. "What about you? You'd be the perfect lawman—and I'd be first in line to speak on your behalf."

Henry hooted with laughter, slapping his palm on the table several times.

Nate grinned at his reaction. "Why is that funny?"

Henry held up two fingers, the same ones that held his cigar.

"Two reasons, my boy. One, I'm too old. These young ruffians would run me over without batting an eye."

Nate didn't agree but let the comment pass. "The other reason?"

"This right here." Still smiling, Henry rolled the cigar between his fingers. "With that man's pay, I couldn't afford these, and I really enjoy them."

After sharing a laugh, Nate slapped his hands on his knees and stood. "Well, I've had about all the fun I can stand for one day." He held out his hand to shake Henry's. "You have a good night."

"Will do. You stay safe."

Nate spent the walk to the hotel looking over his shoulder. He'd never let anyone get the jump on him again. He was new to the job as deputy marshal, but he was learning fast. Most of all, he hated that it came at the expense of learning the hard way.

Chapter Twenty-three
....

Rebekah made her way to the front window for what had to be the hundredth time. She stepped back when more customers entered, smiling her welcome before taking one last glance down the street.

Where is he? She'd asked herself that question almost as many times as she'd peered out the window. And what was with all the patrons today? Did everyone run out of supplies at the same time? Did they all have a big town picnic but didn't invite her family?

Knowing better, she scolded herself for taking her tension out on them. It wasn't their fault she hadn't seen Nate in two days. Her father was to blame for that. Never mind the fact that it was to help poor Mr. Zimmer. But if someone tried to blow up the mill with Mr. Zimmer inside, who was to say they wouldn't do the same to Nate? She mentioned her fears to her father but he only said she was being silly. Why did men always think women silly, when in her opinion, women had far more common sense then men?

After what she'd heard from a good many of the customers who'd been through the store, Cora included, she needed to talk to Nate, and she didn't want to wait another day. But Daddy had Nate spending all of yesterday and again today out at Mr. Zimmer's stamp mill, going over the machinery and equipment. In an attempt to help keep Mr. Zimmer from losing his business, Daddy had Nate making a list of what they could fix and what they might be able to build, despite the fact that he was still fighting for his life. She figured it was also her father's way of making sure Nate had a couple easy days to recover from his beating.

After totaling up the purchases of a couple ladies, Rebekah followed them to the door and bid them a good day, just so she could peek down the street again. The moment all the customers had finished their shopping, she planned to make a dash into the livery to see if Nate had returned without her being aware. She needed to know if the rumors about his near arrest being discussed so freely were true.

Rebekah clung to her last thread of patience as she helped the last of the shoppers pick out fabric for a new dress. At the moment, she didn't care one bit which kind of lace would look best with the chosen material, but she helped Mrs. Stallings finish that small task.

Feeling contrite about rushing the elderly woman out of the store once she'd paid for her purchases, Rebekah charged toward the side door intent on finding Nate. Before she could touch the knob, the door flung open and the man she sought strode through.

Scarcely giving her a glance, Nate gazed around the store, then moved to the back room and gave it a thorough look. "Where's Thomas?"

Stunned, she stared. "What?"

"Thomas. Your father told me he was in here."

She nodded. "He was. He picked up some items and left."

His words were terse, but she ventured a question. "Why?"

"Because I want to know what business he thinks he has up at Zimmer's mill."

Rebekah searched her mind for how to defend Thomas and defuse Nate's temper. "I'm sure Thomas—"

"I have a feeling he's the one who turned my horse loose. I had to walk back here."

Rebekah frowned. Nate was getting a bit ridiculous. "Why would Thomas do something like that?"

"You tell me. You seem to think he's a good man."

She crossed her arms, her own anger starting to ignite. She fought it back, knowing full well they'd never get anything accomplished if both remained irate. "He *is* a good man. He's been a friend to us since we got here." She swallowed hard to fight the rising tears. "I might have burned to death if it weren't for him."

Nate's head reared back at her statement. His anger crumbled right before her eyes as his face smoothed until he almost looked relaxed. "I'm sorry. I didn't know."

She sniffled, then nodded. "I don't understand the tension between you two. What happened to create so much distrust? If I didn't know better, I'd almost think you two hated each other."

In silence, he blinked several times. Then he finally shrugged. "I don't guess I can think of any one thing that started it. But from the moment we met, there seemed to be some kind of strain between us."

As he answered in a calm voice, her own tension eased. "Well, I think you two need to get it worked out before it gets any worse. You both are good men. You should be friends, not enemies." She cocked her head as she remembered why he came in the first place. "And what makes you think Thomas had anything to do with Zimmer's mill or your horse?"

His eyes narrowed, and she knew she'd ignited his anger again, making the bruises on his face darken once more. "A couple men told me they saw him there. The place was completely empty except for me, and apparently Thomas. Who else would have done it?"

She still didn't completely understand his logic. "Why would he have a reason to be at Zimmer's mill?"

"That's exactly what I want to ask him." Nate headed for the door. "I've got work to do. If you see Thomas, tell him I need to talk to him."

"Wait."

They still had something else to discuss, and she wanted to hear his side of the story. When he stopped and turned, she tried to keep her heart from racing. He was already angry. She didn't want to add fuel to the fire, but she had to know.

"I've got a question for you."

His head tilted as he examined her face. "All right."

Despite her efforts, her heart continued to race. She prayed he had a good answer for her. "I've heard rumors from several people that the sheriff nearly arrested you the other night for prowling around and acting suspicious."

There. She'd said it. But his expression told her he knew what she would ask before she got the question out, which didn't calm her heart at all. The rumors must be at least somewhat accurate.

"Funny how that news got out when only two people knew."

A hard knot formed in her stomach. "So it's true?"

He snorted as he shook his head, his mouth twisted in scorn. "Yes, it's true. But the sheriff had no business arresting me. If he took everyone into custody who wandered the streets at night, his jail would be filled to overflowing with half the men in town."

She hated feeling nosey and distrustful, but she had to ask. "Why were you wandering the streets?"

The look he gave her made her feel as though he was trying to see if he could trust her. She hoped he knew he could.

His lips twitched. "I saw someone else sneaking around the streets looking suspicious."

She peered into his eyes, trying to read him better. "Are you teasing me?"

This time he gave her a tiny smile. "No. I saw someone acting strangely, so I followed."

Dare she ask? "Who?"

He hesitated. "I'd rather not say right now."

She decided not to push. He'd tell her if or when he was ready. "I hate to tell you this, but the whole town is talking about it. Especially now that word is out about the threatening notes."

He looked startled. "What do you mean 'word is out'? People know about the notes that Mr. Zimmer and the Peters family received?"

So he hadn't heard. She wondered about that, since he didn't seek her out right away. "They only learned about those notes after one of the mine owners found a note shoved under his front door. He was furious. When he announced it to the town, Mr. Peters confessed that he'd received one too."

"But they don't know about the one to Mr. Zimmer?"

"They must. His name was mentioned."

Nate took a moment to think. "But Mr. Zimmer is still mostly unconscious, so I doubt he said anything. How did they find out about his note?"

She shrugged, now as confused as Nate looked. "I don't know. What I do know is that everyone is thinking you have something to do with the notes."

Air blasted from his mouth as he slammed his fist onto the counter. "Unbelievable. I try to help the town and end up taking the blame for the trouble." As far as she could tell, his expression wavered between anger and disappointment. "I can't help them if they look at me with suspicion."

By his voice, Nate was more hurt than annoyed. She scrambled to think of something to say that would lend comfort. Only one thing kept playing through her mind, but she wasn't sure how he'd react.

"People might start trusting you again if you, well—"

His head tilted slightly as his eyes narrowed. "If I'd what?"

She swallowed. "Come to church with me," she rushed out.

His body stiffened. "I don't know if I want to."

She was afraid of that answer. His voice was tinged with aversion. Still, she wanted him to confess his feelings. "Why?"

He paced, then slapped his hand on the counter. "How could your God allow something like this to happen? Mr. Zimmer's a good man. My dad and brother were good men. And your God let them die."

His pain tore through her. She wished she could wipe it away. "He's your God too."

Nate snorted. "Why would I want anything to do with a God who hurts those He claims to love? There are so many examples of reasons not to trust Him." He pointed a finger at her. "You're one of them."

Rebekah caressed the scar on her cheek. "I don't blame God for what happened to me. God doesn't make people do evil things. We do that all on our own. He gave us the right to choose for ourselves, to do right or wrong, to choose for Him or against Him." She peered into his eyes hoping to make him understand. "Don't you know the joy He feels when we choose correctly?"

Anger still coiled his fingers into a fist, though the irritation had eased from earlier. "And when we don't?"

Sadness put an ache in her heart. "Did your father ever shed tears at a bad decision you'd made?"

She remained silent, watching several emotions roll across his face, from grief to fondness. The smallest of smiles pulled at the corners of his mouth.

"More than once," he finally managed just over a whisper. "I think the worst time was when my grandfather died. I was about twelve, I guess. We were supposed to go to the funeral, but I refused to go." He shook his head. "A couple days before he died, Grandpa had scolded me soundly for something I'd done. Funny thing is, I can't even remember what I'd done wrong. I only remember being so mad at him that I said I hated him."

Nate was so deep into his memory, Rebekah didn't say a word to interrupt or draw him away from remembering. She choked up when she saw his eyes shimmering.

"Dad didn't make me attend the funeral. I sat home by myself, at first still stewing in my anger. Before long, that anger turned to regret. I was eaten up with grief over how I'd acted, knowing that the last memory Grandpa had of me was my angry words." He ran his hand over his face. "It got worse when Dad came home, and I told him I wanted to go to the cemetery. Dad dropped onto a chair, and tears started streaming down his face." Nate's throat worked to swallow several times. "I've never forgotten that day. It's played a big part in how I've reacted in other situations."

The rasp in Nate's voice let Rebekah know how much even now it affected him. She reached to touch his hand. "And after you'd disappointed your father, he still loved you anyway, didn't he?"

Nate let out a slow breath as he nodded.

She let him think about it for a bit. "Just as God still loves us when we disappoint Him, we need to continue loving and trusting Him, no matter what." She stepped close. "Come to church with me, Nate. Not only will it go a long way to show the townspeople the kind of man you really are"—she placed her hand over his heart—"it might go a long way in healing this."

Patting his chest lightly, she gave him a trembling smile before walking away. She'd said all she could think to say. The rest was up to him. He had to make the choice. As she prayed he'd make the right one, she dared not think about how much his decision mattered.

Chapter Twenty-four

....

After tying his horse's reins to a tree branch, Nate stood in front of the church, staring, unsure of whether or not he could make himself enter. The spot over his heart where Rebekah had placed her hand still burned. That warmth was the very reason he'd managed to make it this far. Her words had continued to echo through his mind the last few days until he thought he'd go mad. Worse yet, he knew she was right. She'd only repeated what his mother had told him time and again.

Making a decision, he looked down at his shirt and denims, brushing out a couple wrinkles as though he had to clean himself up to enter. Heart hammering, he took a deep breath and headed for the door, feeling very much like he strode through quicksand with each step.

Once inside, sweat broke out on his forehead as he waited for the reactions of those in attendance. The pastor and Perry both gave vigorous handshakes while clapping him on the back. A few men he remembered meeting did the same while others stood back and watched.

Mrs. Weaver wrapped him in a hug before holding him at arm's length. "Plan on joining us for a picnic by the river."

"I will. Thank you."

He tried not to look around much as accusatory stares stabbed him over and over, but once he saw Rebekah and her wide smile, nothing else mattered. As she placed her Bible and reticule on the pew beside her, he wished she didn't plan to sit so close to the front. But he headed toward her anyway.

"Do you mind if I sit with you?"

Her eyes glimmered with unshed tears. "Not at all." She briefly gripped his hand. "I'm glad you came."

Seeing someone move close behind her, Nate pulled his gaze from her. For the first time, he noticed Thomas standing in the same pew as where Rebekah planned to sit. Nate watched Thomas for several seconds, wondering if he had been at last Sunday's service. Finally, he nodded and extended his hand. "Thomas."

Thomas accepted his handshake. "Nate."

The greeting wasn't much, but it was a start. At the very least, Rebekah seemed pleased with the effort. Thomas moved to the center of the pew with Rebekah following. Nate was about to join them when someone grabbed him around the waist. He turned to find Andrew grinning up at him.

"Hi, Nate. I haven't seen you all week. Where you been?"

Andrew's loud greeting pulled everyone's attention toward them, making Nate tense up again. The last thing he needed was to have all the adults hear a child question his whereabouts. He motioned for Andrew, and the boy nestled between him and Rebekah. Andrew again grinned up at Nate, who couldn't resist ruffling the boy's hair.

"Good to see you, Andrew."

Andrew scowled. "You're supposed to call me Andy, remember?"

Nate winked. "Right. Sorry."

The lady at the piano began playing, ending all further conversation. The off-key notes clashed, nearly making his ears shrivel, yet the exuberant woman acted as though she didn't notice a thing. The pastor motioned for them to stand and led them in singing. Nate had hoped the singing would have drowned out the sour notes, but as the voices rose in song, the woman played louder. He glanced at

Rebekah, who only raised her brows at him as she continued with the congregation. The whole thing became humorous, lifting Nate's spirits as well as the corners of his mouth.

After enduring yet another clamorous song, the pastor asked them to be seated and opened the message in prayer. His mind already wandering, Nate recalled that the piano player had received a note last week. Interesting that she made her way from the piano bench to sit next to an older gentleman. Could he be the man the note spoke about, maybe written in a way similar to the one Cora had received? He'd have to mention it to Rebekah after the service.

The pastor had already started reading Scripture when Nate pulled his mind back to the message. Andrew held Rebekah's Bible so they all could read along. Something the pastor said about not grieving the Holy Spirit grabbed his attention, and he started reading where Andrew pointed.

"Let all bitterness, and wrath, and anger, and clamor, and evil speaking be put away from you, with all malice; and be ye kind one to another, tenderhearted, forgiving one another, even as God for Christ's sake hath forgiven you."

Nate raised his brows as he reread some of the text, feeling as though the verses were talking directly to him. He had often thought the same thing as a youth attending services with his mother. Many times, he'd wondered if his mother had spoken to the preacher about what he should preach on.

"Let me draw your attention to one of the smallest words in those verses," the pastor continued. "Often it's the small words that are the most important." He looked down at his Bible again. "Let *all* bitterness, and *all* malice be put away from you." The pastor pulled off his spectacles and leaned over the pulpit, taking time to scan all the faces. "*All* doesn't mean you can hold on to even a tiny part of your anger. *All* doesn't mean a little bitterness is all right, especially if no one else knows about it. *All* means every last bit and portion."

The drone of the pastor's voice continued as Nate examined his own anger and bitterness. How long had he been holding on to his destructive emotions? Around three years? Trouble was, he was the only person being hurt by them. Or was he?

Andrew squirmed, pulling Nate's thoughts to him and all children. They rarely held grudges or anger. Children were usually quick to forgive, their love evident. Somewhere along the way to adulthood, that important quality was lost, as was trust. What a shame.

The pastor's chuckle drew Nate's attention back to the message. What had he missed? He'd have to try harder to stay focused.

"I have this shirt." The pastor wore a strange smile. His wife put her head down, her body already shaking with laughter. "It's my favorite. You can tell by the condition it's in." He nodded. "It has holes near the collar and on the sleeves. Some places are so worn, there'll be holes there before long too. This shirt is so faded, it's difficult to tell what color it used to be."

Many sitting in the pews were laughing and nodding. Some of the women were bumping their husbands or outright pointing at them for all to see.

The pastor grinned. "I see I'm not the only one who loves wearing the most comfortable shirt I own." He winked at a woman sitting in front. "Much to my wife's dismay, I wear this shirt nearly every day, and I refuse to let her throw it out."

His wife turned to let everyone see her expression as she nodded her agreement.

The pastor chuckled again. "She's warned me that one day someone will see me in this shirt and think I don't get paid enough." He quickly looked up. "That's not a hint, by the way."

The congregation roared with laughter. The pastor smiled, patiently waiting for them to get calm. Then his face grew serious as he leaned over the pulpit.

"How many of us, right at this moment, are wearing our anger, malice, and bitterness like an old comfortable shirt?" He shook his spectacles at them. "Who among us keep our unhealthy emotions because they're comfortable? We've grown used to them. We wouldn't know life any other way because we've kept them close for so long."

The church had grown incredibly quiet, and so had the pastor's voice.

"That's called sin, people." He glanced around. "How many of us would walk around in the middle of summer on the hottest day wearing a blanket? None of us would. We'd want to throw it off as quickly as possible." He tapped the top of the pulpit with his finger. "It should be the same with our sins. Why carry them around and get comfortable with them? We should treat them as a blanket on a hot day and throw them off, begging God's forgiveness."

He looked at his wife again, his love for her evident in his expression. "My wife doesn't know it yet, but when we get home, I'm throwing away this old, worn-out shirt. I don't want to be that comfortable again. Not when I have something new and wonderful waiting to take its place."

Amens echoed through the building. Nate added one of his own. He hadn't been so stirred by a message in a long time. The hard part would be applying what he'd heard to his life. Thankfully, the message ended a few minutes later. He wanted time to think about the pastor's words.

But Andrew wasn't about to let that happen. As soon as the last song had been sung, the boy grabbed his hand, shaking and pulling at the same time.

"Come on, Nate. I brought an extra fishing pole for you. Mama said if we caught enough she'd invite you to supper tomorrow night."

Nate looked at Rebekah and received a nod of affirmation. He tugged Andrew toward him and bent to see him eye to eye, his face as serious as he could muster. "That's an awful lot of pressure. How many do we need to feed all of us?"

Andrew's mouth twisted as he peered into the air for his answer. "I think six ought to be enough." He turned to Rebekah. "Don't you think, Bek?"

"I would imagine that would be plenty." She lifted a shoulder. "I might even accept only five."

Returning to his full height, Nate was about to wink at Rebekah until he noticed Thomas peeking around her. Unwilling to rile the man, especially after hearing that message, he smiled instead.

"All right. I've always enjoyed a good challenge." He put his hand on Andrew's shoulder. "Just let me speak to the pastor first. Then I'm all yours."

After thanking the pastor for a great and thought-provoking message, Nate joined Rebekah and Andrew out by the Weavers' wagon. Andrew already had one of the fishing poles in hand, regaling his sister with a story while pretending to toss out the line and pull in a whale. The idea of spending a fun afternoon with the Weaver family was just what he needed after the week he'd endured. He glanced around for Perry and his wife. Not seeing them, he turned to Rebekah.

"Where's your parents?"

No sooner had he asked than Perry strode around the corner of the church and headed their way. Something about his stance made all of Nate's nerves come alive, his relaxed state suddenly gone.

Chapter Twenty-five

....

Rebekah held her breath at her father's expression, unsure what might be wrong. In this town, one never knew. She prayed it had nothing to do with him or Mama, and especially that a note wasn't involved.

Daddy stopped next to her, putting his arm around her waist. Rebekah wondered if it was to hold her up or him. His gaze encompassed all three of them.

"I'm sorry, but my wife and I need to bow out of the picnic today. Some friends have asked us for our help."

Andrew's mouth dropped open, whether to question or argue she wasn't sure, but Daddy put up his hand to stave him off.

"I don't have time to fill you in on the details. If you three want to go on the picnic, please do. The food is in the wagon." He placed his hand on Nate's shoulder. "Whatever is decided, Nate, I'm leaving my children in your care. Keep them safe."

With that said, Daddy spun on his heel and raced back the direction he'd come. Her own mouth dropping open, Rebekah stood staring at the spot from which her father disappeared. Even Andrew stood in silence. Nate swung around in front of them, drawing their attention away from their father.

"Well." Nate clapped his hands together. "I don't know about you, but I'm starving, and a picnic sounds like exactly what we need right now. On the other hand, I'll do whatever you two want. If you'd rather go home, just say so, and I'll get you there."

Weighing their choices and knowing full well all they'd do is worry if they went straight home, Rebekah finally nodded. "I think you're right. Besides, we had our hearts set on eating fish for supper tomorrow." She placed her hand on her little brother's shoulder. "Right, Andrew?"

For such a young man, Andrew seemed fully aware of the situation. Licking his lips, he glanced one more time the direction his father disappeared, then looked up at them. He smiled, though it never quite reached his eyes like usual. She'd have to work hard to get Andrew to forget his worries.

While Andrew climbed into the bed of the wagon, Nate helped Rebekah up to the seat before tying his horse to the back. After sliding in next to her, Nate steered the horses toward the river. She noticed he squirmed a bit, but she didn't quite know what to do or say to make him comfortable while dealing with her own concerns.

Suddenly, Nate started singing at the top of his lungs one of the hymns they'd sung earlier, hitting every note off-key, much like Mrs. Phipps had done.

Rebekah reared back, at first staring in shock and alarm. Then she couldn't stop her laughter. "What are you doing?"

He raised his brows, looking completely innocent. "What?"

She hesitated. In no way did she want to hurt his feelings, but fact was fact. "You sound awful."

"Really?" His brows puckered. "I thought that's the way you all liked your music—clanging and off-key." He shrugged. "I was just trying to fit in."

Rebekah burst into laughter again as she swatted at him. "Don't pick on that poor woman. She can't help it."

"Really?" He tilted his head. "And here I thought you all liked gnashing your teeth when the notes she played clash worse than two little girls screaming their heads off."

Rebekah shook her finger at him. "I told you, she can't seem to help it. We let her continue to play out of love for her."

"Love?" His brows rose once again. "I think it's gotten to the point where it's bordering on adoration." He winked, making her heart hammer against her chest. "Actually, I do understand the feelings there." He bumped her shoulder with his. "I was just looking for a way to take your mind off your father." He gave her a lingering look. "Did it work?"

Heart still threatening to crack her ribs, she nodded. "It did. Thank you."

When in a playful mood, Nate was so fun. She took a deep breath. And he was very attractive, despite the yellowed bruises still marring his face. At this rate, she'd be hard-pressed to remember that her parents weren't along.

"Your piano player," he began, then smiled when she gave him her scolding expression, "no, I'm not going to keep picking on her. I just wondered about the man she sat with during the service. Was the note she received about him?"

With the wild week they'd had, Rebekah had all but forgotten about that note. "I don't know, but it would make sense. Especially if it was anything like the one Cora received."

The mention of a note made her thoughts return to her parents, making her say another silent prayer for everyone's safety. Would having more details alleviate her worries—or make things worse?

"Let's sing some more." Andrew, his fishing pole still held tightly in his hand, now stood right behind them, peering over their shoulders. "I like the way Nate was singing."

Nate threw his head back with laughter. "Now, you see? Here's the best evidence that your church needs to do something about that woman. She's corrupting your brother's ears."

Jabbing her elbow into Nate's ribs, she grinned at his teasing. "Behave yourself." She turned and put her arm around Andrew. "Which song do you want to sing?"

"The same one Nate was singing, only better."

When Nate's mouth dropped open in mock outrage, both Rebekah and Andrew burst into laughter. Then he grinned and led them in a rousing rendition of the hymn. At one point, Nate's attention seemed caught somewhere over her shoulder. She turned to look and saw a rider in the distance. She squinted, thinking it looked like Thomas, but she couldn't be certain. Wondering if Nate thought the same, she turned back. He'd obviously still been looking but focused on her the moment she faced him, his expression bland. Either he thought nothing of the rider or his suspicion of Thomas had waned.

"Hold up there."

The shouted command surprised them. Nate sawed back on the reins while they all craned their necks to see who'd come up behind them. Henry Gilmore sat atop his horse, his forefinger planted in one ear.

"Well, you all look fine. With the racket coming from this wagon, I thought you were in some kind of horrible pain." He nudged his horse up next to Nate's side of the wagon and extended his hand. "Now I can see it's just that none of you know how to sing."

"Oh." Nate put one hand over his heart. "Now that really hurts."

"Not nearly as much as you did my ears, I'm quite certain." He waved at Andrew. "And how are you, young Andrew? Planning to show the fish who's in charge?"

Andrew grinned wide as he held out his pole. "Yes, sir."

"Tell you what, young man." He patted his pocket until some change jingled. "I've been in the mood for fish. You catch me a good-sized one, and I'll make sure you're nicely compensated."

Andrew's face screwed into a comical frown. "Compen-what?"

Rebekah joined in with the men's laughter. "That means he'll pay you to catch him a fish."

Andrew nodded hard. "Yes, sir. I'll sure catch you a nice big one."

Mr. Gilmore leaned close. "Tell you what. You catch the biggest one," he said and aimed his thumb at Nate, "that means bigger than any Nate can manage to pull in, I'll add a dollar."

"All right." Andrew nearly screeched his cheer, he was so excited.

Much as she didn't want to share Nate's attentions, Rebekah's upbringing made her feel the need to ask. "Would you like to join us, Mr. Gilmore? We have plenty."

"My dear." He tipped his hat. "You do an old man's heart good, but I already have prior plans. Thank you anyway." He peered up at the sun. "In fact, I'd best get moving. You three have a wonderful afternoon."

Tipping his hat one last time, he waved to Andrew and spurred his horse east. They didn't get to sit still long. Andrew thumped them both on the back faster than Rebekah could count.

"Let's gooooo. I gotta catch a lot of fish."

Minutes later, after stopping in their favorite spot by the river, Rebekah began laying out the blanket and food while Nate and Andrew raced to the river, both determined to be the one to catch the first fish. With everything ready, Rebekah took some time to sit and watch the way Nate spoke and acted with Andrew, much like a loving older brother. She had no doubt he'd make a good father. He'd make some lucky woman very happy. If only that woman could have been her.

Unable to help herself, Rebekah stroked her scarred cheek. The words *if only* went through her mind again, but she pushed them away.

A shadow fell over her. She looked up and found Nate standing next to the blanket.

"You all right?"

Her heart warmed at his tender voice. "I am. And I'm hungry. You two about ready to eat?"

Nate glanced over his shoulder. "I know I am, but I'm afraid your brother is determined to catch all, as well as the biggest fish. He told me to save him something to eat, and he'd come later."

Rebekah glanced at Andrew, seeing how much fun he was having. "I'm not about to get in his way. Have a seat."

She glanced at Nate to see if he'd be willing to say a prayer of thanks but was almost certain he'd want her to take care of that task. To her surprise, he didn't even wait to be asked but did the honor. The prayer was brief but heartfelt, and she found herself staring. He opened his eyes and caught her.

"What? We haven't even started eating yet, so I know there's nothing stuck to my face."

Unable to speak, she only shook her head, suddenly knowing without a doubt that she was in love with this man. She knew it as surely as she knew of her love for the Lord. And one day her heart would be broken as she watched him marry someone else or ride out of town. But for now, she'd enjoy her time with him.

She avoided looking at him as she handed him some bread and slices of ham. "You seem different somehow."

He stayed quiet until she met his gaze. "Different how?"

Thinking for a minute, she tried to put her finger on what had changed. "Less angry. More at peace." She shrugged. "I think."

He smiled before taking a bite. Since he didn't seem inclined to talk, she made her own sandwich and started to eat.

"You ever feel like the pastor is talking directly to you?"

She made a face. He just *had* to wait until her mouth was full to ask. She covered her mouth and chewed as fast as she could until she could swallow. Then she noticed his grin.

"You did that on purpose." The twinkle in his eyes only confirmed her suspicion. She shook her head. "I know your mother taught you better."

He burst into laughter. "You're right, she did."

"I thought as much. And to answer your question, yes, I do feel like the pastor is speaking directly to me. Most Sundays, in fact. Today especially."

"Really?" He took another bite but didn't wait to swallow. "Me too." He finished his sandwich before saying another word. Then he motioned to her. "But I would have thought, well, I mean, you don't seem to have any bitterness or ill-will toward anyone. How could you have felt the pastor was talking to you?"

A gust of wind blew one of her curls across her face, and she tucked it behind her ear. "I guess just as my hair won't stay in place, neither do my emotions. Though I try to control bad thoughts or feelings, sometimes things happen to make me have to fight them all over again." Though she really didn't want to talk about herself, she would if it helped Nate in some way. "I thought I had control of my anger about getting burned until I found out Daddy doesn't think it was an accident. Then I had to work on it all over again."

Nodding, he wiped his mouth, then leaned back on one elbow. "I know what you mean. I didn't realize how much anger I'd carried with me about the deaths of my father and brother." He tossed a blade of grass off the blanket. "I guess, if I'm honest, I still want revenge. But the pastor's message this morning really spoke to my heart. I think I finally realize that not only am I hurting myself, but I'm hurting my heavenly Father as well."

"But it's hard to forgive someone when they've done you wrong," she finished for him.

"Exactly."

As much as she wanted to ease his pain, only One could do that. "God is waiting to help you if you'll let Him."

He peered up at her, squinting one eye against the sun. "He's helped you?"

She remembered the peace that filled her every time she allowed God to do His work in her. "Yes. In ways I can't begin to explain. It's my own hard heart and disobedience that makes a mess of things."

His head tilted as he looked thoughtful. "But don't you think what the Lord puts us through makes us bitter?"

His voice held no anger or annoyance. He was genuinely trying to understand. She wasn't sure if her answer would help or hinder, but it was the only thing she could think to say.

"I believe it's all in our attitude. I think God allows us to go through trials to test us, see how we'll handle them. Will we get angry and bitter, or will we allow the trial to refine us and make us stronger so we can be better servants for Him?"

"All because He loves us."

She smiled. "As odd as that sounds, yes. It's not for us to understand why the Lord works the way He does, but we are to remain obedient through all things."

He lay back, propping his arms behind his head. "I can tell you really love Him."

"How could I not when He gave the ultimate sacrifice?"

Andrew raced up and dropped onto Nate's chest, nearly knocking the wind from him. "Come on, Nate. You've got to help me catch some fish, or you can't come for supper tomorrow."

Nate sat up. "What? The mighty fisherman needs my help?"

Completely serious, Andrew nodded. "Hurry before it gets too dark."

Rebekah quickly threw some ham between two pieces of bread. "Make sure you eat, Andrew."

He grabbed it from her with one grubby hand and grabbed one of Nate's hands in the other. Nate sent her a wink as he strolled off with Andrew tugging at him to move faster. She sat watching them and pondering their conversation. If today was any indication, God was doing a work in Nate's heart. Hopefully He'd do a work in her own heart to keep it from being crushed.

Chapter Twenty-six

. . . .

Nate rode away from the Weaver home after making sure Rebekah and Andrew were safely inside their house. Their parents weren't home yet, and that worried him. What had happened with their friends? With no idea where to begin looking for them, Nate made sure Rebekah and Andrew would be protected. He refused to leave until he heard them latch the door. Perry had left them in his care, and he took that responsibility seriously.

Before getting them home, he'd allowed Andrew to stop by Henry's store to drop off the fish he'd caught. Now fifty cents richer, Andrew probably wouldn't sleep tonight for want of examining his new treasure. The thought made Nate grin. He'd been the same way as a kid.

The smile didn't last long. In the midst of all the chaos of the day, he'd seen Thomas in the distance while they were on their way to the picnic. Since he was certain Rebekah had seen him too, he tried to act as casual as possible, though he had every intention of riding back out there in the next day or two to see if he could discover why the man would be heading out that way. It wouldn't do to just ask him. He and Thomas were about as friendly as a bear with a beehive. With a mix like that, one of them was sure to get bit.

In the meantime, Nate had more on his mind than a short, moody man. He cut down a side street to return to Henry's store.

Something about the usually jovial man had seemed different when Andrew had dropped off the fish. Though he'd been personable, a certain tension had emanated from him, unusual enough to make Nate want to go back and check on him before dropping by to see how Grant was doing.

After tying his horse to the railing, he knocked on the door and waited. Receiving no answer, he knocked again, hoping Henry hadn't gone home. Nate had no idea where the man lived. He'd never thought or needed to ask. Preparing to pound one more time, Nate pulled his hand away just as the door opened. The scent of whiskey drifted toward him.

"What?"

The sour attitude surprised Nate. Henry had always been pleasant in the past. Not quite sure what to say, Nate stuck his foot inside the doorway to keep Henry from shutting him out.

"Let me in, Henry."

The two locked eyes for several moments before Henry finally shrugged and stepped back. A glow from the back room told him why Henry had taken so long to answer the door. He may not have heard the first knock. With Henry already headed that direction, Nate closed the door and followed. A cigar smoldered from a tray that sat next to a whiskey bottle and glass. Henry dropped onto a chair and drained the glass of amber liquid.

Nate took the chair opposite him. "What's wrong, Henry? What happened since we saw you this afternoon?"

He poured more whiskey into the glass but didn't take a drink. "I—" He shook his head. "I can't tell you."

Those words made each of Nate's nerves stand on end. He'd heard them too many times. He leaned forward. "Did you get a note?"

Henry's head jerked toward him. "How'd you know?"

Nate hadn't planned on telling anyone what he knew, but he trusted Henry. He'd been a friend since they met, nearly a father figure. "I know a couple others who've received notes too. Trouble followed."

Blowing out a long breath, Henry reached to finger his whiskey glass. "So they told you what the notes said?"

"Some." He leaned back again. "I've never read one. I've just been told what they said."

Henry took a drink, then puffed his cigar before returning it to the tray. "Nate, my boy," he said, wiping some ashes from the table before looking him in the eyes, "I can't afford to pay this person. So, what am I going to do? Wait around for whatever this blackmailer decides to do to make me pay?"

For the first time since they'd met, Nate heard weakness in Henry's voice. He'd always been the strong leader type before. Nate needed to work harder than ever to prevent another tragedy, especially harm intended toward a friend.

"No. I'll help. I don't know how, but I'll do what I can to keep anything from happening to you."

Henry's eyes softened and a smile started, only to be interrupted by shouting outside. Then the word "Fire!" penetrated the walls as boots thumped past. Nate's heart skipped a beat. Shoving back from the table, he ran for the door, praying hard the Weavers were safe.

In moments, Nate realized his prayer had been answered. An orange glow shone just down the boardwalk, revealing several people milling in the street. As he raced their way, he realized where the fire came from—the Peters' boardinghouse. Were they still inside or had everyone made it out?

Once in front of the building, Nate could see the fire wasn't as large as he'd feared but crawled along the front boardwalk, blocking one set of windows and the front doors. The other set of windows had been broken out—probably how the residents had escaped. While Nate joined the water-bucket line, he glanced around for the Peters family and found them huddled together, fear evident on their faces even in the dark.

Another ten minutes of hard work, and they had the fire out. Near as Nate could tell, there wasn't much damage to the majority of the building, though the front would need new lumber. No doubt the Peters would be busy cleaning and washing up a lot of soot and ashes in the morning. He made his way to Cora's side. Her new beau stood with her wrapped in his arms.

Nate held out his hand to the young man. "Will Bradford, isn't it?"

Will accepted his handshake, never taking his other arm from Cora's shoulders. "Yes, sir."

"Is everyone all right?"

He glanced at the family. "Shaken up but no one got hurt, thank the good Lord."

Nate nodded his agreement. "Did anyone see what happened?"

"I don't think anyone's had a chance to ask questions. We were busy making sure everyone got out."

"It's not your business, Kirkland."

He turned and found the sheriff eyeing him. "I just asked—"

"Yeah, well, quit getting in my way, or I'll arrest you for that very thing."

"Leave him alone, Paul." Henry had joined the fray, still weaving from too much whiskey. "If you'd do the job you're paid to do, no one else would feel the need to step in."

Nate moved between the men to stave off a fight, whether it be with words or fists. Henry would normally be more tactful. Putting his arm around Henry's shoulders, he led him back to the tobacco store.

"Go on back, Henry. Stay there, and make sure this same thing doesn't happen to you."

Henry tapped Nate's temple. "Good thinking, boy. Guess it's time I put the bottle away so I can do the same."

He waited until Henry entered the shop before turning back to see if he could help. He didn't get far before the sheriff stepped in front of him and stopped him with a hand to his chest.

"Go home, Kirkland. You stay here and get in my way, and your bed will be behind bars tonight."

Nate crossed his arms, fighting the desire to flatten the man. "What did I do to make you dislike me so much?"

Sheriff Caldwell took another step forward until they were only inches apart. "You're in *my* town and working hard to make me look bad. Leave, or you and me will have a go."

Mouth opening to tell the man he was the only one making himself look bad, Nate stopped himself before the words escaped. He put his hands in the air in a show of surrender and took a step back, doubting the sheriff would stay long enough to ask questions or find out how the fire started. More than likely, the sheriff already knew. As far as Nate was concerned, the sheriff was up to his neck in the blackmailing scheme. He needed to dig a little deeper to find out who all worked with him.

The only other question he had right now was whether the sheriff meant for him to leave town or the area. For now, he'd go check on Grant. By the time he returned, the sheriff would no doubt be gone. Nate could then look around and ask questions undeterred.

Retrieving his horse from Henry's shop, Nate arrived at the doctor's office in minutes. To his delight, he found Grant sitting up in bed trying to eat. Grinning, he headed toward the chair by the bed.

"Well, as I live and breathe."

Grant managed a smile with the spoon in his mouth. He pulled it out. "Yeah, me too."

Laughing, Nate shook the man's hand as he sat. "Glad to have you back, Grant. You gave us a scare."

"Really? I hadn't noticed."

This was the first time he saw Grant's humor, and he liked it. He had to be feeling better. "Perry and I have been looking over your mill. We think we can help fix up a great deal. Everything else you'd need to find someplace else."

All the while he'd been talking, Grant shook his head. He swallowed another spoonful of broth. "Don't bother yourself."

Nate eyed him a moment. He didn't like the change of tone and expression that came over Grant. "Why?"

"I'm not staying."

Nate turned in his chair to look Grant in the eyes. "You just woke up, and you've already made that decision?"

Handing him the bowl, Grant sank back against his pillows. "I didn't just make it. I'd been thinking about it while checking out the equipment. The second blast helped me make up my mind."

"And I can't change it back?"

Grant exhaled. "Look, Nate, I appreciate your friendship and your help, but I'm done. I don't have the means or the desire to continue here."

Nate's heart sank. He'd hoped to help get Grant back on his feet. "Where will you go?"

"My sister and her husband live in California. I thought I'd pay them a visit and decide from there. I have a feeling they'll offer me work."

Certain now he wouldn't change Grant's mind, Nate turned the conversation in a new direction. "Feel up to answering some questions?"

The doctor cleared his throat, but Grant waved him away. "I've got a few more minutes left in me. What can I do for ya?"

Nate glanced over his shoulder to make sure the doctor wasn't hovering. "The day you were hurt, did you see anyone lurking nearby? Someone who had no business being there, even if you consider that person a friend?"

Grant was already shaking his head, but Nate's thoughts jerked to a halt. What if the person who threw the dynamite worked for Grant, giving him easy access and knowledge of the place?

"A couple of my workers came with me since they hadn't found other work, but that's all I saw other than the stars after the explosion."

"Do you trust all your workers?"

A frown marred Grant's face. Nate couldn't tell if it was from disagreement or pain. He waited, giving Grant all the time he needed.

"The men closest to me I trust completely. I can't answer the same about those I hardly know. A lot of the men were hired at a moment's notice because I needed a body to do a job."

"But none of those unknowns were with you that day?"

When Grant rubbed his hand across his face, Nate knew he

needed to end this and let the man get some rest. Maybe he'd get a chance to talk to him one more time before he left for California.

"I only remember two men with me, and they're the type of friends who, if they haven't struck gold by the time I leave, they'll probably leave town with me."

Nate nodded and slapped his hands on his knees. "Well, it's good to have friends like that." He reached to shake Grant's hand. "You get some rest, and make sure you look me up before you head out so we can say our good-byes."

"You got it, Nate. And thanks for helping."

He strode out of the doctor's office, knowing in his heart he couldn't help Grant in the least. But, if nothing else, if he managed to catch the blackmailer, he could help others in town. Intent on doing just that, he led his horse back to the boardinghouse to see what he could discover.

Chapter Twenty-seven

....

Rebekah blew strands of hair from her face as she crawled on hands and knees scrubbing at the soot on the floor inside the Peters' boardinghouse. As much as she hated to admit it, she was glad Cora was too upset to want to talk. Rebekah's parents' best friends had moved away yesterday due to the blackmailing note they received. The news weighed heavy on her mind.

Mama and Daddy had spent the entire day helping their friends pack up their wagon, only to return home to the news that someone tried to burn down the Peters' boardinghouse. Exhaustion rode them hard, but they insisted Rebekah go over and help the Peters clean the home while her parents stayed at the livery and store to keep the businesses running. One of the saddest parts of this whole situation was that her mother had finally started looking happy and healthy again. With her friend leaving town, Mama's eyes had lost some of their gleam and cheerfulness.

And now the threatening notes were no longer a secret. Word had also gotten out about the messages Cora and Mrs. Phipps had received. Talk ran rampant that the author of both types of notes was from the same person. Rebekah wasn't sure she agreed, but she desperately wanted to talk to Nate about the theory. By the look of things, that would have to wait until tomorrow at the earliest, allowing too much time to pass for the rumors to spread and grow with no way to slow their expansion.

* * * * *

The next morning found Rebekah in much the same position as she scoured yet another room of soot and ashes. The scent of old smoke mixed with the water to wipe everything down made her stomach churn and her head throb. Her muscles ached from the day before and now screamed their rebellion at another day of the tedious labor. Much to the Peters' and boarders' delight, they were able to move back in today, making her task that much more difficult as the residents tromped through her work area.

"You look like you're ready to take a club to the heads of the people wandering through here."

Nate's statement was filled with amusement at her expense, but she was never happier to hear his voice.

"Are you volunteering to be first in line?"

He chuckled. "Not on your life. Or mine for that matter." He moved in front of her. "Your father sent me here to see if there was anything I could do to help speed this along so you won't have such a long day."

Pushing to her knees, she shoved loose hair from her face before rubbing her lower back. As sweat oozed from her temples and down the length of her back, she knew she looked a mess but no longer cared much. She was ready to collapse. "How do you feel about washing down the walls?"

"Sounds like my favorite job of the day."

She gave a snort. "You expect me to believe that?"

"Of course. I'll get to work with you again." He reached for one of the rags stacked on the table. "Besides that, I don't have to worry about you walking to the left like Twister or weaving between my legs like Mercy does while I'm working. Plus, this place smells better than the livery."

She laughed. Secretly she was thrilled to spend more time with Nate. He was so much fun. "Well, I'll see what I can do to make you feel at home."

Grinning, he snapped the towel open. "This ought to be interesting."

They'd only worked a few minutes before Nate stopped and turned to look at her. She'd wondered how long it would take him to tire of the mundane task. She was about to tease him when she noticed the concern on his face. Instead of asking, she waited for him to speak his mind.

"Did you hear that news of the notes is out?"

She stood to stretch her legs as well as her back. "Yes, I did." She tucked her stray hair behind her ear and grimaced. "I don't know what the townspeople are saying exactly, and what they're feeling."

Nate's eyebrows rose. "It's awful. They walk around looking over their shoulders. They even seem afraid to wake up in the morning for fear they'll find a note shoved under their doors."

She made a face. "That bad, huh?"

"You'll be able to see the difference, the tension, when you get back amongst the people again. It's pretty much all they can talk about." He shook his head. "I almost feel sorry for them."

"Why almost?"

He leaned against the wall and crossed his arms. "Because if they'd join together and fight against this blackmailer, rather than run and hide in fear, they could end this scheme."

She cocked her head, feeling compassion for the residents. "But you have to understand the fear when you consider the real threats written in the notes, followed up by fires and explosions. People are getting hurt. Besides, that's the reason we hire lawmen, so they can do the rough and scary peace-keeping for us."

Nate snorted and turned back to scrubbing the wall. "A *good* lawman could do that for you."

She lifted an eyebrow. "You agree with my father that the sheriff isn't doing a good job?"

He glanced over his shoulder. "Let's just say I think he could be working harder."

She stared at his back for a moment. "What aren't you telling me?"

Taking his time to rinse and wring out his rag, he finally looked at her. "I'd rather not say until I know more."

She wouldn't get any more out of him. Rebekah knelt to her task again, her mind working much harder than her arms. Then she remembered what she wanted to ask him yesterday. She rocked back on her heels. "Cora told me everyone thinks the love notes and the threatening notes are from the same person. What are your thoughts, Nate?"

He stopped and turned toward her. "I can see why they'd think as much. The notes started showing up at almost the same time. That alone would be a strange coincidence. But unless I get to see them for myself, I'd hate to draw a conclusion on that fact alone."

She peered up at him, seeing him in a new way. "You almost sound like a lawman."

He tilted his head, an odd smile playing on his lips. "Almost?"

Goodness, but he was handsome. "You're certainly smart and perceptive enough to be a good sheriff or marshal. Not to mention tenacious. Daddy is the only other man I can think of who'd spend so much time looking into all that's happened and try to help. I know he'd do more, but he's busy with the store, livery, and trying to help at the mine."

"That's a lot of responsibility." Nate rinsed the rag again, looking thoughtful. "Why did he get involved with a mine? He has two successful businesses. It seems a mine would run a big risk of eating into his profits. Or did the idea of striking it rich with the mother lode play a factor?"

She lifted a shoulder. "I wouldn't doubt that holding a large nugget in his hand might have had something to do with buying into the mine. I mean, the majority of people in town are here because of the chance of getting rich with gold or silver. It's what brought us here. But Daddy also has a big heart. He knew Reuben needed help, and he didn't hesitate to give it."

"And the big dream going bust is the main reason most people are leaving. Anything to do with mining is a risk, both to your bank account and your health." He shook his head. "Mr. Zimmer is leaving as soon as he's well enough to travel."

Rebekah shook her head. "Oh no."

"Yep. And now Mr. Gilmore has received a threatening note." He returned to scrubbing the wall clean. "It's enough to make most people leave."

Her heart skipped a beat. "Is that your way of telling me you're packing up with the rest?"

He glanced over his shoulder. "Not yet. I'm tenacious, remember?"

His wink made her heart thunder before dwindling down to its normal pace at the knowledge he only looked at her as a friend at best, his employer's daughter at worst. She scolded herself over and over in the ensuing silence about getting her hopes up when she'd already resigned herself to life as a spinster. No man would want to look at a scarred face for the rest of his life—especially Nate. He could do much better.

Her thoughts returned to her plan of studying to be a teacher. That way she could be around children every day, though they weren't her own. And after living with her little brother, she might even be able to handle the young boys who played with snakes and frogs and all the other horrendous creatures that delighted them.

"You got quiet."

She looked up to find Nate staring. She forced a smile. "Sorry."

"What were you thinking? You had such an odd look on your face."

"Now I'm odd?"

He shook his head. "Don't try to change the subject."

The rascal. He wasn't about to let her off easy. "I was thinking about life. How it can change at a moment's notice, and we either have to adapt or be miserable."

His brows rose. "Goodness. That's pretty intense. I'll have to remember not to let it get quiet again. No telling what you'll start thinking when it's silent."

She laughed, and true to his word, he kept the conversation flowing for the next couple hours, telling her about his childhood and asking about hers. Time disappeared quickly, as did the soot. They were just cleaning up from finishing the room when Thomas appeared in the doorway. His stony expression made her knees weak.

"What happened, Thomas?"

His expression never changed. "Your daddy sent me to escort you to the store." He nodded at Nate. "He thought you might want to come too."

Feet feeling like they were made of lead, Rebekah couldn't move. Fear and dread had glued them in place. It wasn't until Nate put his arm around her that she managed first one step, then another. As she followed Thomas down the boardwalk, the best prayer she could manage from her frozen mind was very simple.

Lord, help us.

Chapter Twenty-eight

....

The strong and confident Rebekah that Nate had come to know had disappeared as she clasped the silver disk her father had made. In her place was a trembling mass of insecurity, her expression full of fear. He refused to let go of her, sure she'd crumble without his support.

Stepping up their pace, he managed to catch up to Thomas, his annoyance with the man simmering just below the surface. Staying between Rebekah and Thomas, hoping she wouldn't hear, he leaned close to Thomas, keeping his voice low.

"Why didn't you just tell her what's going on? Can't you see what your silence is doing to her?"

Thomas glowered up at him. "Perry told me not to say anything. He wanted to explain everything when we got there."

"So you don't know what's wrong?"

An answer never came, and Nate didn't get the chance to pursue his questions. Rebekah gripped his arm in a way that told him to stop. Her light brown eyes sought his.

"It's all right. I can wait. It's what Daddy wanted."

Somewhere along the way, Rebekah's strength had returned. He could see it on her face and also in her walk. She was an amazing woman. He hoped she'd be able to remain strong when she heard whatever her father had to tell them. He also hoped the problem wasn't what he suspected.

Not another word was said along the way, though the manner in which Thomas carried himself and the glowers he sent Nate's direction spoke volumes. Nate had no doubt that one day he and Thomas would have to face one another, man to man. They'd either come to blows or find some kind of solution to their animosity. With the Weaver family as their common ground, something would have to be done, at least until Nate left town. If nothing else, Rebekah would insist on a degree of resolution.

The livery appeared to be locked up tight as they passed on their way to the store. Residents were bound to notice the Weaver family had closed early. Without a doubt, rumors would be buzzing through town before nightfall.

Once inside, Andrew ran up to Rebekah with a small envelope. "This came for you, Bek."

She didn't even take a look but tucked it into her apron pocket before putting her arm around her brother's shoulders, almost as if she hung onto him for comfort, or maybe support. But Nate wondered who comforted and supported who. Yet, by the look on Andrew's face, he knew nothing about what might be happening. If the boy stayed much longer, he'd more than likely catch on in a hurry.

They waited in silence for the parents to arrive. Once they showed, Perry left his wife leaning against the counter and waved Andrew over. "I want you to go to the livery and check on Mercy. The poor cat looked like he didn't feel well earlier. Just hold him and keep him calm and happy until I get there." He ruffled Andrew's hair. "Can you do that for me?"

Andrew peered up at his mother for several moments before facing his father. "Sure can, Daddy. He'll be good as new by the time I'm done with him."

Andrew raced off, looking thrilled to be a help to his father. Or maybe he thought his mother was upset about the cat and intended to make them both feel better. Once the door slammed behind the boy, Perry pulled his wife close. Her eyes red, she looked ready to either crumple or burst into tears, or quite possibly both. Nate moved to hold Rebekah, just as Perry did his wife, but Thomas managed to get there before him. Wishing he'd have thought to embrace her sooner, Nate stepped back. Now was not the time for a tugging match with another man.

Feeling a bit like an intruder at an obviously stressful time, Nate didn't want to leave. He'd come to love this family, and if he could help in some way, he would. He just prayed it wasn't—

"We received a threatening letter today."

Punctuating Perry's statement was the gasp from Rebekah, the sob from Mrs. Weaver, and the thud of Nate's heart hitting the floor.

* * * * *

Fear nearly brought Rebekah to her knees. Much as she wished she could run to her mother to be comforted, she was no longer a child. Instead, with much difficulty and inner coaxing, she did hurry to her mother, not to be consoled, but to help soothe her mother's dread. They wrapped their arms around each other, both fighting tears and failing. Daddy's hand grasped her arm as he cleared his throat to continue.

"After much thought and discussion, Kate and I have decided to stay. We won't—we can't pay what they're asking, but neither will we let them run us off like they did others." He led Mama to a chair and had her sit, motioning for Rebekah to do the same. "We've come to love Silver City. It's our home. And because it's our home, we're planning to fight this blackmailer and bring his shameful scheming to an end. To my own shame, I should have done something long before now."

The fear of losing their businesses turned to terror for her father's safety. If he went up against this evil man, he could get hurt. She looked at her mother and finally realized the extent of her alarm. Mama wasn't worried about the businesses as much as she was terrified of losing her husband.

Daddy stood behind Mama, his hands on her shoulders. "I plan to spread the word that there will be a town meeting at the church in the morning. Maybe if we all work together, we'll discover who this offender is, and this madness will come to an end. It's time we start living a somewhat normal life again. In the meantime, I've got to try to protect my home and businesses."

Rebekah peeked at Nate. He'd said much the same thing earlier. He acknowledged her look with a subtle nod, his eyes intense and concerned. It still amazed her how much he was like her father.

Thomas moved close. "I'll stay at the livery tonight. Me and my rifle will keep it safe."

"Thank you, Thomas. You've always been a good friend." He reached to shake his hand. "I'll keep an eye on the house, but first I have to get out to the mine and warn Reuben to be careful. I don't want him hurt or caught off-guard."

Nate pushed away from the wall. "I'll protect your family until you get back. Then I'll help get word out for everyone to show up tomorrow."

Rebekah had a feeling he'd do much more than that. He'd no doubt spend the night keeping watch. He was that kind of man.

"Perry, do you have the note with you?" Nate asked.

With no hesitation, Daddy pulled the note from his pocket and handed it to Nate. He unfolded the paper, and she watched his eyes flash back and forth as they scanned the words. He flipped the paper over, held it closer a moment, then turned it back. After another minute of silent examination, he handed it back to Daddy. Nate appeared puzzled. Rebekah wanted to ask him his thoughts, but something held her tongue. Maybe she'd get the chance later.

After finalizing plans for the night, Daddy warned everyone not to let Andrew know of the danger. Then he headed toward the livery to join him and the cat. Oh, to be so naïve and innocent again. But in her maturity—and helplessness—she knew to lean on the Lord. In the minutes they waited for Andrew to return, Rebekah bent her head in prayer.

Chapter Twenty-nine

....

Exhausted after a sleepless night of watching over the Weavers, Nate tied the reins of his horse to a tree branch near the church, then waited to be the last to enter. He probably shouldn't have bothered showing up. Last night, as he'd tried to spread the word for Perry, most residents received him with distrust or eyed him with suspicion, barely slowing to hear what he had to say. Some hurried to the other side of the street to avoid him altogether. Evidently the sheriff's poisonous rumors did the work he'd desired. As Nate watched the stream of townsfolk entering the church, it appeared Perry had more luck. The pews would be nearly full.

Waiting for the last of the latecomers to enter, he once again puzzled over the note Perry had received. The paper it was written on was the same type Perry kept for his ledger work in the livery. He noticed because it was a different texture than what he was used to seeing and using. The only people who had access to that paper were Perry himself, the Weaver family, Thomas, and Reuben. Trouble was, Nate wasn't certain if any other store supplied that same paper. That would be another job for him to tackle today.

Figuring the meeting was about to begin, Nate made his way inside. He hung near the back, so Perry wouldn't have any disruptions because of his presence. Nate scanned the room to see who all came, but most importantly, who hadn't bothered to show. The latter group most held his interest. Anyone who didn't make an appearance would earn a second look by him—and soon.

Recognizing a great many faces, Nate stopped when his gaze came to rest on Rebekah. Kate and Andrew had stayed locked inside their home, but she had insisted on attending the meeting and sat at the front with Thomas by her side. Pale and drawn, she didn't appear to have gotten any more sleep than he did.

Just as Perry called the meeting to order, Sheriff Caldwell entered and strode past Nate toward the front, causing everyone to start murmuring. If Nate were to guess, Perry hadn't run his idea past the sheriff, who stopped near the first pew and crossed his arms. If he meant to be intimidating, he failed miserably. Perry barely gave him a glance before lifting his hand for silence.

"Let's get started, so we can all get back to work." Silence fell as though the pastor was present to give a sermon. Perry skimmed the room, glancing at all the faces. "My friends, by now I'm sure you've heard about all the threatening notes many of us have received over the months, though they've only just come to light in the past few days because of their demand for secrecy." He looked down and licked his lips before facing them again. "My family received such a letter yesterday."

His voice shaking, Perry took a few moments to pull himself together while the room buzzed with the new information. Rebekah's head dipped, and Nate wondered if it were in prayer or from the stress of the situation. He wanted to go to her but held back, unwilling to draw attention to himself and away from the importance of the meeting.

Perry raised his hand again. "Quiet down, please." After a bit, silence fell again. "Thank you. In case you didn't know, several of the town's residents, our friends, have left Silver after receiving a note blackmailing them. The note threatens that they and their business would be protected if they paid a high sum of money, but the blackmailer couldn't guarantee their safety if the money wasn't given."

The hum of whispered voices rose again, but that didn't stop Perry from continuing. "Ladies and gentlemen, it's time we stop letting this person or these people steal from us."

Sheriff Caldwell's arms unfolded, and he propped them on his hips. "Then maybe you should start by firing your hired help and running him out of town."

Nate should have known this was why the sheriff came to the meeting. His heart thumped and his fists clenched as he waited for Perry's reaction. Perry glared down at the sheriff before meeting Nate's gaze. To Nate's dismay, Perry waved him to the front. Nate shook his head, but Perry continued waving him forward.

"Come up here, Nate."

His boots could have been filled with gold bars, they were so heavy as he made his way to the front. Perry would receive nothing but ridicule, but there was nothing Nate could do. Everyone doubted him and his integrity, and now Perry would pay the price for his trust in Nate.

Climbing the two steps, he came to a stop next to Perry, who put his arm around Nate's shoulders and made him face the crowd.

"I want everyone to know right here and now that I have nothing but the utmost respect for this young man. I trust him with my life, but more than that, I trust him with the lives of my family."

The tears that rose in Perry's eyes almost made some start in Nate's own. He dipped his head in humility, feeling undeserving of so much love.

"I'll vouch for the young man too."

Nate looked up. Henry Gilmore stood two rows back, his brows creased in a stern look.

"We need more men like him in this town, so, Sheriff"—Henry turned and faced the lawman square on—"stop badgering this young man and do your job. It's a shame that Perry is the one who had to get this inquiry started when you should have done the same months ago."

Red-faced and trembling with anger, Henry dropped down on the pew. Many an "amen" followed his scolding of the sheriff as the man skulked out of the church. Before the noise managed to get out of control again, Perry called for quiet. They quickly obeyed.

"Thank you, Henry. And Nate," he said and patted his back, "why don't you find a seat, and let's get this done?"

As Nate descended the steps, many moved over to allow him room to sit. He dropped onto the first open spot, mainly because his legs no longer wanted to hold him. Thanks to two highly esteemed men who spoke up for him, everyone saw him in a much different way. Only minutes ago, he was despised. Now, admiration radiated from many eyes. Humbled, Nate knew in his heart it was a work of the Lord. It was time to give back to all of them by investigating harder than ever before.

"I would like to propose," Perry began again, "that if we all work together, we can put this blackmailer behind bars and get on with a decent life."

Perry laid out his plans of how the men could pair up to keep watch on the town and hold any suspicious person until he and the sheriff could arrive to ask questions. While he organized the men, Nate again scoured the faces. He took note of the fact that the two young men who beat him were not present, nor did the sheriff stay to offer his assistance. As his distrust of Thomas decreased, the sheriff and the two men remained highly in doubt.

As Perry dismissed everyone to go back to work, Nate made his way toward Rebekah. He wanted to hear for himself that she'd be all right. But before he got to her, Henry grabbed his arm and pulled him to a stop.

Disappointment trickled through him but only for a moment. He owed a great debt to this man, and he intended to thank him. He grasped Henry's hand in his.

"Thank you for what you said. You've made my life in this town much easier."

"I only spoke the truth."

Nate examined Henry's face. A certain sadness filled his eyes. "Everything all right, Henry?"

The elderly man heaved a sigh. "I'm thinking about leaving town, my boy."

The news hit him harder than when Grant told him the same thing. "What? No. Give us a chance to make this plan work." The words tripped over each other in his rush to get them out. He took a breath to slow his thoughts. "Just don't do anything in a hurry, Henry. Take some time to think it over."

For the first time, Henry looked old. Gone were the stiff back and sparkling eyes. In their place were slumped shoulders, dimmed eyes. Henry didn't speak for a time. Then he nodded. "All right. I won't do anything right away."

Relief flooded him. "Thank you." Nate put his arm around him. "Go to your shop and open for business. I'm sure everything will be fine. I'll be by to check on you in a little while."

Without a word, he nodded and patted Nate on the back. After saying his good-byes to the kind gentleman, Nate again made his way toward Rebekah, thankful she'd not rushed off before he could see for himself she was fine. What he found was a serene woman, much different than when he'd arrived. Whether it came from being in church or being in Christ, he wanted that same peace and felt that much closer just by being near her. He'd thought of spending time with the Lord once this chaos was over, but now he knew he couldn't wait to renew his relationship with the Lord.

Before he could say a word, she briefly squeezed his forearm. "Seems like you've suddenly become quite prominent in this town."

He smiled. "I wouldn't go that far, but your father and Mr. Gilmore certainly did wonders to turn around people's opinion of me."

"Oh, I don't know. I think they might have come to the same conclusion without their help."

He snorted. "Maybe. But not for several months."

Her brows rose. "Does that mean you plan on staying around for a while or that we're all slow to learn?"

It felt good to laugh again. "My, but aren't you feeling a bit spirited today?"

Tilting her head, she gave him a sassy grin. "Not spirited, but full of the Spirit." She tipped her head toward the door. "I've got to go. Walk me to the store?"

His heart tripped over a couple beats. "It would be my pleasure." He offered his elbow and loved the warmth of her hand on his arm. His search for answers could wait another half hour or so. He wouldn't miss out on this time with Rebekah for anything.

With a quick wave to Thomas, then a signal to her dad that she was leaving, Rebekah motioned for him to lead the way. With her in a great mood, he'd like to spend the entire day with her, but he'd already promised himself to work harder to find the blackmailer. He'd see her safely to the store; then he had to get busy. As he pulled the reins to his horse free from the branch and led it as he walked beside Rebekah, a plan formed in his mind. First off, he'd somehow have to get Perry to give him more free time.

There was a definite skip to her step, and Rebekah's teasing continued on their way to the store. "So now that you've gained the approval of everyone in town, I imagine my poor daddy won't get any work out of you."

He frowned down at her. "What makes you say that?"

She returned his look with one brow raised. "How on earth will you manage to get anything done with all the single women vying for your attention?"

Nearly choking on his surprise, Nate burst into laughter. Her accusation was the last thing he expected to hear. Something that should have been flattering made him shudder with the hope Rebekah was completely wrong. He didn't have the time or interest in courting any women right now. Catching a blackmailer demanded his total concentration.

"You've let your imagination run completely wild, I'm afraid. And you wonder why men call women silly."

Her mouth dropped open and something like a squeak emerged. "I can't believe you said that."

She tried to tug her hand away from his elbow, but he held it there, not wanting her to leave his side. "What if I told you I didn't mean it?"

"I wouldn't believe you." She gave a playful toss of her head. "But I'll take into consideration the fact that you don't know women well enough to know how clever we really are."

He laughed again. "Since I've known you, I've been learning fast."

"Well, at least that's some—"

She not only stopped midsentence but midstep, her grip on his arm tightening. He followed the direction she was looking and saw the door of the store standing open. Dropping the reins to his horse, he yanked his pistol from the holster.

"Stay here."

Without waiting to make sure she complied, Nate rushed across the street toward the store.

Chapter Thirty

....

Though Rebekah's ears were ringing from her heart pounding so hard, she heard Nate's command. She managed to obey until he made it to the middle of the street, then her feet, of their own will, moved to follow.

Through a fog, she saw Nate stop at the store front, his back pressed against the wall, his gun at the ready. He swung his head around just enough to see inside, then pushed the door wide and raced in.

A yell and a scream pierced the air.

Rebekah's air froze in her lungs. A part of her wanted to stay outside until Nate told her all was clear. The strongest part ordered her inside. She ran up the steps, crossed the boardwalk, and stopped at the threshold, waiting for her eyes to adjust to the dim interior. Her mother stood behind the counter with one hand over her heart and the other holding Andrew against her.

Nate holstered his pistol. "I'm so sorry, Mrs. Weaver. I didn't think you'd be here today." He motioned toward the door. "When I saw that standing open, I thought someone was in here stealing or—causing some kind of trouble."

"It's all right. You just startled me."

Andrew squirmed out of her embrace, then brushed at his shirt. "I'm all right. I wasn't scared or nothing."

Breaking out of her shocked stupor, Rebekah scooted across the room. "What are you doing here, Mama? You two are supposed to be at home." *Where it's safe*, she added silently.

Mama reached across the counter and grasped her hand. "I know, honey, but we have a business to run if we want to keep eating. Not only that, but after spending the morning on my knees," she said, and looked directly into Rebekah's eyes, "following the example of my daughter, I decided it was time to trust the Lord to take care of me and my family." She came around the counter and stood in front of Rebekah. "My dear, you've been so strong, so faithful. The very person I should have been." She caressed Rebekah's face before pulling her into a hug. "I'm so proud of you."

Tears formed. "I'm only following the example you and Daddy have shown and taught." She pulled out of the embrace. "But you should have stayed home."

Mama's tinkling laugh filled the room. "Probably. I know your father will scold me worse than you have."

Andrew joined them, all but pushing between them. "Why will Daddy scold you, Mama? Did you do something wrong?"

Rebekah had forgotten about Andrew listening. Mama must have done the same. Dismay flashed across her mom's face before she bent to answer him, putting her hands on his shoulders.

"I didn't really do anything wrong, son. I suppose I should have discussed it with your father first. But I think he'll understand when I explain my thoughts and feelings." She moved one hand to cup his chin. "Understand?"

He nodded, his expression serious. Then he moved to Nate's side. "Nate and me will keep you safe, won't we?"

All these weeks, Andrew hadn't said a word about what was

happening in town, yet he knew. What all he knew, Rebekah had no idea, but if he had questions, they were best answered by them.

She knelt on one knee in front of her little brother. "Is there anything you want to ask us, Andrew?" She kept the question simple, unwilling to divulge the extent of the danger if he wasn't aware.

A tiny frown creased his brows. "Is Daddy gonna be all right?"

Nate knelt next to her and took one of Andrew's hands in his. "Your father is strong and smart. He'll be just fine."

Rebekah figured hearing those comments from a man was just what Andrew needed. His confidence returned with a vengeance. "I'm strong and smart too. I'll help Daddy."

Nate ruffled the boy's hair as he stood. "I know you will." He turned to Rebekah. "If you two feel, uh"—he glanced down at Andrew—"comfortable here, I'm going to head out, check on a few things."

Andrew jutted his chin. "We're fine."

"We'll be fine," Rebekah said at the same time as her mother.

Nate nodded. "If I see Perry, I'll let him know where you are." He tipped his hat and left.

Mama winked at Rebekah. "He's a good man."

Her heart skipped a beat before hammering out. "I think so."

"Who? Nate?" Andrew made the motion of casting his line out and pulling it back in with a jerk. "He's not that good. I caught more fish than him."

Exchanging a look with Mama, Rebekah moved around the counter and grabbed a rag from the back room. "Well, since we're here, we might as well get something done."

She went to work wiping down the shelves, cans, and jars, all the while feeling her mother's eyes watching her every move. Mama had to know how she felt about Nate. No doubt she and Mama would have a talk before long. She glanced back at her mother. Maybe it was time. And maybe her mother could teach her how to deal with the bitterness of inevitable loss.

How would she get over the heartbreak of losing the man she loved? Rebekah returned her gaze to the task at hand, rubbing at a spot on the counter through a blur of tears.

* * * * *

After retrieving his horse, Nate's first stop was at the livery to make sure Thomas had arrived to keep his word and watch over the place. The wide doors were still latched, so Nate moved around to the side door, which opened easily. Thomas sat on a bench petting the cross-eyed cat nestled on his lap. His rifle rested against the post next to him. He stared at Nate without saying a word.

Deciding not to enter any farther, Nate leaned against the door-frame. "Just thought I'd check to see if you needed anything."

Thomas took his time answering, never even blinking. "I'm fine."

Not knowing what else to say, Nate nodded. "All right. I'll try to check in again later." He started backing out, closing the door at the same time.

"Nate?"

He pushed the door back open. "Yes?"

Thomas opened his mouth but said nothing. Finally, he gave a slight shake of his head. "Thanks for stopping by."

Slightly confused, Nate inclined his head. "Sure thing."

For the second time today he questioned his suspicion of Thomas and decided to walk so he'd have time to think. He continued down the street, cutting through an alley, on his way to see how Henry was faring. With a little luck, some prayer, and lots of pleading, he might be able to persuade the man to stay in Silver.

Though a bit less boisterous than usual—the people seemed much more wary as they glanced around—the town still bustled. Many of them waved or shouted a greeting, making him feel welcome for the first time since he'd arrived in Silver.

Funny how two men could change the opinion of an entire town. Stranger still was the fact that in just under a month he'd taken to shortening the town's name like the long-time residents always did. He nearly stumbled when he came to realize one thing—when did he start thinking of Silver as home?

The interior of Henry's tobacco shop looked dark. Nate tied his horse to the post, then tried the knob and found the door unlocked. He pushed through and glanced around. Except that Henry wasn't sitting in his chair on the boardwalk or puffing on one of his cigars while perched behind the counter, all looked normal.

"Henry?"

A loud thump echoed from the back room. Nate headed that way, but before he could get there, Henry appeared in the doorway.

"Tell me you're here to buy tobacco. I'm beginning to think everyone in this town has quit smoking."

Nate's concern grew. If Henry didn't sell anything, he'd pack up and leave, and there wouldn't be a thing Nate could say to stop him. "You haven't had any customers?"

Henry wagged his gray head. "Not a soul. Might as well close up for the day again."

The disheartened tone increased Nate's worry, yet he had no idea how to help. He couldn't force men to come in and spend their money. "Don't give up yet. It's still early. They're probably just getting their pipes going good."

Henry's face finally lightened. "You're a good man, Nate." He closed one eye. "I don't suppose I could talk you into learning to smoke."

Laughing, Nate shook his head. "Tried it once and nearly choked to death."

"That's what I figured, but you can't blame a man for trying." Henry chuckled and clapped him on the back. "You don't need to hang around and hold my hand, son. You've done plenty by caring enough to stop by and check on an old man." He pushed him toward the door. "I know you've got more to do than waste your time around here, young Nate. Go on and win the heart of that pretty Weaver girl. You two would be lucky to have each other."

Mouth wide open, Nate stood mute while Henry closed the door in his face. The echo of the elderly man's chuckle hung in the air.

With nothing more to do than get back to work finding the blackmailer, Nate grabbed the reins of his horse and headed toward the sheriff's office. He intended to trail the man around, hopefully without being seen.

His horse gave a snort and shake of the head, making Nate feel sorry for him. The poor thing hadn't had a good run since he'd arrived in town. He'd have to take care of that soon. He reached and patted the horse's neck. "Just a little longer, Rusty. We'll get to have a run soon."

Nate's thoughts didn't linger there long. Henry's comment about Rebekah wouldn't shake loose from his mind. Why would he think there was anything between him and Rebekah? What did Henry see that—

This time Nate did stumble to a stop. He spun around toward the tobacco shop, his thoughts tumbling over themselves, all finally landing on one probable idea. Henry was the man who wrote the notes to Cora and Mrs. Phipps, informing each that someone was interested in them. Except Henry had completely missed the mark when it came to him and Rebekah. He enjoyed her company, but that was all. She was brave and funny and would make some man a fine wife. But playing the role of a husband hadn't even crossed his mind. He wasn't ready for that kind of commitment. Maybe Rebekah wasn't either.

A grin spread slowly across Nate's face. All the hours Henry sat in front of his store allowed him to observe what no one else saw. The insightful old gentleman, though alone, still wanted to make sure others had a chance at loving someone. Someday he'd have to ask Henry what had happened to his wife. In the meantime, he had a job to finish.

Trying to get focused, Nate climbed onto the saddle and nudged Rusty toward the sheriff's office. He doubted the sheriff would be there this late in the morning, but Nate had to start somewhere. Since the lawman didn't seem to enjoy doing his job, there was a chance he might be sitting in his chair with his feet propped on the desk. If not, Nate would have quite a task ahead of himself trying to find him. His gut told him the sheriff was involved in the blackmailing scheme. The best places to keep an eye on him would be where the last notes had shown up—at Henry's and the Weavers'.

As he passed the saloon, Nate's mind wandered back to the day he'd arrived in town and helped the sheriff arrest the two drunken men. Something about the whole event didn't sit right. First, the sheriff didn't try hard to stop the boys from continuing their mischief, and second, he didn't keep them in jail long. If he remembered right, the sheriff claimed he had let them out that same night because their fines had been paid. Was that something the sheriff said to keep from raising suspicion, or did someone really come up with the money? If the second, who paid the fines?

Still a distance from the sheriff's office, Nate reined Rusty to a stop, trying to see if the lawman's horse was tied out front. A man striding along the boardwalk across the street caught his attention. The worn and floppy hat looked familiar. Just before the man reached the alley, Nate caught sight of his scruffy beard. He couldn't be sure, but the man certainly looked a lot like the one who'd shot at him and Rebekah the first time they'd met the Loomis family. There was only one way to find out.

"Hey! You there!"

At his shout, the man looked his direction. The next second he hefted his rifle and took a shot at Nate before ducking into the alley.

Chapter Thirty-one

....

Nate launched from the saddle and used his horse as a shield. He peeked under its neck, but the shooter was nowhere to be seen.

Climbing onto the saddle again, Nate reined his horse toward the alley. Seeing it was empty, he raced to the other end, stopping before he reached the end.

Searching both directions, Nate saw no sign of the shooter. The man could disappear faster than a mouse being chased by a cat. He'd done the same thing the first time he shot at him and Rebekah, but how? The most important question of all—why was the man using him as a target?

Nate dismounted, his frustration building. He explored every building, boardwalk, and bush. Finding nothing, he jumped onto the saddle and headed into the hills, doubtful he'd find any trace of the man.

An hour later, empty-handed, he rode into town straight toward the sheriff's office. If the sheriff was in, he'd confront him with the news he'd been shot at. He'd be interested to see how the lawman reacted.

Minutes later, Nate stood on the opposite side of the desk from Sheriff Caldwell. He knew before a word was spoken he'd get no sympathy or concern. With the snarl on the man's face, he'd be lucky if he heard him out.

"What do you want? I've got work to do."

A sarcastic reply burned on his tongue. Nate swallowed it back. The Scriptures said a fool utters what's in his mind but a wise man keeps it in. "Someone shot at me."

Sheriff Caldwell sat back in his chair and crossed his arms. "Did you get a good look at the shooter?"

"I think so."

"So you know who he is?"

Just as Nate thought, the sheriff was about to start twisting the circumstances to make him look bad. "I don't know his name, but he shot at us once before." The moment the words left his mouth, he wanted to grab them back.

"Us?"

Dumb. A slip of the tongue. Inexcusable for an investigator. "Me and Rebekah Weaver."

The glower deepened. "And I'm just now hearing about it?" He grunted and leaned his forearms on his desk. "You trying to get the young lady killed?"

He fought his temper. "Of course not." The sheriff didn't say another word, so Nate went on the attack. "Are you planning to do anything about this shooter?"

"Like what? You don't know who it was."

"But I know what he looks like. Don't you want a description?" He propped his fists on the desk, bringing him to within an arm's reach of the lawman. "Or do you already know about the shooting and know who did it?"

One corner of the sheriff's mouth curled up. "And how would I know who did it?"

Now this was the reaction Nate figured he'd get—the smug, calculating attitude. "Maybe you had something to do with it."

The sheriff shoved to his feet, toppling his chair. "You better watch your mouth, boy. Accusations like that could land you into big trouble, like getting hurt in a bad way."

Nate narrowed his eyes. "Is that a threat, Sheriff?"

The way the sheriff's jaw moved, Nate wondered if he was gnawing on his tongue. He'd definitely struck a nerve. Now that he'd gotten the reaction he wanted, it was time to move along.

"I'll check back later to see what you've found out about the shooter." Nate tipped his hat. "I'm sure you'll do your job and go looking for him."

Not waiting for a response, Nate strode out the door and closed it a bit too hard. He could have handled that better, but considering that he wanted to slam the man to the ground, he'd done pretty well.

The next step was to find a place to keep an eye on the office and follow the sheriff if he left. If he was guilty, the sheriff would seek out the shooter to talk, not to arrest him. At the slight possibility he'd actually try to do his job, there was a good chance the sheriff knew who the shooter might be and go after him. Either way, Nate would find the man trying to kill him.

He reined his horse down the street in the direction of his hotel, hoping the sheriff would call it a night. Several buildings down, he turned into a narrow alley and dismounted, crouched, and leaned against the wall, ready to wait as long as it took. If he guessed correctly, the sheriff would show in no time.

Minutes later, Perry strode past. He stopped in front of the sheriff's office and tried to enter but slammed into the door. Perry tried the knob again and frowned. He cupped his hands at the window and peered inside before returning to the door and pounding with his fists. Then, with hands on hips, he stood on the boardwalk, looking up and down the street.

Concerned that something was wrong with the family, Nate left his hiding place and raced down the street toward Perry. "Everything all right?"

Perry turned, his face showing relief the moment he saw him. "Nate! There you are." He jumped from the boardwalk and scrutinized Nate head to toe. "Mr. Peters hunted me down and told me he'd heard a rumor you were shot at."

"Lucky for me, the guy's a bad shot."

"Who is?"

Nate shrugged. He'd already gone over this once, and now his mind was on where the sheriff disappeared without being seen. "I don't know who he was. I went after him, but he managed to vanish before I could catch up." He pointed toward the sheriff's office. "He's not in there?"

Perry glanced over his shoulder. "That man is never where he's needed."

"Funny." Nate had never taken his eyes from the door. "I just came from his office. How'd he get away without me seeing him? Is there a back door?"

"Probably. Tell you the truth, I've never spent much time in there to know." He cocked his head. "Why were you watching the place?"

Unsure how much he should tell, Nate glanced around, hoping to come up with a logical explanation.

"Let's have it, Nate." Perry's brows creased in a deep frown. "What's going on?"

Nate shuffled his feet and then looked into Perry's eyes. He could trust the man completely, he decided. "Have you ever wondered if Sheriff Caldwell is an honest lawman?"

Mouth dropping open, Perry stared for several long moments. Finally he admitted, "I've always thought he was lazy and didn't deserve to wear the badge, but it never crossed my mind he was a scoundrel." He lifted his hat and scratched the top of his head. "Now that you mention it, it sure would explain a lot, wouldn't it?"

"I think so." Nate jabbed his thumb over his shoulder. "I hid out back there, hoping to follow him when he left, but he slipped away somehow."

"Where did you think he'd go?"

Nate hesitated. He had no solid proof to support his accusations. "Not sure, but I thought he might know who shot at me."

Perry's brows nearly reached his hairline. "That's quite a claim. You got anything to back it up?"

"Not really. More a gut feeling than anything."

Perry secured his hat back in place and nodded. "Right about now I'd trust your gut over anyone else around here." He clapped Nate on the back. "Come on. Kate's got supper waiting."

Nate didn't move. Much as he'd love a warm, tasty meal at the Weaver home, he was much more interested in keeping them and their businesses safe. "I appreciate the offer, Perry, but if you don't mind, I plan to spend the night in your store. Thomas is covering the livery, and you'll be home. That leaves only one place unprotected."

Even in the low light, Nate was certain he saw Perry's eyes water up. "I appreciate that, young man. More than you know." He held out his hand. "There's food in the store. You get hungry, you help yourself."

For the first time in many hours, Nate grinned. "You may regret that offer."

Perry shook his head. "Not even a little."

Nate held out the reins. "Take my horse. You've got a longer walk than I do."

They walked together until they reached the store. Then Nate pulled his rifle from the scabbard, and with another handshake, they parted company with plans to meet up in the morning to decide what needed to be done next.

Locking the door behind him, Nate prowled the shelves for something to eat. If he waited much longer, his stomach would curl up in a ball for good. Trouble was, most of what Perry sold in his store needed to be stirred in with other items in order to be edible, and other than roasting a rabbit over a fire, Nate wasn't much of a cook. Thankfully, he found some dried meat behind the counter.

Trying to ready himself for another long, sleepless night, Nate hunkered down on the floor with his back resting against the counter and began gnawing at the meat. Looking around the room, he saw signs of the Weavers everywhere, mostly of their faith in God.

As he stared at the large wooden cross above the door, he remembered his conversation with Rebekah at their last picnic. She'd been through so much, yet she trusted Him to love and take care of her. The faces of his dad and brother wavered in his memory. Until their deaths, Nate had trusted God too. Or at least thought he had. If a hardship could make him turn his back on God, did he ever really have faith in Him? In his mind's eye he could see his mother, hear the lilt in her voice as she told him the story of Job. Even as a boy, he couldn't grasp Job's blind trust in God.

Thinking back on all that had happened since he arrived in town, Nate could feel his heart soften. Even with the burn marks on her beautiful face, Rebekah trusted God. And in his own case, the Lord had shown Himself faithful over and over, from saving his life to leading him in the direction he should go. One of the best gifts God had given him was friendship with the Weaver family, Rebekah in particular. Her example of trusting without understanding amazed him.

Running all the thoughts through his mind again, he could no longer hold his head up. Broken and remorseful, he moved to his knees and closed his eyes.

Heavenly Father, I beg You to forgive me for being angry with You. And not just that, but I pray You'll forgive me for all my many sins. I'm undeserving of Your love, yet I know that even now, after I've turned my back on You, You continue to give Your love freely. When I had given up on You, You never once gave up on me. You've waited patiently for me to return and made certain I met those who would lead me back to You. Dear Lord, I can't promise that I will never get angry again, but I can promise You this. Though I won't always understand Your ways or like what You do, I will never again turn my back on You. I will remain Your faithful servant.

Spent, Nate rolled back and rested his back against the counter once more, then wiped the moisture from beneath his eyes. Though exhausted, he felt peace again for the first time in years.

Chapter Thirty-two

．．．．．．．．．．．．．．．．．．．．．

Rebekah paced from one end of the house to the other, stopping only to peer out the window for a minute before moving across the room again. She knew Mama watched, but Rebekah wasn't in the mood to talk, at least not until she knew if Nate was safe. Andrew looked up from time to time from his playing. He never commented, though his grim expression let her know of his growing concern.

She paused at the wall. When Daddy heard about the shooting, he insisted they all return to the house and lock themselves inside. Except that once they were home, Daddy ordered them to lock the door behind him because he wanted to try to find Nate and make sure he wasn't hurt. She felt relief that Daddy went to find Nate, but now she had to worry about two men she loved.

At her last thought, her breath left her in a gush, and she marched across the floor. Yes, it was true, and she'd no longer fight her feelings. She loved Nate, and though she'd never have him to herself, she prayed that he'd live a long and happy life. Long enough to be a husband and father.

Stopping in front of the window again, she dropped onto a chair, propped her elbows on the sill, and rested her chin on her hands. After the way the morning went, with everyone at the meeting coming to like Nate, why would anyone shoot at him? Surely the shooter wasn't at the meeting and hadn't heard the news that Nate was a good man.

Rebekah sat up straight as she remembered this wasn't the first time someone had tried to kill him. Was it the same man? She closed her eyes.

Lord, please protect Daddy and Nate.

The quick prayer was the best she could muster without bringing herself to tears. Hands suddenly gripped her shoulders. She looked up and found Mama standing over her.

"Come help me finish the meal. It'll give you something to do with your hands. Sometimes keeping busy helps me get through a rough patch."

Rebekah nodded and followed her mother to the kitchen—the room farthest from the front window. The distraction would either help her or tear her in half. By the time they'd finished preparing the meal, night had fallen, and Daddy still hadn't returned.

"Let's go ahead and eat so Andrew can get to bed. I'll keep a plate warm for your daddy."

The words were no sooner out of her mouth than someone knocked at the door. They all exchanged a look, yet no one moved.

Another round of pounding rattled the door latch. "It's me, Kate. Let me in."

Smiling, Mama dashed toward the door and swung it open wide. Without a word, she rushed into his arms. Daddy held her close, landing kisses on her forehead. Moments later, he held her at arm's length.

"I found Nate. He's fine. Thomas is watching the livery, and Nate insisted on staying in the store to make sure nothing happened to it." He hugged Mama again, his voice husky. "God blessed us with good friends."

Andrew pushed between them and peered up at Daddy. "Why wouldn't Nate be fine?"

Rebekah's heart went out to her father for having to explain his words. Then it went out to Andrew, because they'd kept him in the dark about all that had been going on. She wondered just how much her father would tell.

Daddy crouched down, put one hand on Andrew's shoulder, and looked him in the eyes. "We don't know why, Andrew, but someone tried to shoot Nate. They missed, thank the good Lord, but no one had seen him since then. I found him, and he's not hurt."

Tears shone in Andrew's eyes. Rebekah could tell he was trying to be a big boy and not cry. He heaved several deep breaths, his bottom lip trembling for a time, then wiped his sleeves across his eyes. He clasped his hands together under his chin and clamped his eyes closed.

"Thank You, God, for saving Nate," Andrew said in a small voice. Opening his eyes, he leaned against Daddy and wrapped his arms around his neck.

Daddy held him a full minute before patting Andrew's back, then held him away enough to see his face. "Better?"

Andrew nodded, his eyes rimmed in red. Daddy stood but lifted Andrew's face to his with fingers under his chin.

"Keep praying, little man."

Solemn-faced, Andrew nodded again, and Daddy put his arm around Mama. "How about we eat and call it a day. I'm tired and hungry both. I'd eat in my sleep if I could."

His words lightened the mood as all moved to the table. With very little said, the meal didn't last long. Once Andrew was in bed, Rebekah sent Mama off with Daddy, offering to clean up the kitchen by herself. In the silence, she shed her own tears and said her own much longer prayer, then fell asleep moments after her head hit the pillow.

* * * * *

Hearing heavy footsteps pounding back and forth through the house, Rebekah opened her eyes and realized she'd overslept. When she heard the door slam, she threw back the covers, grabbed her robe, and put it on as she headed toward the kitchen. Mama stood at the window wringing her hands as she stared outside.

Dread started in Rebekah's roaring ears and moved down her spine. Knowing something was wrong, she moved to Mama's side and put her arm around her waist.

"What happened?" The question came out in a whisper, as though anything louder might make Mama crumble.

Sniffling, Mama pulled a handkerchief from her apron and wiped her nose. "We can't find Andrew. Your father's going out to see if he's in the barn."

Rebekah's heart stopped beating, then slammed to a start. Trying to fight the terror filling her, she tried to reason with herself. Andrew always went outside to play while he waited for breakfast to be ready. Surely today was no different.

Mama wiped her nose again. "Daddy should have told Andrew not to leave the house."

She gave Mama a squeeze. "We were all so tired last night. None of us were thinking clear enough. And Andrew knows nothing about all the trouble in town, not to mention the note we received."

"I know."

But Rebekah could tell her words didn't make her mother feel any better than they did her. Daddy appeared from the barn door with Nate's horse but without Andrew. The way he strode toward them, head swiveling every direction, let them know Andrew hadn't been found. Mama started crying in earnest while Rebekah ran to the door. Daddy met her gaze and grasped her hand while giving a slight shake of his head on his way to comfort Mama.

He pulled her into his arms. "I'm going into town to see if he's there. I can't believe he'd leave without telling us, but after the way he reacted to Nate getting shot at, I think he might have decided to run to the store to check on Nate for himself."

Mama's eyes grew wide as she examined Daddy's face. "You really think so?"

"It's the only thing that makes sense."

Rebekah raced toward her room. "Wait for me, Daddy. I want to go with you."

"Now, Rebekah, you should stay with your mother."

She slid to a stop, heart dropping.

Mama put her arm on Daddy's. "Let her go, Perry. She doesn't need to be here to watch me fret. I'll be fine."

He looked at Rebekah. "All right, but you'd better hurry. I won't wait but a minute or two."

Dressing faster than ever before, Rebekah followed her father from the house and waited as he retrieved Nate's horse, hoping she'd put herself together well enough to keep from being embarrassed. She patted her hair to make sure some of the tresses weren't sticking straight in the air.

As they headed toward town, Rebekah nearly ran to catch up to her father's long strides. She needed to talk. Much as she hated asking the question, she wanted to know her father's plans. She veered away from Nate's horse and made it to Daddy's side. "What are you going to do if Andrew's not at the store?"

When she saw the alarm on her father's face, she wished she'd kept her mouth shut.

Without slowing his steps, he took a few moments to answer. "I don't know yet, sweetheart."

That answer was not what she wanted to hear. "Then we'll go to the sheriff, right?"

"I doubt it."

Shocked, she grasped his arm. "Daddy?"

He never slowed.

"Why not?" she ventured.

Something like a growl came from his throat. "That man doesn't know how to work. Better to do it ourselves than go to the sheriff."

The fear she'd been fighting so hard began to win. She'd never heard her father talk about Sheriff Caldwell that way before. If they couldn't go to a lawman, how would they find Andrew? Out of breath from how fast Daddy was walking, she couldn't question him any further. She'd wait until they got to the store and catch her breath.

Giving another growl, Daddy stopped and climbed onto the saddle, then reached one arm down. "I know you don't like riding this way, honey, but we've got to move faster. Give me your hand and I'll pull you up behind me. Then just hang on tight."

What she liked and didn't like no longer mattered. They had to find Andrew. Obeying her father, she gave a little screech as he yanked her behind him. He placed her arms around his waist and patted her hands.

"Hold on."

He nudged the horse's ribs with his heels, and they were off at a gallop.

Minutes later, Daddy unlocked the door of the store and pushed it open, only to look down the barrel of Nate's pistol.

* * * * *

Hearing the doorknob rattle, Nate leapt to his feet with pistol in hand, his heart hammering. Much to his regret, he'd fallen asleep, and now someone was trying to break into the store. Ready to pull the trigger, Nate lifted the gun away once he saw Perry and sagged with relief. In his sleep-fogged stupor, he'd nearly shot his friend.

"Good grief, Perry. Warn a man before you come barging in." But the look on Perry's face woke Nate up in a hurry, especially when Rebekah entered the store with the same expression. "What's wrong?"

Perry scanned the store. "Andrew's not here?"

Nate frowned. Why would Andrew be here? "No. Why?"

"He's gone."

As Perry said those words, he raced toward the livery. Exchanging a glance with Rebekah, Nate followed, dread filling his chest. He and Rebekah waited while Perry unlocked the livery door; then they all rushed inside.

"Thomas?" Perry hollered while he ran to the center of the building.

They all looked around and called for Thomas again, receiving no answer.

Nate climbed the ladder to the loft. "He's not up here either." Back on the ground again, Nate stood in front of the two Weavers. "What happened?"

Shoulders sagging, Perry dropped onto a nearby bench. "When we woke up, Andrew was gone. We can't find him anywhere."

Heart racing, Nate knew going to the sheriff was useless. He'd have to take matters into his own hands. "Saddle up. We'll get the rest of the town looking."

He strode toward the big doors and shoved them open. As they swung wide, the gust they created caused something to flutter. Nate leaned down for a closer look. Nestled in the dirt lay a piece of paper. Perry had received another note, and in his heart, Nate knew this one would be worse than the last.

Chapter Thirty-three

....

Nate grabbed the paper from the ground and turned to Perry, who sped across the livery and snatched it from his hand. He stood back while Perry unfolded the paper and read the note. A dazed look crossed his face as the paper dropped back to the dirt.

Glancing at Rebekah, Nate scooped it from the ground. Rebekah moved to his side and together they read the words.

> *We've got your son. You'll pay for trying to turn the town against us. If you want your son back unhurt, you'll come up with three hundred dollars. Once you have the money, paint a long white line on the doors of your livery and you'll soon receive a note of where you can leave the money and where you'll find your son. Do it by the end of the day if you want him back alive.*

Rebekah collapsed against her father, sobs shaking her shoulders. Nate read the note once more. Never before had the blackmailer kidnapped someone. But to take a child was pure evil.

He held the note in front of Perry. "Do you recognize the handwriting?"

Perry wiped his eyes and took the note from him. After examining it for several moments, he handed it back. "No."

Nate held it in front of Rebekah. "How about you?"

In much the same manner as her father, Rebekah dabbed at her eyes so she could see. "I don't think I've seen it before."

Frustrated, Nate wanted to crumple the paper. He thought surely they'd say it looked like Thomas's handwriting. When they came in and found Thomas gone, instead of watching the livery, Nate shoved aside his good will for the man. Thomas could be involved with the sheriff in this wicked scheme. He would have had the easiest time leaving the note behind.

"What about the type of paper? I've noticed it's different than any I'd seen before. Is this something everyone uses or a kind only you sell in town?"

Frowning, Perry looked again, then rubbed the sheet between his fingers. He shrugged. "I just assumed it's common. I order it out of my catalogue to use it in the livery, but I sell it too."

That wasn't the answer he'd hoped for. If only Perry sold this particular type, it would have painted Thomas as an absolute party to the scheme. For now, he'd keep his suspicion to himself. No need to upset the Weavers further.

Rebekah clasped her father's arm. "Let's go to the sheriff, Daddy."

Nate caught Perry's eye and gave a slight shake of his head. He didn't trust that man any more than he did a cat with a limping mouse.

Perry finally grasped Rebekah by the shoulders and looked her square in the eyes. "I want you to lock yourself in the store."

She was shaking her head before he finished. "No, Daddy. Please. I want to help look for Andrew."

"But, honey—"

"No, Daddy. It'll kill my soul to have to stay here and not help." Tears flowed down her cheeks.

Nate watched Perry weaken and finally nod. "All right, but only if you promise to stay close to one of us. I can't have you getting taken too."

Nate's heart clenched with fear. He'd feel much better if Rebekah stayed with her mother.

Before he could suggest just that, Perry chimed in with another comment. "In fact, you stay with Nate until I can let your mother know what's happening."

Coming close to demanding Rebekah go with her father, he bit back the words when he saw the relief on her face. With her along, he wouldn't be able to move very fast, but at least he'd know she was safe.

"Perry," he called before he disappeared out the doorway, "let's meet up in about half an hour. The two of us will check with everyone along Washington Street while you ask those down Jordon Street. We can meet on the other end."

"Good plan." Perry gave a wave and was gone.

Nate dipped his head to gaze into Rebekah's eyes. "You sure you're ready for this?"

She put her fingers over his lips, making his heart lurch. "Don't even try to talk me out of this. I'll go without you if need be. I want to help find Andrew."

Nate grasped her shoulders. "Either you promise me you'll stay by my side, or I'll toss you over my shoulder and take you to your mother." He put his face inches from hers. "Do I have your word?"

Blinking several times, she nodded her agreement. She looked so adorable with her messy hair hanging in limp curls, he had to force himself not to pull her close and plant a kiss on her lips. He released her and took a step away to fight the urge.

With his hand on his pistol, he escorted Rebekah to the first building on their street. Just as he was about to enter, she stopped him by grabbing his elbow.

"This would go much faster if we split up and each took one side of the street."

The idea of her going off on her own about stopped his heart. He leaned down to make sure she understood. "Don't even try it, Bek. I'll carry out my threat of throwing you over my shoulder and have you halfway home before you can even think about screaming."

Mouth open, she stared up at him with surprised wonder in her eyes, yet not a word was said. Returning her gaze, he couldn't take it any longer.

"What? You don't think I'll do it?"

Slowly shaking her head, she never took her eyes from his. "You called me Bek."

Stunned, he stood up straight. "I did?"

She nodded.

He raised his brows. "Was that bad?"

The sweetest smile crept across her face. "I guess not."

When they found Andrew, he and Rebekah needed to have a talk. Or at least spend time alone so he could sort through the feelings racing through him now. In the meantime, he gave her a wink and a nod.

"Let's find your brother."

He pushed open the door and questioned the owner about whether or not he'd seen Andrew. Over and over, as they worked their way along each side of the street, they received the same answer.

No one had seen him. Several of them didn't even know of Andrew. Most of them asked what was wrong, but Nate refused to be tied down answering questions. They didn't have that kind of time.

He stopped and grasped Rebekah's hand. "You doing all right? Do you need to stop and rest or anything?"

"No. Let's keep going. I won't go home without Andrew."

He nodded. "Let's go then."

When they arrived at Henry's shop, the door was locked. Nate cupped his hands and peered through the big front window. No light shone from the back and Nate couldn't see anyone moving inside. He hoped Henry was just opening a little late. The alternative was that Henry had decided to go ahead and move away, and Nate wouldn't accept that. Henry was too good a friend. Once they found Andrew, he planned to find Henry next and make sure he stayed in town. If Nate caught the blackmailer, Henry wouldn't have to pay the money they demanded, which meant he wouldn't lose his business.

They continued down the street until they reached the end, everyone having given the same answer. No sign of Andrew. Empty-handed and with no more information than when they started, they went to meet Perry. They only had to wait a few minutes for him to arrive, but he wasn't alone. Kate had joined him.

Together once again, Perry motioned toward his wife. "Now you can see where Rebekah gets her stubbornness. I couldn't persuade my Kate to stay behind. You find out anything?"

Nate shook his head. "Not even a little bit. You?"

"No. Now what?"

Before Nate could come up with a suggestion, Kate stepped in front of her husband. "Call another meeting, Perry. You've got to get everyone looking for Andrew. We can't do this alone."

Perry stared at her face for several moments, then pulled her into a hug. "You're right. We'll get started immediately." He turned to face Nate but still held Kate with one arm. "Nate, go back down that street again and tell everyone to meet up at my livery. Tell them it's important, that it's an emergency." He drew a deep breath. "You tell them whatever you need to get them moving. We need the help of every breathing soul in this town."

Not waiting for an answer, Perry marched back down Jordon Street, still holding Kate's hand. He stopped at a shop, pounded on the door, and asked questions in his desperate attempt to find his son.

Nate glanced down at Rebekah. Tears in her eyes, one hand covered her mouth as she watched her parents. Nate reached to take her hand, telling himself it was to make sure she stayed close and wouldn't get hurt. Then he, too, marched toward Washington Street to alert the town to the new trouble facing them.

Taking time to explain to the business owners and residents about the kidnapping and getting back to the livery took much too long, especially when Nate saw that Henry was now in his shop. He tapped on the window to gain his attention before opening the door and allowing Rebekah to enter ahead of him.

"Good morning, Henry. You had me worried."

"I did?" Henry struck a match and held it to the end of his cigar, puffing several times until it glowed. He shook the match, extinguishing the flame. "About what?"

Nate shook his head. Henry and his cigars. He sure started early in the morning. "We were by earlier, and you weren't here."

Henry lowered his head, then dropped heavily onto the chair next to him. "I had a rough night. Drank too much when I started thinking about this blackmailer." He made a helpless gesture with his hands. "I don't know, young Nate. I'm not sure I can stay here."

Before Nate could respond, Rebekah crossed the distance between them and knelt in front of him, putting her hands on his. "We're going to stop him, Mr. Gilmore. Give us time. Don't leave just yet."

Nate stayed back and let Rebekah do the talking. If it was possible to get Henry to stay, she could get it done. She had a way about her, a certain something he couldn't explain. He could see by the softening expression on Henry's face that he also thought so.

Henry reached out to caress her unscarred cheek. "My dear, you've been through so much and yet you still care what happens to someone as worthless as myself."

Nate could see moisture shimmering in Henry's eyes. All the hardships were making him suffer. Nate had to get this blackmailer stopped before he hurt anyone else.

Rebekah covered Henry's hand with hers. "You're not worthless, Mr. Gilmore. You're a leader in this town, a model for others to follow."

Henry shook his head, but Nate stepped up to speak before he could deny Rebekah's words. "She's right, Henry. Don't do anything yet. Give us some time. This town needs you. I need you. Look what you've done when it comes to people's opinion about me."

Rebekah stood next to Nate. "And we won't take no for an answer."

With a chuckle, Henry finally nodded. "You two are good for a man's soul."

"Great," Rebekah said before Henry could change his mind. "Now, in the meantime, we need your help. My brother is missing." Her voice broke.

Henry's bushy brows touched as he frowned. "What do you mean, missing?"

Nate put his arm around her and took over explaining. "Perry received another note from the blackmailer. He says he has Andrew. If the Weavers want him back alive, they have to come up with a lot of money. We're getting everyone in town together to see if they'll help find Andrew. That's why we're here. Everyone is meeting at Perry's livery."

Henry pushed to his feet. "Then why are we still standing here talking about me? Let's get going."

Nate had Henry escort Rebekah on to the livery while he notified everyone else down the street. He found them several minutes later and moved to Rebekah's side. If it were possible, she seemed both strong and fragile. She gave him a tiny smile when he stood next to her and her mother. Perry decided to wait awhile to give everyone a chance to arrive so they'd have to explain the situation only once.

All the curious chatter of the crowd produced a buzz like that of an angry beehive. If Nate had his way, he'd swat the residents away the same as he would the bees. In his opinion, getting everyone involved would do nothing more than create more confusion. But since Andrew was the son of the Weavers, they had every right to reach out to anyone they wanted. He hoped their plan worked.

Perry jumped onto the back of a wagon he'd pulled from his livery and whistled for everyone's attention. They all fell silent.

"By now I'm sure you've all heard at least bits and pieces of what's happened. Now you're going to hear everything, and when I'm finished, I hope I can count on each of you helping me and my wife."

He motioned for Kate to move closer, and she came to stand

right in front of him. He crouched down and placed his hand on her shoulder.

"As most of you know, we received a note telling us to pay two hundred dollars if we didn't want anything to happen to our businesses. We called a meeting asking everyone to help fight the blackmailer."

He lowered his head for a moment, giving it a slight shake before lifting it again to face them. "Because I called that meeting, that blackmailer decided to take my boy and ask for even more money. I—" His voice broke, and Nate saw his throat working to swallow. "I'm asking each and every one of you for your help once again. We've searched our home, businesses, and the town for Andrew, and haven't been able to find him or any information about his whereabouts." He paused. "I'm hoping—no, I'm begging all of you to help us search for our son."

Henry's fist went into the air. "We'll get your boy back for you, Perry."

Cheers went up from most of the crowd.

Cora's father stepped up to the wagon. "We'll all close for the day. Then we need to put together a plan—who all is going to look in which directions. If we spread out, we'll cover more area."

Perry reached to shake Mr. Peters' hand. "Thank you, Carl. Will you help with getting everyone going out in the right directions?"

"Sure will." Carl Peters waved his arms to get everyone quiet. "I need eight men willing to lead search groups."

Several men crowded toward the wagon, ready to get their instructions. As they leaned down to watch Mr. Peters draw in the dirt, an explosion made each of them drop to the ground.

Chapter Thirty-four

....

Heart thundering, Rebekah stooped and covered her head. As the blast echoed through town, she rose and looked to the west. A thin spiral of smoke climbed in the sky. She turned to her father, who'd also stood and looked at the smoke.

Daddy pointed. "That came from the direction of my mine."

Mama grabbed his arm, her face filled with terror. "Andrew might be in there."

Rebekah's heart tripped over a couple beats before slamming to a start again. Eyes wide, Daddy gathered Mama close. "And now it's probably closed up tight." He glanced around. "I need everyone who can dig to come with me. I think that explosion came from my mine, and my boy might be inside. I know my partner is in there."

Rebekah stood back as everyone opened Daddy's livery and grabbed horses and mules, wagons, shovels, and anything else that might help dig Andrew out of the mine. Daddy and Mama climbed onto the wagon seat.

Nate ran for his horse, only to be stopped by Daddy. "I need you to stay here with Rebekah."

Rebekah ran up to her father. "But I want to go. I want to help."

Daddy handed the reins to Mama, jumped to the ground, and took her by the arms. "Sweetheart, I need you here more than I need you out there."

"But—"

"Listen to me, Rebekah. If another note shows up, I need you here to find it and let me know what it says. You have to stay, for Andrew and for us. Please don't fight me about this. We don't have the time."

Nate moved to Rebekah's side and put his arm around her shoulders. "We'll stay. We'll do whatever we can from here."

Rebekah didn't get a chance to respond. Daddy nodded at Nate and climbed back onto the wagon and slapped the reins against the rumps of the horses. In seconds, they disappeared behind the livery along with most of the town's residents.

She stared at the spot she'd last seen her parents. Her heart ached so much, she thought it might explode and cave in like the mine. "What if Andrew really is in there?" Her words came out in a hoarse whisper.

Nate gave her shoulders a squeeze. "If he is, they'll get him out."

Horrible visions went through her mind. "But what if—"

Nate stepped in front of her, dipped his head to look into her eyes, and put one finger over her lips. "Stop right there, Bek. It's never a good thing to think the worst. Pray and ask God to protect him until we get him back."

The tears she'd been fighting finally won and ran down her cheeks.

Nate's gaze softened. He put his hands on her cheeks and wiped away her tears with his thumbs.

"Oh, Bek," he whispered as he held her against his chest. "We're going to find little Andy and get him back to you. I won't stop looking until he's safely back home and throwing snakes and frogs at you again."

Rebekah laughed through her tears. "I'd give anything right about now to see Andrew tossing a snake at me."

Nate held her away and gazed into her eyes. "You're going to eat those words when we find him."

Rebekah dabbed her face with her sleeve, sucked back a sob, and nodded. Like a balm, Nate managed to soothe her raw emotions. The fear remained, but with him by her side, she'd get through this awful day. He took her hands in his and bowed his head.

"Dear Lord, we ask that You watch over Andrew and keep him safe, along with all those looking for him. Give us wisdom and strength as we continue fighting the evil in this town. In Jesus' name, amen."

Rebekah nodded. "Amen." She wanted to hug Nate for his thoughtfulness. Instead, she peered up at him. "Now what?"

He released one of her hands but kept hold of the other as he led her toward the store. "Now, you'll lock yourself inside and not open it for anyone until I get back."

Her heart thumped. He was leaving her. "Why? Where are you going? I can come with you."

He never stopped walking, nor did he look at her. "Nope. Not this time."

Something was wrong. She could feel it. "Why, Nate? What are you going to do?" she called after him. He didn't answer so she caught up to him and pulled him to a stop. "What are you thinking, Nate?"

He looked at her for several long moments before blowing out a loud breath. "I think Thomas is involved, and I'm going to find him and learn the truth once and for all."

Stunned, Rebekah yanked her hand free of Nate's. "I told you he's a good man." She huffed several times, ready to explode again. "What do you have against him that makes you keep attacking him?"

He reached for her, but she pulled away. "I don't have anything against him, Bek, but you've got to see it from where I stand."

"I can't see it that way because you're wrong about him. You've not liked him from the start. And you're wasting your time while you can be searching for the real blackmailer."

He shook his head and released a sigh. "Would you at least hear me out?"

She crossed her arms, ready to do battle on behalf of Thomas. Because of his small stature, he'd always been picked on, but never before had he been accused of something so awful. "I'll listen, but I won't believe you."

Nate motioned to the steps in front of the store. They moved there and sat. She made sure there was plenty of distance between them. His touch always worked its way to her heart, and she didn't want him making her weak in any way.

He cleared his throat. "Thomas has almost always been seen where something bad happens."

She opened her mouth to refute his words, but he held up a finger to stop her.

"I'm not finished. Let me state my case. He was there when you and I were shot at. I saw him sneaking around town right after Mr. Zimmer's mill was blown up. He has the perfect opportunity to move around at night without being seen, because he stays at your father's livery. But what I think is the most important fact is that he was supposed to be here this morning guarding this place, and he was nowhere to be found." He motioned around them. "And he's still not here—and we can't find your brother."

She glared as if it would change Nate's mind. "That doesn't mean he took Andrew."

"Then why isn't he here to help?"

That question had her stumped. In the past, they could always count on Thomas to help them through anything. Regardless, she still refused to believe Thomas had anything to do with Andrew's kidnapping. He loved her family as much as they loved him.

"I don't know." It was all she could think to say.

"Exactly. And that's why I intend to look for him and find answers to all my questions." He stood and helped her to her feet. "Now go inside and lock yourself in. Don't let anyone in but me or your father." He leaned close, his nose almost touching hers. "Not even Thomas."

Defiant, but too bewildered to disobey, she stomped through the doorway and slammed it closed. After waiting a moment, she moved so she could peek out the window. Nate stood there with his arms crossed.

"I didn't hear the door lock."

Men! The word screamed over and over in her head. Gritting her teeth, she reached and turned the lock. "Satisfied?"

"Yep. Keep it that way."

With that said he jumped off the boardwalk, climbed onto his saddle, and rode off.

She stood at the window, fuming long after he'd disappeared. Why was he being so stubborn? Why wouldn't he listen to her and believe Thomas was a good man? She paced in front of the window, running all Nate had said through her mind. After several minutes of silent arguing, she couldn't convince herself that Thomas had anything to do with the blackmailing or Andrew's kidnapping. What scared her most was how strongly Nate believed just that, and because he did, he might hurt Thomas as he dug for the truth. He was wrong, and she had to convince him of that fact.

With that thought repeating itself with so much intensity, Rebekah could stand it no longer. She rushed to the counter, grabbed the pistol they hid there, and dashed out the side door. Knowing full well Nate would kill her when he found out she'd defied his command, she made a face and pushed away her fear, while praying there was at least one horse or mule left.

Chapter Thirty-five

Not quite certain where he'd find Thomas, Nate decided to begin where they'd first run into trouble with him—at the Loomis home. Or at least near there. Nate couldn't quite swallow the tale Thomas spun about why he didn't hear the rifle shot that could have killed him or Rebekah. Anyone would have heard a rifle shot over the chopping on a tree.

If he didn't find Thomas there, he'd continue on to where he saw him the day of the last picnic he'd shared with Rebekah. Why Thomas would be out there, Nate couldn't fathom, but he aimed to find out.

Rebekah. Seemed like everything in his life lately involved that woman. So much so that she invaded almost every thought and dream. That is, whenever he managed to get some sleep. Maybe that's why he couldn't get clear thoughts or feelings about her. If he could get some rest, he could think clearly.

He rode into the Loomis's yard and reined to a stop. "Hello in the house."

He didn't have long to wait for a response. The children raced out of the house like they were thrilled to have a visitor. The boy he'd given the top to tugged on his boot and motioned for Nate to pick him up. He couldn't resist the longing in the boy's eyes and reached down to scoop him from the ground.

"You ain't taking him, mister."

Nate looked up to see the mother standing on the porch, leaning against the pole just like the first time they'd met. "No, ma'am, I'm not taking him. I just thought he'd like to see the world from up here."

She tipped her head. "I reckon that's fine."

Pretending to be engrossed in the boy, Nate glanced at Mrs. Loomis out of the corner of his eye. Odd that she'd think he was taking the boy. Had she heard about Andrew? Or was she a part of his kidnapping? He tried to examine her face without being obvious in order to gain an answer, but she was harder to read than a book in the dark. He didn't have time for guessing.

"Have you seen Thomas today?"

She cocked her head. "Why?"

Nate tried hard not to look suspicious of her, but that task was getting more and more difficult, especially since she seemed so protective of Thomas. "There's a problem in town, and we were hoping for his help."

"What kind of problem?"

He gritted his teeth. This woman sure wasn't making this easy. He cleared his throat. "Look, I'm kinda in a hurry. We're running out of time. Have you seen him or not?"

Narrowing her eyes and studying him for a bit, she finally shook her head. "Nope. Not today."

Praying she was telling the truth, he ruffled the boy's head and set him back on the ground. Tipping his hat, he reined the horse around. "Thank you, Mrs. Loomis."

Nudging his horse into a gallop, he headed east to look in the area he'd seen Thomas days ago. So much had happened lately that he couldn't remember how many days had passed since he and

Rebekah went on the picnic, nor did he want to muddle his thinking with Rebekah again. She was safe at the store and hopefully from his mind as well.

Almost to the tree line, near the stream where Nate fished Andrew and Rebekah from the water, he caught sight of someone disappearing into the trees. Slowing to a trot, then to a walk, he headed to that same spot, certain it had to be Thomas. Who else would be in this area? Almost everyone was out at Weavers' mine.

Once he reached the trees, he dismounted and tied his horse to one of the branches. Too much noise might give him away, and he hoped to see what Thomas was up to before cornering him. After listening for rustling and breaking twigs, Nate headed off in the direction of the sounds. A few minutes later he spotted Thomas, crouched low next to the stream. Nate couldn't tell what he was doing, but he hoped he didn't have Andrew. When he stood and started walking along the bank, Nate moved to stop him, unwilling to take a chance on losing his prey.

Nate rushed toward him, stopping when Thomas turned and spotted him. "Wait right there, Thomas." When all he received was a grimace before Thomas moved on again, Nate put his hand on his pistol. "I won't ask again."

This time Thomas obeyed but with obvious reluctance. He turned and faced Nate, crossing his arms. "What do you want? I've got work to do."

"I bet you do." He'd never disliked Thomas more. "Where's Andrew?"

Thomas frowned. "What?"

Nate took a step forward. "You heard me. Where is he? Where'd you put him?"

Thomas tried to mislead him with an innocent look. "Nate, I don't know what you're talking about. Andrew isn't at home?"

Patience all but gone, Nate grabbed his shirt. "You know full well he isn't at home. Tell me where he is."

Thomas shoved his hand away. "I told you. I don't know."

Nate started to waver, no longer confident in his judgment of Thomas. Then a look that wasn't quite sincere flashed across Thomas's face, and Nate's certainty returned. He grabbed Thomas by the shirt front and shoved him against a tree.

"I know you're lying, Thomas. I saw it in your eyes." Thomas pushed against him, but Nate had the advantage of height and weight. He thrust him back once more. "I can't even imagine the amount of evil it takes to do this to someone who's treated you so well. The Weavers are an incredible family, and Perry's done nothing to deserve losing a son. He's a great man, and I intend to give him his son back. Now tell me where he is."

Grabbing his wrists, Thomas shook his head, but Nate couldn't tolerate any more of his denial. It was time for the truth. Holding Thomas against the tree with one hand, he pulled out his gun. "Stop it, Nate!"

He heard Rebekah's voice but refused to believe she was actually behind him. He'd specifically told her to stay at the store. Turning, he found her standing next to one of Perry's mules with no saddle, a pistol in her hand. What in the world was she thinking?

"Rebekah, I told you to—"

"Leave Thomas alone. You're wrong about him, so stop your threats and holster your gun."

Still holding Thomas by the shirtfront, Nate wasn't about to give up. He just knew Thomas was involved. "But Rebekah—"

"No! Let's take this to the sheriff. We can straighten this out in front of him. But I won't let you continue to harass Thomas like this."

Nate released Thomas as he holstered his gun, then looked fully into Rebekah's face. The disappointment he saw there cut him deeply. He shifted his gaze to Thomas and saw confusion in the man's eyes. In his love for the Weaver family, and his desire to get Andrew back to them, Nate had allowed anger to cloud his thinking. He had never been the same since the murders of his dad and brother. The unfairness ate at his soul—the need to avenge, relentless. This time he'd gone too far.

Nate shrugged. "Just trying to help." Who was he kidding?

As much as he distrusted the sheriff, maybe he'd misjudged him as well. Maybe God had put the lawman in his path to help him see himself more clearly. And just maybe the answers he sought would be sorted out in that office, face to face with the sheriff.

Hanging his head, he moved in front of Rebekah. "I'm sorry." He turned slightly to include Thomas. "I could try to give excuses for my behavior, but when it comes right down to it, there is no excuse except that I wasn't trusting God to lead my decisions."

Rebekah nodded. "Good. Now you're back to the Nate I—" She sighed. "We need to get moving. We still don't know if Andrew is safe."

Nate wagged his head. "I'm still not sure about Thomas here. His comings and goings have been suspicious since I got here, and—"

"Thomas?" Rebekah looked from Nate to Thomas. "Do you have anything to say to Nate?"

Nostrils flaring, he shook his head. "Nope. I don't trust him either."

Mouth dropping open, Nate was about to ask what he'd done to earn distrust, but Rebekah made a growling sound deep in her throat. Nate couldn't be sure, but he thought he heard her say "men" under her breath.

She moved to climb onto the mule. "Then let's go to the sheriff. Now. We can't keep wasting time."

"Sounds like a good plan to me." Thomas helped her up, then started walking.

"Climb up behind me, Thomas. Walking is too slow."

In no time, Nate was left standing by himself. He hurried to catch up, running to where he'd left his horse. He wasn't ready to let Thomas off so easy. He had questions that needed to be answered first.

Chapter Thirty-six

....

Squirming almost from the moment she'd landed on the mule's back, Rebekah tried to get comfortable. She should have taken the time to hitch the beast to a wagon, but she didn't want Nate to get too far ahead of her or she'd never find him. She'd always hated riding on the back of an animal, but at the moment, it kept her from dwelling on Nate's actions.

Thomas took the reins and held them in front of her. "You keep wiggling like that, this mule will buck us both off."

"Well, this isn't exactly the most comfortable ride I've ever been on."

He chuckled. "I'm glad you came, though. No telling how that mess back there would have ended up." He nudged the mule, but the animal refused to go faster. "What happened to Andrew? Nate didn't tell me anything."

She turned around to examine Thomas's face and found what she sought. She knew he was innocent. "He was gone when we got up this morning. We couldn't find him anywhere. Then we found a note in the livery demanding money for his safe return."

Thomas sagged in the saddle. "A note in the livery. I knew I should have stayed. No wonder Nate suspects me."

Nate galloped up to them, keeping them from chatting further, mainly because Thomas refused to talk in front of him, the fact made obvious by his stiff back and tight lips.

She'd had enough of these two men acting like children. "You know, if you two would just open up and talk to each other, maybe we could get to the answers we all need a whole lot faster."

The frown on Thomas's face went so deep, the furrow between his brows could hold water. "That reminds me of my other question I meant to ask. Why doesn't the sheriff know about any of this?"

Rebekah drew her head back in surprise. She didn't know the answer. "I have no idea." She looked at Nate. "Do you?"

He looked everywhere but at her.

"Nate?" A sick feeling stirred in her belly. "You know why the sheriff doesn't know about Andrew, don't you?"

He shifted in the saddle. "Maybe."

Rebekah waited for more, but he was just like Thomas. She'd have to pry the answer from him. "Well? Do you plan to tell me why?"

After a few moments of fidgeting, he finally looked at her. "Because I don't trust him."

Thomas snorted. "You don't trust many people, do you? I hope you have a better reason for not trusting him than you do for me."

Nate craned his neck to see Thomas. "Look—"

"All right, you two." Incredibly frustrated, Rebekah wanted to grab them by their earlobes. "You're getting worse than Andrew. And he's supposed to be the only one we're concerned about right now, so stop it." She leaned to see Nate's face and caught a glimpse of his anger. Maybe he'd talk more freely in a temper. "So why don't you trust the sheriff?"

He held up one finger. "One, he never does his job, as though by allowing others to break the law, it will cover the fact that he is too." A second finger rose. "Two, I thought it odd that he released those two young men only hours after he'd arrested them—the very same men who told me to leave town after beating me. That tells me the sheriff might be friends with them." He added a third finger. "Three, he tried to arrest me because I was on the street after dark, then didn't plan to bring me to his office but led me in the opposite direction. I have no idea what he had planned, but I'm thankful Mr. Gilmore stopped him." He blew out a loud breath. "There's more, but hopefully you'll take my word that he isn't the kind of man this town needs to uphold the law."

Rebekah stared, more than ready to take his word, trusting his instincts completely. But what else were they to do but go to the sheriff? In this situation they needed the law, and the sheriff was all they had.

Nate frowned. "What? You don't believe me?"

She shook her head. "Just the opposite. So, what do we do?"

His expression softened. "We go to the sheriff."

Shocked, her mouth dropped open. "But you just said—"

He smiled. "I know what I said, but this might let us see the man's reaction, maybe even give us a chance to trap him in some way. So when it comes right down to it, you had the best idea."

Thomas adjusted his position. "Does this mean you trust me now?"

Nate eyed him for a bit. Rebekah noticed his mouth open and close a couple times.

Finally Thomas growled and nudged the mule to go faster. "Never mind."

Nate reached out and snared the mule's reins. "Hold up a minute. Can we talk without getting mad at each other?"

Not about to interrupt the two of them coming to an understanding, Rebekah thought it was about time they talked. But they needed to get it done soon. They were almost to town. Before they could say another word, though, the man they'd been talking about rode up to them, his badge glinting in the sun.

"What's going on around here? There's almost no one in town."

He motioned to Thomas and Rebekah. "And why are you two riding like that?"

Nate closed one eye as he looked at the sheriff. "You been sleeping or out of town?"

Rebekah held her breath. Nate seemed to know just what to say to get people angry. She could almost see the steam radiating off the sheriff's head. Before the sheriff could spew any wrath, Nate put up a hand to stop him.

"We were just on our way to your office to talk to you."

The sheriff lifted his hat and wiped the sweat from his forehead. "Then let's get there and out of this sun."

Rebekah caught the look Nate sent her way. Why hadn't she noticed the sheriff's lack of effort and responsibility before? Probably because she never had much to do with him. Her father handled anything to do with the law. Confused, she kept her mouth shut, as did everyone else. The remainder of the ride to town was silent except for the clip-clop of hooves and the squeak of leather of the saddles whenever Nate or the sheriff moved. The sounds should have been soothing but only served to add to the mounting tension.

The sheriff didn't wait for any of the others but walked on into his office and plopped onto his chair. This was Rebekah's first time inside the building, but by the look of it, he spent plenty of time inside. His chair was worn, and a spot on the desktop revealed that the sheriff's boots spent a great deal of time propped there. She didn't dare stare at the dust and trash covering everything, or she wouldn't be able to stay. If the sheriff didn't uphold the law, what exactly did he do around here? Finally understanding what Nate meant, she turned to glance at him.

Tipping back in his chair, the sheriff bumped his hat farther up on his forehead and then crossed his fingers across his plump belly. "Now, what's this all about?"

Rebekah noticed Nate give an almost imperceptible nod at Thomas before turning to answer the sheriff.

"Andrew's been kidnapped, and I think Thomas had something to do with it."

Nate's bold and direct statement almost made Rebekah choke. She noticed Thomas was in the same condition, his face now red, his cheeks puffed out with unspent air.

The sheriff leaned forward over the desk, his expression revealing his shock as his eyes shifted to her. "Perry's boy's been kidnapped?" He switched his gaze toward Thomas and thumped his fist on the desk. "Did you do this, Thomas?"

The breath Thomas had been holding exploded in a gust as he started pacing. "I'm full up sick of being accused of this. I've had more than my fill of being blamed for all that goes wrong in this town. I'm outta here."

As Nate stepped in his way, the sheriff pulled his pistol, cocking the hammer at the same time.

Thomas spun around to face him, his hand going out in front of him. "Now, hold on there, Sheriff."

Nate moved between the sheriff and Thomas. "I don't think that's necessary, Sheriff. Thomas will stay and talk." He turned. "Won't you, Thomas?"

Thomas nodded nervously. "Yeah, sure."

Rebekah's heart pounded. This wasn't what she'd expected. They were supposed to alert the sheriff to Andrew's kidnapping.

"Sit." The sheriff motioned to a chair beside the desk. "I won't have you running off again."

Once Thomas occupied the chair, the sheriff holstered his pistol and returned to his seat. Instead of questioning Thomas, Sheriff Caldwell turned to Nate. "What makes you think Thomas had anything to do with the Weaver boy disappearing?"

Nate's eyes narrowed just a bit. Rebekah had gotten to know him well enough to realize he didn't like something the sheriff said. She could almost see his thoughts spinning.

Finally, he strolled closer to the desk. "Because I've accused him of several things, and he hasn't denied even one."

The sheriff leaned back again as he eyed Thomas. "Accused him of what?"

"First and foremost, that he took Andrew."

Rebekah's heart nearly stopped. She knew Nate thought Thomas had something to do with Andrew's kidnapping, but she now realized she'd never heard Thomas deny the accusation. Her mind scrambled back to their ride. He did seem unaware that Andrew was missing.

Thomas's face turned red again. "I didn't take the boy."

Nate leaned close. "But you either know who did or where he is, don't you?"

Holding her breath, Rebekah waited for his answer, while feeling shame that Nate had her doubting her friend.

Arms crossed, Thomas remained silent.

Nate stood upright again. "All right, let's try this one. You've been the man leaving notes at night, haven't you?"

Rebekah gasped, then covered her mouth. Why would Nate think that? But the way Thomas jerked his head up in surprise, suspicion crept in once again, especially when his mouth bobbed open and closed but not a word came out. His silence declared his guilt.

Chapter Thirty-seven
....

The sheriff leaned forward, looking just as surprised as Rebekah felt. "You've been leaving the notes?"

"No. Well, I—"

This time, Nate thumped the desk. "Spill it, Thomas. You've basically just confessed."

Thomas glared at Nate and clamped his mouth shut. Heart aching, it was time for her to help get the truth out in the open. She moved to Thomas's side and crouched, then grasped his forearm as she peered into his eyes.

"Please, Thomas, if you know anything at all, tell us. Andrew needs us. You've been our friend and helper since we've known you. Please help us again, right now."

Tears formed—for fear of possibly losing Andrew and the pain of possibly losing a friend—and began to roll down her cheeks.

Thomas stared into her eyes for several long moments before sighing and putting his hand over hers. "All right. I'll tell you what I know. Then I'll tell you what I think."

Confused at his last statement, she let it pass. Time was running short, and Andrew needed them. "Thank you."

He gave a slight shake of his head. "I have been writing notes."

The sheriff released a low whistle while Nate blasted out a growl, then mumbled, "I knew it."

Thomas tensed and leaned forward. "Let me finish." When

everyone was quiet again, he relaxed a bit. "Like I said, I have been writing notes, but they were love notes."

Brows raised, Rebekah couldn't help but smile. "You wrote those notes to Cora and Mrs. Phipps?"

He nodded. "But I only wrote those kinds of notes. I never wrote any threatening ones."

Nate leaned against the desk. "So the rumors about the same man writing both kinds of notes—"

"Are wrong," Thomas finished for him with some force in his voice. "I wouldn't hurt anyone in this town, especially the Weaver family. I only wanted to make sure..." Thomas looked away.

Rebekah knew him well enough to know he was embarrassed. "To make sure of what, Thomas?"

Still avoiding her eyes, Thomas ran his hand across his whiskers, the stubble creating a scratching sound against his palm. He blew out another breath. "I don't want the people I like to go through life being alone just because they're too shy to let someone know they care."

Throat closing from so many emotions, Rebekah's eyes filled with tears again. She'd known since he kept her from burning to death that Thomas had a soft heart. She gave him a hug.

"This is all well and good," the sheriff's gruff voice boomed, "but we're still nowhere near finding the Weaver boy. What else do you know, Thomas?"

Wanting to strangle the unfeeling wretch, Rebekah turned and stared at the sheriff. The way he pulled his head back, she knew her emotions were apparent. She decided not to scold the brute.

Thomas changed his position but kept hold of Rebekah's hand. "I don't *know* anything else. The rest is all what I've come up with by noticing things and pure guessing."

Before anything else was said, Nate pushed away from the desk, retrieved a chair from the far corner of the room, and brought it to Rebekah. Pulling a kerchief from his pocket, he wiped the dust from the seat. When she'd smiled her thanks and sat, Nate motioned to Thomas.

"Let's hear what you've noticed."

The fact that he emphasized the last word didn't get past Rebekah or Thomas. She couldn't believe Nate still didn't trust Thomas. Silently, she threatened with her eyes that he'd better watch himself or she'd give him the scolding she didn't give the sheriff.

Thomas tilted his head up toward Nate. "I've noticed that a couple young men strut around here like they own the town. And very likely, they soon may, if my guess is right. I'm also pretty sure they aren't trying to own the town alone. And lastly, I heard a couple men talking as they passed the livery this morning." The confidence left Thomas's attitude. "They're the reason I left the livery. I wanted to follow them."

Nate leaned forward. "Do you think they have Andrew?"

Thomas shrugged, looking miserable. "I don't know. Maybe."

Pushing away from the desk, Nate faced the sheriff. "One more question, Thomas. Is the sheriff involved?"

Sheriff Caldwell reared back. "What? Me? Hold on there." He rose to his feet, his hand going to his pistol.

Nate beat him by pulling his, then motioning the sheriff's hand away. "Put your gun on the desk, Sheriff."

"But I didn't do anything."

"Then you shouldn't mind giving up the gun for a while." Nate motioned one more time, and the sheriff finally pulled the gun and tossed it onto the desk.

"Now, have a seat."

His anger evident, the sheriff dropped onto his chair. Rebekah's head spun with all that had happened. When did Nate learn to pull his gun so fast? What was he going to do to the sheriff? And why did he sound so much like a lawman?

Nate picked up the sheriff's gun, then holstered his own. "Where were you this morning, Sheriff?"

"What do you mean, where was I? I was right here."

"And what about last night after I left? Where'd you go then?"

The sheriff suddenly acted nervous, not looking at anyone. "I didn't go anywhere."

Nate moved to stand behind the sheriff. "Then why didn't you answer the door when Perry came by?"

Swallowing hard, the sheriff slouched in his chair. "Perry came by? I didn't hear anything."

"Then where'd you go?"

Slumping forward and putting his head in his hands, the sheriff shook his head. "I didn't go anywhere. I was right here all night." He yanked out the bottom drawer of the desk and pulled out a jug. "Thanks to this, I slept through everything."

Rebekah's mouth dropped open, as did Nate's. That certainly explained a lot.

Nate moved to the sheriff's side. "Where'd you get that?"

A miserable expression on his face, Sheriff Caldwell sat back in his chair. "From those two men I arrested that day you came to town. They said they'd keep me well supplied if I let them have some fun in town without giving them trouble. Then when you showed up, they wanted me to give you a bad time so you'd leave."

Rebekah couldn't believe what she was hearing. What kind of man was the sheriff to allow such activity, not to mention risking the lives of those in town by drinking too much?

Nate put his hands on the desk. "And the night you tried to arrest me?"

The sheriff nodded. "Those men wanted me to bring you to them."

Disgust for the sheriff almost glowed from Nate's face. He paced a few moments before he stopped again. "Well, that explains a lot, but we still have to find Andrew. Do you know where we can find the ruffians, Sheriff?"

The sheriff shook his head. "I tried to find them a couple times when they didn't bring me my jugs. I never did find out where they stayed."

"I might know where they are."

At Thomas's words, everyone turned to him. A spark of Rebekah's anger lit. Why did he wait until now to say something? He knew she was afraid for Andrew's life. How dare he keep information from her? She grabbed Thomas's arm.

"Where's Andrew, Thomas?"

He turned to her. "I honestly don't know. But I might know where those boys are."

Rebekah stood, pulling on his arm. "Then what are we doing sitting here? Let's go."

Nate moved to her side. "I agree."

Thomas stood, looking Nate dead in the eyes. "Not you. I still don't trust you."

"What?" Both Rebekah and Nate responded at the same time, but Nate took a step forward.

"Why? What have I done to make you say that?"

"It's in your eyes." Thomas stood as tall as he could stretch his spine. "I've been watching you along with everyone else, and there's something you're hiding." He moved a step closer. "Tell me I'm wrong."

Rebekah examined the shock on Nate's face and knew Thomas was right. Her heart shriveled. What could he be hiding and why?

Nate took a step back and sat on the corner of the desk, stunned disbelief on his face. When he remained silent, Rebekah stood in front of him.

"Out with it, Nate. It's obvious you've kept something from us. What do you know?"

Shaking his head, he pulled a leather pouch from his pocket. Slipping a piece of paper from inside, he opened it and held it out for them to see. "It says I'm a deputy marshal. I've been assigned here to find out who's been burning and exploding the businesses in and around town."

"What?" The sheriff stomped around the desk and grabbed the paper from Nate's hand. He took a few moments to read it, then shoved it against Nate's chest. "Why didn't you tell me? I'm the law here. I had a right to know."

Nate folded the paper and replaced it in his pocket. "Like it says in this letter, I'm supposed to be undercover, mainly because you were named as a suspect."

The sheriff's mouth dropped open. "Me? Who pointed the finger at me?"

Nate shrugged. "My boss didn't say—only that I was to keep an eye on you."

"I wrote the marshal's office." Once again, Thomas managed to shock them. "You gotta admit, Sheriff, you've been acting a bit odd lately."

Patience gone, Rebekah grabbed Thomas's shirt sleeve. "Where can we locate those men? We need to get Andrew."

"Right." Thomas moved to the door and held it open. "We'll need to find me a ride."

"No, we won't." Nate strode out the door and untied the reins to his horse. "Rebekah isn't going. You can use her mule."

Temper flaring, Rebekah marched across the boardwalk and loosened the mule's reins. "I'm going. Andrew's my brother, and if he's with them, he'll be scared, and I want to be there for him." She faced Nate, daring him to argue. "And you can't stop me."

He moved to within inches from her. "I can if I take your mule and leave you on foot." He grasped her by the arms. "This could be dangerous, Bek, and I don't want you getting hurt."

She pulled free. "I won't get hurt, and I will be going, even if I have to borrow someone's horse."

Nate took two steps away, his hands curled into fists. "How does your father deal with you?" He turned back to face her. "All right, but only if you stay behind us. I want your word, or I'll lock you in one of those jail cells."

"You wouldn't dare."

He strode up to her and leaned down until their noses bumped. "Don't tempt me, Bek. I'll do what's necessary to keep you safe." He motioned to Thomas. "Let's get to the livery and find you a ride. We need to get moving."

Though anger boiled below the surface, Rebekah had never loved Nate more. When she caught Thomas grinning at her, she made a face and determined not to look at him again. Emotions swirling worse than the river water during spring melt, she allowed Nate to help her onto the mule, then followed him without another word.

Chapter Thirty-eight
....

As they all rushed toward the livery to find Thomas a ride, Nate wavered in his decision to allow Rebekah to join them. He'd never forgive himself if something happened to her. But if the look on her face was any indication, she'd find some way to follow.

While Thomas ran inside for another mule, Nate helped Rebekah to the ground so he could put a saddle on hers, knowing it would be more comfortable than riding bareback. One look at the sheriff, wobbling in his horse, told Nate the man wouldn't be much help.

Joining Thomas in the livery, Nate slid to a stop when he almost ran into Thomas standing in the middle of the building.

"What's wrong?"

Thomas motioned to one of the stalls. "The only mule left is Twister." He turned a helpless look toward Nate. "If I ride him, we won't get to leave town."

Any other day, Nate would have found the situation humorous. Today, his mind scrambled for answers. "Saddle him."

"What? Nate—"

"Just do it, Thomas. I think if I keep to his left and hold his bridle, we can get him to walk a straight line."

By the time Nate had Rebekah's mule saddled, Thomas had Twister ready and was struggling to get him out of the livery. About to help Rebekah up, she stopped him.

"Wait. We need to check for a note before we leave."

He'd forgotten all about that. "Wait here. I'll look."

Racing through both buildings, Nate didn't see any sign of a note being shoved under the doors. He returned and, at Rebekah's questioning gaze, shook his head. He lifted her onto the saddle, then climbed onto his own. Nudging his horse next to Twister's left side, he leaned and grasped the left rein.

"All right, which way, Thomas?"

He pointed west. "Toward the river."

With a nod, Nate headed that way, certain they'd end up in the area where he saw Thomas the day of the picnic. Fighting Twister all the way, the trip took them much longer than Nate had figured. They had to cross the river at a low, and Twister all but landed everyone in the water with his weaving and curling and tossing of his head. Finally on the other side, Thomas grabbed Nate's elbow.

"There's a shack a short distance up that hill. I think they might be in there. If not, they're back by the Loomis home."

Nate couldn't believe his ears. That was the exact opposite direction of where they were right now. Frustrated, he nudged his horse forward, wishing Thomas had mentioned the other place earlier. "Let's get moving." Catching an odd look on Thomas's face, he frowned. "What?"

His mouth opened, then he shook his head. "Nothing."

With no time for another discussion about mistrust, Nate pushed Thomas from his mind. They'd find Andrew first. A few minutes later, Nate spotted the shack through the trees. He motioned for everyone to stop and to remain quiet. Dismounting, he crouched for a better view, taking time to figure out the best approach. He didn't bother asking the sheriff. They were fortunate he managed to stay in the saddle on the ride there.

Thomas knelt next to him. "Any ideas how to get in there without anyone getting killed?"

"I got one, but it's not great." Nate faced Thomas. "I'll need your help."

He nodded. "You got it, whatever it is." He paused, that odd look on his face again. "Nate."

He was already examining the shack. "Do you know what the back side looks like? Any windows or doors?"

Thomas shook his head. "I never went back there. I was nervous just getting this close. Them boys scare me. They're pretty rough."

Remembering the beating he took, Nate nodded. "Yeah, they are. We may be in for a fight, but I don't want Andrew hurt." He pointed to the far side. "I'm going to work my way back that way. When you see I'm there, give me a few minutes to get set, then I want you to walk Twister up to the front."

Eyebrows high, Thomas stared. "Are you sure? That seems mighty risky."

"I know, but it's the best plan I could come up with." Nate motioned toward the door. "I want you to stay away from that door. Just holler for anyone inside." He grimaced. "And if you hear someone cocking their gun, hit the ground fast. No matter what happens, I'm going to get inside soon after you holler. Got it?"

Thomas blew out a long breath and rubbed the back of his neck. "I guess so."

Nodding, Nate patted Thomas on the back. At least he could count on someone—he hoped anyway. He headed to the sheriff.

"I want you to stay back here with Rebekah. Keep her safe. Thomas and I will handle anyone inside the shack." He turned to Rebekah. "I want your word you'll stay back here."

Expecting an argument, he was surprised to see her nod. Then he saw the fear on her face. Her lips trembled. He wanted to comfort her but didn't have the time. Squeezing her hand was the best he could do for now. Giving her a smile, he turned to leave, but she tugged him back.

"Be careful."

His smile dissolved. "I will." He pulled away. "Thomas? You ready?"

With a hesitant nod, Thomas moved to Twister and grabbed his reins. Nate held up two fingers.

"Two minutes *after* I get back there."

"Right."

Taking a moment to examine the front of the shack one more time to make sure he saw no movements, Nate took a deep breath and headed toward the back. Trying to keep the trees between him and the building as much as possible, he made it behind the shack without anyone taking a shot at him.

After silently thanking God for his safety, he examined the back to find the best way inside. That's when he saw a horse tied some distance away, its swishing tail grabbing his attention. He squinted for a better look, thinking he'd seen the horse somewhere before. Since he was in a hurry, he pulled his thoughts back to the shack. He didn't have much time to decide how he would get in. In two minutes, Thomas would be shouting to whoever was inside.

There were two windows, one at each end of the building. There also appeared to be a door between them, but it blended so well with the worn wood, he couldn't be sure, almost as if it was supposed to be hidden. He'd have to wait until the last moment to decide which access he'd choose.

"Hello in the house."

Hearing Thomas's shout, there was no more time for thinking. Nate rose and sped toward the shack. Seconds before he reached the back, the door became obvious. He aimed for it and, with his shoulder, blasted against the wood. The door splintered under his weight.

Pistol in hand, he rolled to a stop and leapt to his feet. Seeing who stood at the opposite window, Nate nearly dropped his gun.

Chapter Thirty-nine

....

Lifting the barrel, Nate aimed the gun again but wished for the first time he hadn't become a lawman. With a glance around the room, he spotted Andrew on a chair against the far wall. Ropes lay at his feet like he'd once been tied up, but otherwise, he looked fine.

With his free hand, he waved Andrew over. The boy charged toward him, wrapping his arms around Nate's waist. Nate held him close, his heart swelling and breaking at the same time. So many questions swarmed his mind, yet he couldn't think of anything to say.

Finally, one question landed on his tongue. "Why did it have to be you, Henry?"

The elderly gentleman lowered his head and gave it a slow shake. Then he looked up at Nate. "I'm sorry. I was just trying to do something good, but it went all wrong."

Nate frowned. "Something good? How can stealing and kidnapping be good?"

"Nate?" Thomas called from outside. "Everything all right?"

"Yeah. Come on in."

Thomas shoved through the door, his own gun in hand. He glanced at Henry but stared at Andrew and broke into a smile.

Nate gave Andrew a light push. "Go to Thomas." The boy ran and grabbed Thomas much like he had Nate. "Take him to his sister, Thomas."

Andrew took a step back. "Bek's here?"

Without waiting for an answer, Andrew raced from the shack, hollering Rebekah's name. The joy of the siblings reuniting filled Nate's heart.

"Thomas, go get the sheriff's cuffs. Mine are still in the hotel room."

With a nod, Thomas glanced between Nate and Henry, then followed after Andrew. Keeping his gun aimed at Henry, Nate retrieved the chair Andrew had occupied and placed it in the middle of the room. Then he motioned to Henry.

"Have a seat."

Henry stood staring him down for a while before he nodded. He took a step, then flung a bottle from the windowsill at him before lunging for the door. Nate ducked, and the bottle missed him. When he looked up, Henry was gone. He ran outside, ready to shoot, then slid to a stop.

In his rush to escape, Henry must not have noticed the mule he tried to steal was Twister. The two trotted in circles, Henry yanking on the right rein and kicking the mule while Twister continued to the left. Cursing, Henry finally flung the reins away and raised his hands before sliding from the saddle to the ground.

"Stupid beast."

Nate finally smiled. "Oh, I don't know, Henry. He looks quite a bit smarter than you at the moment."

Thomas rushed up to them, the cuffs in hand.

Nate motioned toward Henry. "Put them on him. Then we'll have us a little talk."

Once Thomas had Henry cuffed, he led him to the steps and forced him to sit. Then Thomas returned to Nate, his expression one of guilt.

"I got something to tell you, Nate. Something I tried to say before but didn't know how. Didn't figure you'd believe me anyhow."

Nate frowned. "What is it?"

Thomas kicked at a stick then looked up at him. "I was pretty sure Henry was involved. But with you two being such good friends, at first I thought you might be in with him. Then I just couldn't tell you." He shrugged. "Sorry."

Putting his hand on Thomas's shoulder, Nate gave a squeeze. "It wasn't all your fault, Thomas. I accept some of the blame for being such a fool." He patted his back and headed toward Henry. "We can finish this later. Right now I need some answers."

Before he could ask his first question, Rebekah, Andrew, and Sheriff Caldwell joined them. As much as he would have liked to do this alone, all the others had a right to know what Henry had to say.

He looked from Rebekah to Andrew. "You two all right?" When they nodded, he turned back to Henry. "I've got a lot of questions, Henry, and I hope you'll do the right thing and answer truthfully."

By the look on Henry's face, all the fight was gone. All that seemed to remain were shame and sorrow. He peered up at Nate. "I'll tell you anything you want to know, but first"—he swung his gaze to Rebekah—"I need to apologize to this little gal."

Confused, Nate frowned. Maybe he just wanted to express his regret for taking Andrew and causing her to be upset.

Tears filled the old man's eyes, but he didn't try to wipe them or look away. "I'm partly to blame for your burns, Miss Weaver."

As she gasped, Thomas lunged for Henry's throat.

Stunned, Nate stayed back. Henry deserved whatever happened to him. Then, as though God's Spirit gave him a shake, Nate moved to drag Thomas away.

Thomas charged at Henry again, but Nate had no trouble pulling him off.

"Let me go, Nate. At the very least, he's earned a good beating."

Wavering in his decision, Nate figured it was about time he started listening to the Lord more than his gut. "I want to agree with you, Thomas, but under God's law and that of our country, I have to stop you."

As if slowly waking from a bad dream, Thomas looked up at him, his body relaxing. When Nate was sure he wouldn't attack Henry again, he let the man go. Nate immediately took the few steps to check on Rebekah. He lifted her chin with his fingers. Seeing her tears, his heart clenched, and he wrapped her in his arms.

Andrew put his arms around them both, and Nate reached down to put his hand on Andrew's head. These two had been through so much, and all at the hands of Henry. How could he have been so wrong about the man?

Nate bent to look into Rebekah's eyes. "Will you be all right?" When she nodded, he crouched to face Andrew. "How about you, young man? You doing all right?"

Andrew hugged his neck, then nodded and returned to Rebekah's side.

Nate headed back to Henry. "How about you explain yourself? Tell us how Rebekah was burned."

He met Nate's eyes. "I didn't set that forge so it would flare, but the boy who did it worked for me. He was angry with Perry because he kept the boy from seeing Rebekah."

"Cole."

The surprise in Rebekah's voice made Nate turn to her, but Thomas had moved to her side to comfort her, so he pushed Henry to continue.

"Yes, Cole. He thought that if he got Perry out of the way, he could see Rebekah all he wanted." Henry shook his head. "The fool had no idea Rebekah would be the one to stoke that fire." He blew out a sigh. "I went to confront him, and he pulled his gun on me. I had no choice but to shoot him."

After all this time, Rebekah finally had her answers. He hoped they helped. Now it was time for more.

"Tell me about the blackmailing and all the fires and explosions. You weren't making enough money in your tobacco shop? You had to steal from other hard-working men, nearly killing some of them?"

Nate took several deep breaths, trying to calm his temper. He didn't know if he was more angry with Henry because of all he'd done, or with himself for believing Henry to be a gentleman.

After wiping his forehead with his sleeve, Henry shrugged. "I didn't do it for me."

Though Henry's voice sounded broken, Nate had all the lies he could stomach. "Oh, come off it, Henry. Who else would you want that money for? You told me you had no family." He paused. "Or was that a lie too?"

Henry stared into Nate's eyes. "My men were my family. When they died, their families became part of mine too." Tears fell as his eyes took on a faraway look. "Almost five years ago, I watched those blue coats cut my men down after burning them out of that field." He raised his cuffed hands, making slashing motions. "They shot, stabbed, or slit the throat of every last one of them, and I just stood back in the trees and watched." He wiped at his eyes again. "I thought the only way I could gain their forgiveness was to take care of their wives and children."

Nate stayed quiet. This was the man he'd come to know. The man who cared for and about others. That other man, the man who stole and kidnapped, was a stranger. "Why blackmailing, Henry? Why take Perry's son?"

Henry gestured to the hills around them. "All this gold and silver. These men didn't need all they found, and I had no money of my own. Taking some from them was the only way I could think of to take care of my men's families."

With a weary shrug, he continued. "After the war was over, I met up with some other commanders. They felt the same as me, so we came up with this plan when we heard about the gold rush in Colorado. When we got there, we'd threaten them until they gave us money, then send the money to families without husbands and fathers. But when they started killing some of the hold-outs, I broke away from them and moved here to start over."

Nate frowned, his mind spinning. "Killing people at the gold rush in Colorado? Do you know if they're the ones who killed my dad and brother?"

Henry shrugged one shoulder. "Couldn't say for sure, but it wouldn't surprise me." He blew out a long breath. "Anyway, the plan was going well here until I asked for help."

Nate squatted, resting one knee on the ground, to better see Henry's face. "Help?"

Henry nodded. "Getting old slowed me down, made moving from place to place a lot harder. One of my men had two grown sons and a brother. They were more than willing to help me, said it was a good thing what I was doing. They were good help, right up until they got greedy and wanted to keep the money for themselves."

The faces of the two young men he'd helped arrest came to mind, followed quickly by the old man who'd taken a shot at him and Rebekah. "So those two boys and their uncle, did they take over your scheme, or did you still play a part all along?"

After shaking his head, Henry lowered his head into his hands.

"I was a part of it at first. The three of them mentioned lighting a couple fires to scare the owners into paying whenever they refused. I agreed. And it worked. But then they became more violent. When I tried to stop them, they told me to either leave them alone, or I'd end up one of their victims." He looked up at Nate, the tears still flowing. "They threatened to kill me. Then, when I wanted to leave Silver, they said I had to stay or they'd hunt me down and kill me anyway. And if I stayed here, they'd make sure I kept my mouth shut."

Grasping the situation, Nate rubbed his forehead as though it would relieve the tension. "So kidnapping Andrew?"

"Was all their idea. I had no part of it." Henry turned to the boy. "I knew about this place. We used it for money drops several times. I knew I'd find Andrew here when I found out he was missing. I slipped away from the group going to Perry's mine and came here. I was still trying to figure out how to get out of this mess without getting either of us killed when you showed up."

Nate motioned Andrew over and put his arm around the boy. "Is that true, Andrew?"

The boy nodded. "Them men tied me up so tight it hurt. Mr. Gilmore came and took off the ropes."

"Good." He inclined his head to Henry. "Thank you for that. Now, where can I find these other three?"

Henry shook his head. "They're mean, Nate. You be careful."

"Where are they?"

Thomas stepped up. "Are they in that cabin out by the Loomis place?"

Henry reared his head back. "You know about that?" Thomas nodded, and Henry waved his cuffed hands. "Yeah, well, that's where they are. And will you do me a favor?" He didn't wait for a response.

"Watch over the Loomis family. They came here because of me. I've been helping them. They know about the blackmailing but promised not to say anything since I've been giving them some of the money."

Feeling he had all the answers he needed, Nate stood. "How far from the Loomis cabin, Thomas? In what direction?"

When Thomas finished, Nate turned to the sheriff. "Can you get Henry back to town and locked in your jail? I'm going after…" He looked at Henry. "What's the name of this family?"

"Moreland. The uncle's name is Roy. The boys are John and Adam."

Nate put his hand on Thomas's shoulder. "I need you to get Rebekah and Andrew safely back home, then go out to Perry's mine and let them know what happened."

Rebekah approached and touched his arm. "You're not going after them alone, are you?"

He motioned around. "There isn't anyone else. I have to."

"No, you don't. Wait for—well, come with us to town, then take Thomas and the sheriff with you."

He took her hands in his. "I'll be fine. Besides, the sheriff needs to stay with Henry at the jail."

She turned to Thomas. "You can't let him go alone."

Nate made her face him. "We're out of time, Bek. Who knows what else they'll do before I stop them. Go back to town. I'll let you know when I get back." He wasn't about to let her argue with him. She was stubborn enough to try to follow him. "Thomas, Henry left his horse behind the shack. Andrew can ride with Rebekah. I've got to get going."

Before Rebekah could say a word, he ran to his horse, jumped onto the saddle, and rode hard to the west. Every step of the way, he prayed for God to give him wisdom and safety in what he was about to do.

Following Thomas's directions, he found the cabin just as he'd described. Dismounting far from the cabin so as not to alert them to his presence, Nate tied his horse, pulled out his pistol, and slipped up to the door without making a sound. With his back to the front wall, he waited to catch his breath. Without cuffs or rope, this wouldn't be easy, but he had to finish the job. Saying one more prayer, Nate grabbed the knob and rushed inside.

Prepared for a gun battle, Nate slid to a stop at the sight before him. He smiled. God had gone before him and handled the situation. Both boys were passed out drunk and snoring, each with a jug still in hand. The uncle started to stir, so Nate rushed to him and stuck the barrel of his gun in his ear.

"Don't move if you want to live." He slid the rifle from the man's hands and tossed it onto a cot and out of reach. Looking around, he found a piece of rope at the end of the cot. "Lay on the floor."

The man's eyes, filled with hate, bored into his own. He moved to obey, then lunged at him.

Nate slammed the gun handle against the man's temple. He crumpled to the ground. Not sure how long he or the boys would be out, Nate rushed to get all three tied up tight. Unwilling to take any chances, he pulled the boots from their feet and secured their ankles with rope.

After saddling their horses, Nate tossed each one on a saddle and tied them to it so they wouldn't fall off. As he rode into town, the men were just starting to rouse from their stupor. Cursing, they demanded to be released.

With the jail in sight, Nate breathed another prayer of thanks to the Lord. That arrest could have been deadly, but God blessed him and kept him safe. Once he'd stopped in front of the jail,

Perry ran out. He nearly pulled Nate from his horse, pumping his hand with an enthusiastic shake.

"How can I ever thank you, Nate? You saved my family."

Nate shook his head, humbled. "No, sir, it wasn't me. Thank the good Lord. I know I sure am."

They hustled the three men into the cells next to Henry and returned outside, glad to let the sheriff watch the men. Nate would have a talk with him in a bit, but at the moment, he wasn't in the mood.

"How's the family, Perry?"

Tears filled his eyes. "Never better, my boy. Never better. Kate insists you come to supper."

"How's Reuben?" He avoided answering the invitation. Not only was he weary, but he needed time alone.

Before Perry could respond, Reuben came running up to them, covered in dust and dirt. Perry met him and grabbed him by the arms. "You all right, Rube? You look near dead."

Reuben grinned, his teeth gleaming through the grime on his face. "Not dead, Perry. Alive. Very much alive. I found silver. More than you can count."

Perry stared. "What?"

Reuben howled with laughter. "Silver, man. We're rich. Near as I can tell, the explosion shook it loose."

Still staring, Perry started to smile. "Reuben, my friend, you never stuttered a single one of those words." He gave the man a shake. "Praise God." He whooped and punched his fist through the air. "Praise God."

In all the excitement, Perry forgot Nate and left him standing in front of the jailhouse as they raced toward home.

Nate didn't mind. He was praising God along with Perry and Reuben. He'd spend the night doing much the same.

Chapter Forty

....

Rebekah wiped off the counter for the third time, then glanced around for something else to do. Boredom ate up her insides. She'd rather be flooded with customers than have to sit idle, but since her father and Reuben found silver in the Florida Mountains, half the town hiked out there every day, trying to do the same. And now she and Mama had fewer patrons.

When she thought of Mama, happiness filled her heart. They'd all been worried about her, but now that the blackmailing and threats had stopped, Mama's sad disposition had also ended. Now Mama's smiles always lurked near the surface and at the ready.

She abandoned the dust cloth and looked around. Where'd she put the broom? At the very least, she could sweep the floor and boardwalk again.

As much as she tried to fight memories of Nate, he found a way back into her thoughts, like right now. If only he'd said good-bye before taking Mr. Gilmore and his friends to Boise for their trial two weeks ago...

No, she wouldn't allow herself to dwell on that. Most men didn't know how to say a proper farewell. Maybe Nate feared that she'd cry—but she wouldn't have. She'd known from the get-go he'd be in Silver for a short stay. No need to take his departure personally. That she'd fallen in love with the near-perfect stranger was absurd. As she searched every inch of the store for the elusive broom, Rebekah repeated, "Lord, take captive my every thought."

Finally, she spied the broom, not two feet from where she'd stood behind the counter. Breathing hard, she narrowed her eyes. She only had to locate a hammer and nail. Once she had that nail pounded in the wall, she could hang the broom on it and never have to hunt for it again.

Finding what she needed in the livery next door, she returned to the store, decided where the broom should hang, and took aim at the nail's head. Three whacks later, the nail tip had barely made a dent. She slammed it harder hoping she wouldn't damage her hand.

"You trying to kill the nail or your thumb?"

Swinging her head around at the voice, she did hit her thumb. Rebekah dropped the hammer, brought her thumb to her mouth, and glared at Thomas for causing the accident. It didn't help that he fought a laugh. He moved behind the counter with his hand out.

"Here, let me see."

Tucking her hand in her apron pocket, she narrowed her eyes. "I don't think so. You're the reason I'm hurt. Don't you know you shouldn't sneak up on someone with a hammer?"

His chuckles finally escaped. "I wasn't sneaking. You just weren't paying attention."

She narrowed her eyes. "I was paying attention—to what I was doing." Her hand brushed a scrap of paper in her pocket. She pulled it out. "What's this?"

Thomas's eyes widened as he reached for the paper. "Let me see."

She jerked her hand back. "I don't think so. At least not until I look at it." Unfolding the note, she instantly recognized the script and looked at Thomas. "You wrote this." He'd sent her one of the notes like he'd given Cora. "When did you give it to me?"

She started to read, only to have Thomas reach for it again, forcing her to pull it away once more.

"Don't read it, Rebekah."

His eyes begged her to listen, but her curiosity was too strong. Taking a few steps back, she started to read aloud.

> *"You often dwell on thoughts of Nate,*
> *and maybe dream he'll be your mate.*
> *But long before you reach that goal,*
> *be sure to look deep in his soul."*

Searching Thomas's eyes, she felt disappointment. He still didn't like or trust Nate.

"Look, Rebekah, I wrote that weeks ago, before I got to know Nate better. Don't pay it no mind." When she still stared, he shook his head. "I was just trying to make sure you knew him before you lost your heart to him. But I think I sent it too late, didn't I?"

Too late? Thomas's warnings or anybody's would've been too late from the moment Nate had rescued Andrew and her from the river. Rebekah ran her fingers over the lumpy scar on her cheek, then wagged her head. "It's not your fault, Thomas. I—"

Boots clomping on the boardwalk kept her from finishing. The shop door swung open. Nate strode happily inside.

"Thomas, there you are. I've been looking everywhere for you."

Rebekah stared, the sight of Nate stealing her breath. He'd never looked so good, so happy, so at peace. She shoved the warning note back into her pocket.

Thomas reached to shake his hand. "Welcome back. I take it by the look on your face that all went well."

"It did. I ran into no trouble at all." Nate aimed his smile at Rebekah and nearly made her knees give out. "Hello, Rebekah."

His deep voice had softened when he spoke her name. Her smile trembled. *Oh, Lord, but I love him so. Please help me.*

Hands shoved into his pockets, Nate dropped his gaze to the floor before returning it to Thomas, his expression humble. "I've been needing to apologize to you, Thomas." He waved away Thomas's attempt at denial. "Over the last few weeks, I've had a lot of time to think and pray, and I came to a very saddening and humiliating conclusion. I've been wrong about the way I choose my friends. By looking at a man's outward appearance instead of his heart, I did a poor job at selecting friends. I let Henry's proper speech and stature fool me into believing he was a gentleman, while I judged you and looked at you with scorn." With a woeful shake of his head, Nate turned pleading eyes on Thomas. "I can only hope you'll forgive me."

Thomas stood in silence for a few moments, his own eyes turning red. Then he reached out his hand to shake Nate's. "Done." His voice gruff, he cleared his throat. "You're a good man, Nate. You've become worthy of our Rebekah."

That said, he clomped out of the store, leaving her alone with Nate. She sought his eyes, then looked away, embarrassed that Thomas would presume to say such a thing. When Nate remained silent, she chanced a glance at him.

His expression serious, he moved her way. "Is that true?"

"Is what true?" The question came out in a raspy whisper. Heat crawled up her neck, warming her face.

Nate stopped at the end of the counter. "That I'm worthy of you."

She looked away, her hand going first to her scarred cheek, then to the silver disk at her throat. "Yes. Sure. Of course. You—you're worthy of all the women in town."

He crossed the distance separating them and held her by her arms. As much as she wanted to lean against him, breathe in his scent and feel his heartbeat against her own, she resisted, still holding the disk like a shield that would save her life.

"Look at me, Bek." When she complied, he pulled her closer. "Why do you keep mentioning all the other women in town?"

Was he really unaware? Worse, was he being kind to the girl with the scarred face? The thought soured her stomach. Didn't he know his good looks made all the ladies stare? "Because now that you're back, they'll go out of their way to get your attention."

Frowning, he still held her tight. "But I don't care about getting their attention."

What did that mean? If he'd let her go, maybe she could think more clearly. "Does that mean you plan to leave town?" How would she manage to say good-bye to him forever?

With a quiet groan, he drew her closer. "No, Bek. That means it's your attention I've been trying to get."

Leaning her head back so she could see his face, she searched his eyes to see if he was serious. "What?"

A slight smile lit his face. "How can someone so beautiful be so slow to understand?"

The first part of his question was all she'd heard. Once again, she lifted her hand to cover her scarred cheek, hurt that Nate could be so cruel. "Don't make fun, Nate. I can't help that I'm scarred."

Her throat thick with unshed tears, she could barely speak. She tried to pull away, but he wouldn't release her. Then his hands slid from her arms to her cheeks. He tilted her face up until she was looking into his eyes.

"I'm not making fun, Bek. I think you're the most beautiful woman I've ever laid eyes on."

His husky voice sent shivers over every part of her skin. "But my scars…"

He shook his head. "I haven't seen your scars for weeks, Bek. All I've been able to see is your heart, the most beautiful and caring heart in the world." Rubbing her cheekbones with his thumbs, he dipped his head low. "And just so you know, I think your face is incredibly beautiful too."

Tears erupted from her eyes. Words escaped her. She could only shake her head, unable to believe what he'd said.

He kissed the tears, first from one eye, then the other. Then he moved to her lips and touched them lightly with his own. She felt him tremble. He released her, and she took a step forward to keep from falling.

She looked up at him and found him with that incredible smile. He reached down and took her hand in his.

"I know you don't believe what I said, and just so you know, I've resigned from my post at the marshal's office and accepted the position of sheriff here in town. When I'm not arresting lawbreakers, I'll be working full-time at convincing you of my love and trying to get you to fall in love with me." He leaned down until his nose bumped hers. "Because I do love you, Rebekah Weaver."

His words were the most beautiful music she'd ever heard. Grinning, she rubbed her nose against his. "Then you can resign from that job too, because I already love you."

Giving a whoop, he wrapped his arms around her. He lifted her feet from the ground and twirled her around. As he slowly lowered her back to the ground, he again touched his lips to hers, this time claiming them as his own.

"Oh, yuck. That's nasty."

They both turned to find Andrew standing in the doorway, disgust on his face. He pulled a snake from behind his back.

"I'd rather kiss this snake than do something as yucky as kiss a girl."

Rebekah gasped at the sight of the vile creature and reached for her broom. "Andrew Robert Weaver, you get that thing out of here."

Her brother's eyes went wide as he looked at Nate. "She used my middle name."

Andrew didn't move until Rebekah took a step toward him, then he ran from the store yelling like she'd actually hit him. She glared up at Nate, shaking the broom and pointing at Andrew.

"There's your first lawbreaker. Go arrest him."

Before she could take a breath, Nate hooked her around the waist with one of his arms and pulled her against him, roaring with laughter.

"You'd better get used to that, sweetheart. I want a lot of sons just like him."

Her heart soaring higher than ever before, she tried to look repulsed. "Oh, really? Don't I get a say in the matter?"

"Yep." He leaned down and gave her another kiss. "As long as you say yes."

She wrapped her arms around his neck, feeling richer than if she owned the ore in all the mines around Silver City. "Yes."

About the Author

....

Born and raised in southern Minnesota, Janelle Mowery spent hours reading a great many books in her childhood years. Her love of history, mystery, and stories led her toward her dream of writing novels. She began writing her first story in 2001, became a member of American Christian Fiction Writers in 2002, and signed her first contract in 2006. In 2008 Janelle released her first novel, *Where the Truth Lies*, a mystery she co-authored with Elizabeth Ludwig. Books two and three of the mystery series, *Died in the Wool* and *A Black Die Affair*, respectively, are slated for release in 2011. And the first book of Janelle's Colorado Runaway trilogy will release in 2010. When Janelle is not writing, she loves reading, watching movies, researching history, and spending time in the great outdoors. She now resides in Texas with her husband of twenty-one years and their two sons.

www.janellemowery.com

Want a peek into local American life—past and present?
The *Love Finds You*™ series published by Summerside Press
features real towns and combines travel, romance,
and faith in one irresistible package!

The novels in the series—uniquely titled after American towns with unusual but intriguing names—inspire romance and fun. Each fictional story draws on the compelling history or the unique character of a real place. Stories center on romances kindled in small towns, old loves lost and found again on the high plains, and new loves discovered at exciting vacation getaways. Summerside Press plans to publish at least one novel set in each of the 50 states. Be sure to catch them all!

Now Available in Stores

Love Finds You in Sisters, Oregon
by Melody Carlson
ISBN: 978-1-935416-18-0

Love Finds You in Charm, Ohio
by Annalisa Daughety
ISBN: 978-1-935416-17-3

*Love Finds You in Bethlehem, New
Hampshire* by Lauralee Bliss
ISBN: 978-1-935416-20-3

*Love Finds You in
North Pole, Alaska*
by Loree Lough
ISBN: 978-1-935416-19-7

Love Finds You in Holiday, Florida
by Sandra D. Bricker
ISBN: 978-1-935416-25-8

*Love Finds You in
Lonesome Prairie, Montana*
by Tricia Goyer and Ocieanna Fleiss
ISBN: 978-1-935416-29-6

Love Finds You in Bridal Veil, Oregon
by Miralee Ferrell
ISBN: 978-1-935416-63-0

*Love Finds You in
Hershey, Pennsylvania*
by Cerella D. Sechrist
ISBN: 978-1-935416-64-7

Love Finds You in Homestead, Iowa
by Melanie Dobson
ISBN: 978-1-935416-66-1

Love Finds You in Pendleton, Oregon
by Melody Carlson
ISBN: 978-1-935416-84-5

*Love Finds You in Golden, New
Mexico* by Lena Nelson Dooley
ISBN: 978-1-935416-74-6

Love Finds You in Lahaina, Hawaii
by Bodie Thoene
ISBN: 978-1-935416-78-4

*Love Finds You in
Victory Heights, Washington*
by Tricia Goyer and Ocieanna Fleiss
ISBN: 978-1-60936-000-9

Love Finds You in Calico, California
by Elizabeth Ludwig
ISBN: 978-1-60936-001-6

Love Finds You in Sugarcreek, Ohio
by Serena B. Miller
ISBN: 978-1-60936-002-3

*Love Finds You in
Deadwood, South Dakota*
by Tracey Cross
ISBN: 978-1-60936-003-0

*Love Finds You in
Carmel-by-the-Sea, California*
by Sandra D. Bricker
ISBN: 978-1-60936-027-6

COMING SOON

Love Finds You Under the Mistletoe
by Irene Brand and Anita Higman
ISBN: 978-1-60936-004-7

Love Finds You in Hope, Kansas
by Pamela Griffin
ISBN: 978-1-60936-007-8

Love Finds You in Sun Valley, Idaho
by Angela Ruth
ISBN: 978-1-60936-008-5

*Love Finds You in
Camelot, Tennessee*
by Janice Hanna
ISBN: 978-1-935416-65-4

*Love Finds You in
Tombstone, Arizona*
by Miralee Ferrell
ISBN: 978-1-60936-104-4

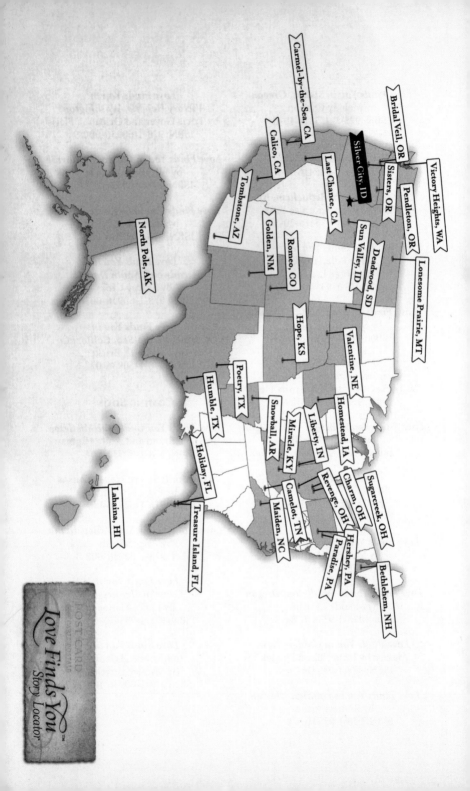